"Now then, what art shall we make of him?"

Grant saw the man's strange blaster come into his field of vision.

"What about inside art?" Antonia proposed. "Red things, the color of life."

Hugh pressed his weapon to Grant's gut and pulled the trigger. With a hum, the odd-looking blaster emitted an orange beam of heat that Grant could feel even through his shadow suit.

Grant screamed as pain racked his body, vibrating his very atoms as he juddered in place, quivering on the ground like a jumping jack. The scream passed in a moment, and after that he strained to cling to consciousness as the pain pressed against his chest.

Grant was unconscious when the pain finally stopped as Hugh switched off the heat beam. "It doesn't work, Algie," Hugh said. "Your heat brush doesn't work."

"It repelled his bullet, didn't it?" Algernon called from where he stood before the fallen figure of Shizuka. She was barely conscious, looking up at him from her position sprawled on the floor.

Other titles in this series:

James Axler
Outlanders®

IMMORTAL
TWILIGHT

A GOLD EAGLE BOOK FROM
WORLDWIDE®

TORONTO • NEW YORK • LONDON
AMSTERDAM • PARIS • SYDNEY • HAMBURG
STOCKHOLM • ATHENS • TOKYO • MILAN
MADRID • WARSAW • BUDAPEST • AUCKLAND

Recycling programs
for this product may
not exist in your area.

First edition August 2013

ISBN-13: 978-0-373-63879-6

IMMORTAL TWILIGHT

Copyright © 2013 by Worldwide Library

Special thanks to Rik Hoskin for his contribution to this work.

Art is the only serious thing in the world. And the artist is the only person who is never serious.

—Oscar Wilde, "A Few Maxims for the Instruction of the Over-educated", *Saturday Review,* 1894

"All war is art."

—First recorded words of Hugh Danner, 1895

The Road to Outlands—
From Secret Government Files to the Future

Almost two hundred years after the global holocaust, Kane, a former Magistrate of Cobaltville, often thought the world had been lucky to survive at all after a nuclear device detonated in the Russian embassy in Washington, D.C. The aftermath—forever known as skydark—reshaped continents and turned civilization into ashes.

Nearly depopulated, America became the Deathlands—poisoned by radiation, home to chaos and mutated life forms. Feudal rule reappeared in the form of baronies, while remote outposts clung to a brutish existence.

What eventually helped shape this wasteland were the redoubts, the secret preholocaust military installations with stores of weapons, and the home of gateways, the locational matter-transfer facilities. Some of the redoubts hid clues that had once fed wild theories of government cover-ups and alien visitations.

Rearmed from redoubt stockpiles, the barons consolidated their power and reclaimed technology for the villes. Their power, supported by some invisible authority, extended beyond their fortified walls to what was now called the Outlands. It was here that the rootstock of humanity survived, living with hellzones and chemical storms, hounded by Magistrates.

In the villes, rigid laws were enforced—to atone for the sins of the past and prepare the way for a better future. That was the barons' public credo and their right-to-rule.

Kane, along with friend and fellow Magistrate Grant, had upheld that claim until a fateful Outlands expedition. A displaced piece of technology…a question to a keeper of the archives…a vague clue about alien masters—and their world shifted radically. Suddenly, Brigid Baptiste, the archivist, faced summary execution, and Grant a quick termination. For Kane there was forgiveness if he pledged his unquestioning allegiance to Baron Cobalt and his unknown masters and abandoned his friends.

But that allegiance would make him support a mysterious and alien power and deny loyalty and friends. Then what else was there?

Kane had been brought up solely to serve the ville. Brigid's only link with her family was her mother's red-gold hair, green eyes and supple form. Grant's clues to his lineage were his ebony skin and powerful physique. But Domi, she of the white hair, was an Outlander pressed into sexual servitude in Cobaltville. She at least knew her roots and was a reminder to the exiles that the outcasts belonged in the human family.

Parents, friends, community—the very rootedness of humanity was denied. With no continuity, there was no forward momentum to the future. And that was the crux—when Kane began to wonder if there was a future.

For Kane, it wouldn't do. So the only way was out—way, way out.

After their escape, they found shelter at the forgotten Cerberus redoubt headed by Lakesh, a scientist, Cobaltville's head archivist, and secret opponent of the barons.

With their past turned into a lie, their future threatened, only one thing was left to give meaning to the outcasts. The hunger for freedom, the will to resist the hostile influences. And perhaps, by opposing, end them.

Prologue

The widow wore black. A tribute to their love eternal, Queen Victoria had worn black since the death of her husband, Albert, in 1861.

She had sat on the British throne for as long as Major Fortesque-Penwright could remember. Her reign had already broken records, with no sign of her stepping down. Some had speculated that she might abdicate when Albert died, but that was thirty-four years ago now and yet the queen stayed on the throne. Queen Victoria ruled not just Great Britain but also the vast British Empire, which circled the globe. Empress of India, head of the Colonial Conference of 1887, she was a magnetic force around which everything on Earth seemed to revolve.

The queen followed Fortesque-Penwright as he led her through the arched doorway and into the vast research theater. The archway was wide, like a train tunnel from the underground system, and the room beyond was wider still, with high rafters and pools of light aimed in cones at the various units in use there. The room was dominated by what appeared to be a vast aquarium along with bubbling cylinders and whirling centrifugal separators like some strange parody of a fairground, with desks and overflowing bookshelves arranged along three walls. Over in one corner of the chamber, set far back from the unfathomable operations, was a small loungelike area with a rose-red rug laid down across the stone floor and four accommodating leather chairs arranged in a crescent around a low table with a gas lamp behind. Incongruous with the rest of the laboratory, it looked strangely comfortable to Victoria as her eyes darted around the room.

There were people here, too, over a dozen men wearing their finest suits for the royal visit, their shoes shined to mirror clarity. To a man, they looked awkward and scruffy despite their best efforts—scientists, Victoria realized.

"God save the queen," one of the men announced as Victoria and the major stepped into the room. Around him, his fellows voiced their agreement with the sentiment, waiting patiently for either the queen or the major to give them their instructions.

"One is delighted to visit," she finally announced, her voice strong despite her advanced years; she could still command a room, even at seventy-six. Her words echoed around the chamber for a moment, bouncing back from the hard surfaces of the wall and ceiling. The room was underground, hidden beneath a great army complex on the outskirts of Windsor in Berkshire, England. No one but her most trusted aides knew that the queen was here. Indeed, if any had asked, the existence of this visit would have been denied.

Once excused, the laboratory men went back to their tasks, checking on the bubbling tank that dominated the room. All except for one man; he remained by the bank of desks, waiting patiently for his audience with the queen. The man was dressed more casually than the others, his hair a little longer, his pants not quite matching his jacket. He was taller than average, with tanned skin, his hair and sideburns black as india ink.

Fortesque-Penwright introduced him, leading the

queen to him by a gesture, deigning never to touch Her Majesty. "Professor Howard, Your Highness."

"Obliged, Your Majesty," Howard said, tipping his brow with his fingers. His accent clearly marked him as an American, an outsider among this group.

"Which part of the United States did you travel from, Professor?" Victoria asked.

Howard looked surprised, caught off guard by the sheer ordinariness of the question. "Texas, originally," Howard recovered. "Then a little all-over for a while before I landed here in merry England."

"One is informed that you are something of an expert in your field," the queen continued, standing before Howard and glaring up at him. "Artificial evolution, from what one understands."

"That's right, Your Majesty," Howard agreed in his Texan drawl. "Biogenetics is what I call it. It's a discipline of science that explores the extreme possibilities of the body, both human and animal."

Victoria shot the man a fierce look. "Do you then consider humans and animals to be interchangeable, Professor?"

"In strict terms of biology, there's not that much difference from a scientist's point of view," Howard admitted uncomfortably. "Though, I don't want you to get the wrong idea about my work. It's very respectful of the human body. I'm seeking to improve, not to hurt." As he spoke, Howard reached across the desk behind him and took up his hat, a dun-colored Stetson with a band of silver coinlike circlets around the base of the crown.

"What success have you achieved, Professor Howard?" the queen asked.

Howard fiddled with the brim of his hat, unsure whether he could wear it in the presence of British royalty. It remained in his hands as he spoke. "I had some success with rats and other rodents, a dog that could run faster than anything you ever saw on my pappy's farm." He looked embarrassed. "Um...which is to say..."

Queen Victoria brushed away his explanation. "We have dogs in this country, Professor," she said archly. "Your meaning is quite clear. Please continue. How is it you have ended up on this side of the Atlantic Ocean?"

"Once I realized the applications of my procedure, I approached the U.S. government to determine their interest levels in my work," Howard said. "There was some interest, what with the longevity and the medicinal implications of..."

The queen stopped him with a wave of her black-clad hand. "A little slower, if you would, Professor, and perhaps a remedial step for the benefit of an old woman's comprehension."

Howard did a hard swallow, realizing for the first time how nervous he was. His funding depended on this aged woman—his funding and his career. Together, the professor and the queen walked across the room, making their way toward the bubbling aquarium. "Ahem. My background draws from both biology and veterinary practice, Your Majesty. I began by experimenting on various mammals, rats and what have you, in an effort to determine what could be done to make them stronger and more resilient—kinda like the way a horticulturalist will crossbreed strains of flowers to make a new rose.

"Now, once that was in place, the implications became obvious. If I could make a stronger rat that was resilient to disease—and I did—and if I could make a cocker spaniel that could outrun its fellows by some considerable margin and never get tired—and, once again, I did—then it only takes a small leap of the imagination to realize what might happen if I were to apply those same techniques to the human form."

The party had stopped before the glass-walled tank in the center of the underground room. Twenty-five feet on its longest side, the aquarium-like tank was thirteen feet high and had been secured to the floor by cast-iron bolts. The tank glowed with ultraviolet light, turning the liquid within an iridescent green hue. Equipment hooked to the tank fed it with chemical compounds and rigorously monitored its makeup. Each feed was printed out by a wavering needle that showed the peaks and troughs of the components, a little like a seismology unit recording earth tremors. The glow from the tank painted the floor in a green wash, while the liquid itself clouded and parted like the London fog, revealing its contents in snatched glimpses.

"Imagine human beings that were resilient to all disease," Professor Howard continued. "Humans of fearsome intelligence who could outmaneuver their contemporaries in every field."

Taking a step closer, the queen eyed the emerald tank with interest. There were shadowy forms within, people floating in the liquid murk, upright as if standing. They were tall, with long limbs and trailing hair that caught in the green liquid like clouds of ink swirling about their heads. For a moment, one figure was revealed in all its majesty—a woman with an oval face and trailing hair the color of molten gold. She hung there like a mermaid, naked in the glistening waters of the tank, her mouth open as if in sexual arousal. Behind her, a man floated, his musculature like a Greek statue, his nakedness a thing of beauty.

As the queen watched the man floating there, Major Fortesque-Penwright stepped forward, blushing a beetroot-red behind his bushy mustache. "I do apologize, Your Majesty," he blustered. "I had no idea that this...show would be so obscene...."

Her eyes still on the naked figures in the tank, the queen spoke in her most regal tones. "One was married for twenty-one years and has had nine children, Major. It takes rather more than a naked figure to offend."

Howard smiled at the put-down, feeling a growing admiration for this old woman on whom his very reputation depended. Around them, white-coated men bustled about the lab, referring to notebooks as they checked bubbling cylinders and rolling printouts.

"You asked how I ended up on this side of the pond, Your Majesty," Howard said, "and that's a mighty fair question. At first I tried the U.S. authorities, and the Army folk were interested, make no mistake. They saw potential here to create some kind of special soldier, strong as an ox and invulnerable to disease, a soldier that never became tired. That didn't sit so well with me, but research of this nature takes funding—a lot of funding. Thing is, Your Highness, they couldn't meet the budget I needed."

"So you came here, Stetson in hand," the queen suggested, fixing Howard with her intense gaze.

"That's how it worked out," the professor admitted, gazing down self-consciously at his hat.

Major Fortesque-Penwright took up the discussion, addressing Queen Victoria. "Now, it should be clear that we, too, are looking into the military implications of this, Your Majesty," he began. His was a voice that always sounded as though he was shouting, no matter how quiet he tried to make it. "The empire would benefit greatly from these...immortals, as Professor Howard has dubbed them. And there are medical applications, as well, down the road as it were. As such, the top people felt it was judicious to invest in Professor Howard's little project."

Howard balked at the derogatory term, but he held his tongue. Funding first, he reminded himself. Always funding first.

The queen looked from Fortesque-Penwright to the professor. "You called them immortals? Like Mr. Wilde's story of Dorian Gray."

Howard looked bemused. "I must admit, I've not had the opportunity to read it, Your Majesty."

"No matter," the queen dismissed. "Show me these Dorian Grays you have been growing."

Howard led the way around the tank, indicating the five figures that floated there. They were full-grown humans, each one a work of art, perfect examples of the human form. They hung like wraiths in the dark liquid, slowly rotating with the currents in the tank. "The first batch is still at test stage," Howard explained, "Our Adams and Eves, if you will. But we're happy with their growth, and initial analysis is proving encouraging."

"They arrive fully grown," the queen observed.

"Well, we take a fertilized egg and we use pressure to make it grow to our requirements," Howard told her. "What you're looking at here may appear to be adults, but they're still fetuses, really. They're no more alive yet than a bubba in its mother's tummy.

"We can teach them at this stage, bring them up to speed and plane off any hard edges we don't like. It's a learning process just now, but we're getting there."

"How long will it be before your immortal supermen are ready to come to life?" the queen asked.

"Twelve weeks," Howard estimated, "give or take a day or two. We'll move them to the U.S. before then.

There are some final preparations I'll need to do and I can only really do those at my proper laboratory."

The queen raised an eyebrow in surprise. "You are unable to obtain such supplies here?"

Before the professor could answer, Fortesque-Penwright interposed in his best hushed tone. "The top bods agree it would be best if this operation moves to America for now. Saves on culpability should anything go awry."

The queen gazed over the major's shoulder at Professor Howard, who stood fidgeting with the brim of his hat. "Will anything go awry, Professor?"

"No, Your Majesty," Howard said with the swagger of an American on foreign soil. "This time next year you'll have the first platoon of superintelligent, super-strong supermen."

"And they'll be standing shoulder to shoulder to defend the borders of the empire," Fortesque-Penwright added proudly.

Chapter 1

"You know what the difference is between grave robbers and tomb raiders, Milo?"

"I dunno— to get to the other side or something…?" Milo replied uncertainly in his deep, rumbling voice. A big man, Milo leaned down with a shovel in his hand, working at the hard soil of a hillock some twenty miles outside what used to be the ville of Beausoleil.

Standing beside Milo, Jake was thinner with a girl's shoulders and a pencil mustache. His dark hair, thinner now at forty than it had been at twenty, though the style remained unchanged, was slicked back.

It had been over three hundred years since Queen Victoria met with Professor Howard in the underground bunker at Windsor, three hundred years during which the whole world had been devastated by two World Wars before an apocalyptic third, in 2001, had turned the United States of America into the radioactive Deathlands. The population was culled to one tenth of its size, and the survivors struggled to eke out their lives in an irradiated wasteland where muties roamed the dust-swept streets of abandoned cities. For some, that era had seemed to go on forever, but eventually humankind had clambered out of that self-made hell pit. Under the Program of Unification, civil North America was governed by nine ruthless barons who split the land into great chunks, which they oversaw. Each baron commanded a ville named after him- or herself—and all demanded absolute loyalty from their subjects. But in the past few years, the balance of power had been upset when the barons had revealed themselves as reborn Annunaki, a race of lizardlike aliens who had walked the Earth once before at the dawn of man, when they had been revered as gods. The Annunaki had planned to take control of the decimated populace, the thinned herd that the nuclear exchange had created two hundred years before, but their plan had crumbled thanks to a combination of infighting and the intervention of a brave band of rebels working under the banner of the Cerberus organization. With the barons-turned-Annunaki now departed, the world itself seemed up for grabs, a future just waiting for guidance. And perhaps that guidance would come from a most unlikely source.

"'To get to the...' What?" Jake spit, glaring at his broad-shouldered companion in disbelief. "What the fuck are you talking about?"

"I dunno," Milo admitted. "It's a joke, right?"

Jake's withering look was lost in the faint illumination of the overhead stars. "I swear to Cobalt, you are one dumb son of a mutant. I've had dumps that showed more intelligence than you."

Milo looked up, offended.

"Just keep digging, huh," Jake told him. "I'm trying to make a point here."

Milo got back to digging, working at the spot that Jake had indicated. It was located amid a thick group of trees. It was the kind of place you'd go to bury a body, and the thin crescent of moonlight did nothing to assuage that feeling in Jake's mind. He wondered when was the last time anyone had actually walked up here, between this particular cluster of trees, way out beyond the farmland.

"So, what is it?" Milo asked as he shunted another shovelful of earth aside. He was a strong man and, even though they hadn't been here ten minutes, already he was down four feet into the heavy soil and showing no signs of tiring. Jake had to credit the guy with that—whatever he lacked in brainpower, Milo worked like one of them old-time slaves; that's why they remained partners long after Jake had become permanently impatient with the dumb son of a bitch.

"The difference," Jake explained, waving his arms theatrically in the air, "between grave robbers and tomb raiders is the reward. See, Joe Grave-Robber, all he cares about is the money. He finds a nice gold wrist-chron or a pretty necklace and he figures he's made a big score. But for tomb raiders, it's all about the history. We don't do it for the money, Milo, my friend, we do it so that the people of the future can look back at the past and go, 'Hey, those old people wore clogs on their heads. Who knew?' You get me?"

Milo shook his head but didn't slow down his digging. "Not really, Jake. I thought you said that we'd be paid handsomely for what was waiting in this place."

"That we will," Jake assured him, "but we ain't in this for the money, are we?"

As usual, Milo was confused. "We ain't?"

Jake clapped his hands together and smiled. "Men like you and me, we're better than that. We seek knowledge, understanding, great…things. And if we happen to discover a treasure trove of artifacts that we can sell on, well—that's the almighty baron's way of telling us we done good, we deserve it. See?"

Milo didn't see, but then more often than not he didn't really have a clue what his partner in crime was talking about. Jake was the brains and he was the brawn; that was the arrangement they had always had, and Jake had always seen him right once the sweat work was over and they cracked open whatever the heck it was that Jake had heard about through his admirable network of contacts. One time they'd gone diving to a shipwreck off the Samariumville coast where they'd found so much gold they hadn't had to pull another job for eighteen months. But funds dried up eventually, so here they were again, looking for another big haul. How had Jake described it? A man had offered him a map, something military, he thought, that showed an ancient redoubt, the kind of place where the prenukecaust people would hide armaments, vehicle specs and crappy food that had turned to dust. It wasn't a shipwreck, but it was something.

Clunk!

"Found something," Milo muttered, his beaming smile shining in the filtered moonlight. This kind of work was best done by moonlight, as it didn't pay to attract attention when you were acquiring unclaimed property. There were too many groups around, these days, from one-man operations all the way up to big outfits like the Millennial Consortium, all of them wanting a piece of the historical pie. Those Millennial bastards were the worst, Milo knew—he and Jake had gotten themselves mixed up with those whackjobs once, and Jake wound up losing a thumb and two fingers during the interrogation before he had finally squealed about their find. That was a long time ago now, back when Jake had still been married. What was her name? Belle? Was that it?

Jake snapped his fingers in Milo's face. "Hey, wake up, dumbbell." He was leaning forward, his other hand pressed against his thigh as he studied the thing that Milo's shovel had clanged against. The object glinted mysteriously as it caught the moonbeams.

"I can't see shit in this light," Jake muttered, reaching into the breast pocket of his jacket. A moment later he produced a penlight, running its narrow beam across the hole that Milo had just finished digging. Beneath the pencil-thin beam the two men saw a metal plate that seemed to bulge a little out of the soil.

"Hey, help me move this stuff, huh?" Jake ordered, kneeling down on the slope and brushing away loose soil.

Milo brought his shovel down against the metal plate, working over it in sweeps that gradually uncovered more of its surface. Revealed, it was roughly three feet across, circular with a convex design that brought the center up in a raised mound like a shallow, upturned cone. There were rivets around the edge of the circle, and beyond its lip was a second circle of steel, this one much thinner than the top, reminding Milo of a sink plunger sitting in a drain. In the center of the circular "lid" was a handle, a simple bar like the kind you might find on a fire door, next to which was an inset panel that showed six interlinked cogs. The workings were black with dirt.

"Move these," Jake muttered, running his hand over the cogs, "to open that. Simple."

"Looks like a door on a submarine," Milo opined as Jake worked the cogs, testing how they interacted. "You know what you're doing, right, Jake?"

Jake looked up at him with that winning smile he used on the ladies. Milo always liked that smile; sometimes it meant he'd get laid, too, if he kept quiet while Jake worked his charm. "Hey, 'course I know what I'm doing. Just need to think it through a little, that's all. Why? You in a hurry?"

Milo laughed. "Heh-heh, not me, Jake. No, sir."

Jake worked the combination for a few minutes, figuring how each part affected the others until finally he heard a click and knew he had the door unlocked. His old man was a jugger—a safe-cracker—and he had shown him the tricks of the trade. Mostly, it was down to patience and a steady hand; that's what Jake's old man had told him.

"You want to give me a hand with this?" Jake asked, working dirt from the ridge around the sunken manhole.

Milo leaned down, and in a few minutes the two of them had the door free, wrenching it out of the ground with a groan of ancient hinges. The door pulled out a few inches before folding back on a sliding mechanism. The mechanism jammed a couple of times, but Jake used a little canister of oil to work it free, and Milo's brute strength did the rest.

Below, it was dark, and Jake played his tiny beam over the gaping hole, running it back and forth until he saw what appeared to be tiled floor beneath. Looking down there reminded Milo of the old wishing wells his late mom had taken him to sometimes, and he laughed. "Want to make a wish, Jake?" he asked.

Jake glared at him, muttering something under his breath. "I'll go down first," he said, "and you follow."

"I dunno," Milo said. "Looks like a big jump."

"That's why I'm going first," Jake told him. "You're good for a lot of stuff, Milo, but you've got the agility of a brick, I swear."

Milo didn't argue, but that was mostly because he didn't understand. Besides, Jake always went first—that was their arrangement.

IT WAS A DROP of twelve feet to the floor, not a lot for a tall man like Jake, and once he was down there he saw the ladder-style rungs that worked up the curved side of the wall. Milo followed, clambering like a monkey to reach for the rungs as Jake speared them in the spotlight of his flash.

They were in an alcove, a tight square room with barely enough space to hold two grown men, a little like the narthex lobby of a church. Milo's shoulders brushed against the wall as he endeavoured to give Jake "room to think." There was no door to this area, which was delineated purely by a short flight of steps that led down into a lower tunnel. Jake peered down the steps, listening carefully to the echoes. There was no reason that anyone should be down here—hell, that combination lock on the door above them had been sealed for centuries —but it didn't pay to get reckless.

Jake couldn't hear anything coming from the narrow tunnel, so he led the way along it with Milo dogging his heels, the little penlight illuminating the careful brickwork of the tunnel in a tiny, moving circle.

"What do you think is down here?" Milo asked eagerly.

"Your grave if you don't button your lip," Jake warned him in a whisper. "Keep it down, okay?"

The brickwork was neat, creating a low arch that ran along the full ceiling of the tunnel, finished in a sandy yellow color. There were markings on the walls here and there, perfect sketches of the female form rendered in intricate pencil. Jake played his penlight over the pictures, and Milo let out a low whistle when he saw them. The sketches looked ancient, the delicate lines worn to a muted gray that reminded Jake of cobwebs.

There was a sharp bend in the tunnel and then it widened. Suddenly, Jake and Milo were standing in a much wider tunnel. This one had a more gentle curvature to the ceiling, wide enough to hold two Sandcat vehicles side by side. And the strange thing was, a whole series of lights ran the length of this tunnel, illuminating the tiles and the grand painting that dominated one wall.

Milo walked across to the mural, examining it with widening eyes. It was a scene of nymphs at play by the waters. A great horse-drawn chariot emerged from the stream in a cascade of water, each droplet perfectly rendered in gouache. The nymphs were shown naked, some of them artistically draped with silks or flowing water. The illustration was life-size.

"Phew," Milo muttered as he stood, hands on hips, before it. "Some ladies, huh, Jake?"

Jake ignored his partner. He was more concerned with the lamps that illuminated the scene. They were gas lamps, ornate brass stems holding onionlike bowls that flickered with a warm yellow glow. "Someone's lit these," Jake said as he reached into his jacket pocket.

"What?" Milo asked, still admiring the women in the painting.

"Milo, wake up," Jake growled as he pulled his pistol free from its hiding place in his pocket. "Someone's here—they lit the lamps."

Milo scratched his face in thought. "The door was locked," he reminded Jake.

"That it was," Jake mused.

"Could be something automatic then," Milo said, grinning.

The two of them had scouted an ancient military redoubt once before, where they had discovered the lights worked on an automated circuit that activated whenever anyone entered the place. Jake looked around, his eyes following the line of lamps that ran along one long wall, flicking across to take in the mural. Maybe it was automated, like Milo said. Could be.

Jake checked the safety on his blaster, a snub-nosed .38

based on the old Smith & Wesson design. The six-shot weapon drew a little to the right on firing, he recalled. One time Jake had used it on a map collector who had discovered Jake rifling through the locked drawers of his study. There had been a flash of light, a shout of discharge and the old man had sagged to the floor clutching at his chest. Jake still thought of the man now and then. He hadn't wanted to kill him. His safe-cracking dad would have called that a complication, and an unprofessional one at that.

Jake steadied himself, flicking on the safety. He would keep the blaster out, right on show in case they bumped into any trouble. But he didn't plan to use it unless he absolutely had to.

Milo was back admiring the mural. "You reckon we could take this with us?" he asked. "I mean, it's really pretty. Someone would probably pay a lot for it."

Jake glanced at the artwork. Milo was right; it was an excellent piece of work, though the stylized figures looked almost three-dimensional. "What are we going to do? Chip it away piece by piece? Come on, there's probably some other stuff down here, the kind we can put in a sack and haul back up to the surface for now."

Milo nodded, pulling himself away from the river nymphs.

The two tomb raiders followed the tunnel where it burrowed through the earth, detecting a subtle downward slope as they walked its grand length. The passageway ended in a wall where two smaller tunnels diverged, each narrower and with a lower ceiling, but still wide enough to accommodate three or four men abreast. Jake picked one, holding the gun up close to his shoulder as he strode gingerly down the sloping corridor. Like the broad tunnel, this one was lit by gas lamps, their flickering illumination making shadows play across the pale walls.

A few steps in, Jake stopped and held up his free hand to warn Milo to silence. "You hear something?" Jake whispered.

Milo thought about it, making a grand show of looking this way and that. "Like what?" he asked.

"Like 'I don't know' is like what," Jake growled. "What am I, a bat? It's a sound, like the sound of a movement. You hear it or don't you?"

Milo listened again. At first he didn't hear anything, but he strained, stilling his breathing as he peered down the flickering corridor. There was something. Not a movement sound—it was more rhythmic, almost like music. Unconsciously, Milo began tapping out the rhythm against his leg. "It's a tune," he said. "Like... uh...la-la, la-la-la..."

"Yeah, okay thanks, Chopin," Jake hissed, commanding Milo to silence. "Enough already."

They continued warily down the curving tunnel, and saw a side door waiting to the left. The door was open and whatever lay beyond was dark. Jake stepped over to it, bringing the snub-nosed .38 up in a ready position.

"Jake," Milo urged. "I don't like this."

"Me, either," Jake whispered, peering into the darkened doorway. Beyond it lay a room, twelve feet in length and cluttered with junk. The room was mostly dark, just a small table lamp lit in the far corner, where a figure sat.

His shoulder pressed against the door frame, Jake peered at the figure from his hiding place. It was a man with long dark hair that reached down past his collar. He wore a swallow-tailed velvet jacket the rich red color of sunset, and beneath that a white shirt with an open collar, dark pants and shoes. The shoes had been polished to catch what little light was cast by the flickering table lamp. Evidently unaware of the presence of the spy, the man was toying with something in his hands, and for a moment Jake took it to be a child. He stifled a gasp, focused his eyes on the thing in the man's hands as he placed it on the floor. A moment later the figure began to walk, taking three steps forward before moving back again like a film on rewind. It was a puppet, Jake realized, the kind that hung down on strings from a rig held by its operator. Weird.

"Jake, look," Milo whispered, pointing at something in the room.

Jake's heart stuttered at Milo's words and it took him a moment to recover. Then, shooting a look of warning at his partner, he peered where Milo was pointing. There were frames there, burnished gold with tooling, like picture frames. And not just one or two—there had to be a dozen in the stack Milo was indicating, and ten times that scattered around the rest of the room. Paintings. Paintings that could be sold, maybe.

Jake scanned the area more carefully as he remained hidden beside the door. Initially, he had been distracted by the man, so it was the first time he properly looked over the stuff he had at first dismissed as "junk." There were paintings there and statues, delicate alabaster carvings of figures draped in silks and robes, some wearing nothing at all.

Jake had a good eye for this stuff, and he was already assessing the room for items of value. Maybe it was junk, but it was artsy junk and there was always a market for that—especially these days with the fall of the baronies leaving so many people resettling in different spots as if they were starting from scratch. All those planners and designers and doctors, all of them wanting their new place to look wealthy like the places they lived in back in Beausoleil and Snakefishville. Yeah, he could sell this stuff if he could get it out of here. But as long as the puppet master over there was waiting, it was a definite no-go. Best to come back, deal with this when the place was empty.

"Why don't I know you?" It was a woman's voice, sharp with an accent like cut glass. His eyes fixed on the puppet man, Jake couldn't process it for a half second.

"What—?" Jake said, turning.

There was a woman standing there, just eight feet down the corridor. "You, I don't know you. I've never seen you here before." She was beautiful with flawless skin that made the vexation on her brow all the more charming. She had blond hair that trailed halfway down her back and she was wearing the kind of dress that Jake associated with fairy-tale princesses, splaying out at floor length with a cinched waist and a low-cut bodice that drew the eye to her milky pale cleavage. "Well?"

Beside him, Jake could hear Milo trying to speak. "W-w-we…"

"Look, sister," Jake cut in, stepping in front of Milo protectively with the gun held loose in his hand, "your crew got here first, we get it. Salvage rules, we both respect that. But there's plenty here, just in that room alone. Maybe we can split it, you know? Cut a deal."

"What are you talking about, you strange, creepy little disease of a man?" the woman demanded, taking a brisk step toward him. Behind her, a little farther around the bend in the corridor, Jake spotted another man approaching, blond like the woman and wearing a puffy white shirt with a lace-up collar, dark pants that clung to his legs as if they'd been sprayed there. Neither the man nor his girlfriend looked much older than twenty, maybe twenty-five at most.

"Look…I—I—I… What did you just call me?" Jake

asked. Already he was raising the .38 in his hands, bringing it level with the woman's forehead as she took another step, thumbing the safety.

The blond-haired woman reached out in a blur, swiping the weapon aside with such force that it leaped from Jake's startled grip. "I asked who you were," she said, the words perfectly formed by her pretty mouth. "You cannot answer a question with a question. That's not the way the game's played, is it, Algie?"

Behind her, the blond-haired man in his shirtsleeves shook his head. "No, Cecily," he averred. "It's a simply beastly way to upset the game."

"Game?" Jake spit. "What damn game? What the fuck are you two…?"

The woman's hand was around his throat in a flash, the grip so tight that suddenly Jake could not breathe. "What deplorable language to use in front of a lady," she said. "Shame on you."

The woman called Cecily shoved Jake away and he staggered back, his hands reaching to his burning throat. "Wh-wha—?" he began, before sinking into a fit of coughing.

As Cecily rounded on Jake again, Milo stepped in, interposing his bulk like a prison door. "Hey, you don't just…"

Cecily turned her attention to Milo and her face held a thin smile. "You're a large one, aren't you? Do you like girls or boys?"

"Um…wh-what…?" Milo began.

"Honk!" the blonde woman shouted in his face, her smile becoming broader, a malicious twinkle in her eye. "Hesitation. You mustn't hesitate—it's against the rules."

Jake saw what happened next but he couldn't quite process it, not straight away. The woman lashed out with her arm, moving it so swiftly that it actually hummed as it cut the air. Only, it didn't just cut the air, it cut Milo, too, splitting between the slats of his rib cage before emerging from somewhere close to his spine. Her hand was covered in Milo's blood, wearing it like a scarlet glove as she pulled her arm back out of his body.

Holed like a ship, Milo sank down the wall in a splutter of blood. Bubbling, foamy red liquid appeared between his clenched teeth as he collapsed to the floor, the red stain blooming across his ruined shirt. The woman stood over his fallen figure and smiled.

"It was hesitation, wasn't it, Algie? Do please tell me it was."

Still standing by the bend in the tunnel, the blond man nodded his head slowly in agreement. "It was."

"Good," the woman replied, "because I don't think he'll be able to play again. I think perhaps I broke him."

"What the hell?" Jake muttered as the woman turned her attention away from his fallen colleague and back to him. He was scared now, more scared than when he had shot the map collector in his own home, more scared than when those millennial bastards had taken his fingers.

"Let's try again, shall we?" Cecily cooed as she wiped Milo's blood from her hands on the beautiful silks of her skirt.

Jake sobbed, assuring her he would answer everything.

"And no st-st-stuttering this time," the blond-maned Algie taunted.

Chapter 2

Brigid Baptiste was wired on glist with her foot rammed hard against the accelerator of the Turbo 190. There was a sweet taste in her mouth, like something from her childhood. The drug buzzed in her veins while the engine roared all around her, its sound like caged thunder as it rumbled through the chassis of the cherry-red sports car while the car's life pulse beat a tattoo against the sole of her foot where it held the accelerator down against the floor.

"Keep heading north," she reminded herself through gritted teeth. "Remember the plan."

Brigid was a beautiful woman in her late twenties with flame-red hair and bright emerald-green eyes. Her full lips suggested a passionate side, while her high brow inferred intelligence. In reality, Brigid encompassed both of these traits, though it was her fearsome intellect that had gotten her into this jam. A warrior for the Cerberus group, an organization established to protect humanity from threats both extra- and intraterrestrial, Brigid Baptiste was an ex-archivist from Cobaltville who had stumbled upon a conspiracy to delude the public about man's history. Her eidetic—or photographic—memory allowed her to retain information in precise detail, even after just a glance, and it was this ability that made her such a force to be reckoned with.

Right now, however, she was racing down the busy

streets of an Australasian city called the Hoop, urging more speed from the roaring engine of the Turbo, even as the glist surged through her blood. Around her, neon signs blurred as she sped past them through the ville's central square, a tribute to futurist architectural design.

It was daytime, the sun high in the sky, and she was tearing along one of the Hoop's broad streets, weaving through the moving traffic as if it was stationary, her eyes fixed on the road. Like the car's a part of me, Brigid told herself as she pumped the accelerator, urging even more speed from the powerful engine. What was it, eight hundred horsepower? Like eight hundred stallions caged beneath the hood, each one straining at the reins.

People and neon rushed by in a flickering display of shadows and brightness, advertising hoardings, an intensity of trivial information, over and over.

People.

Neon.

. On and on.

Her hands felt slick in the driving gloves, sweat clinging there in glistening, silver rivers. But that didn't matter. She was one with the automobile right now, a techno-organic synergy of thought and speed.

The Turbo 190 took the corner at speed, charging at the on-ramp and hurtling up its incline in a growl of barely restrained power. Around it, the city had become a blur, the other automobiles something sensed as much as seen. A wag swerved aside as her cherry-red sports car whipped by, the driver hurling obscenities at her as he mounted the sidewalk.

Behind Brigid, three security vehicles were following, gunning their way through the traffic, sirens wailing, their thick bullbars knocking aside anything that didn't move out of their path in time. They were armored like tanks, with triple axles to carry the weight without compromising their speed. Their sirens echoed across the elevated off-ramp, their Doppler song bouncing from the hard concrete barriers that lined its edges. Brigid ignored them. She could think two, three moves ahead, anticipate what the other vehicles would do, where the next pedestrian was coming from.

This high up, Brigid could see the edge of the coast where it abutted the ville's limits. The elevated street made a shallow curve toward it before banking back again. She gunned the engine, teasing another notch of speed from those eight hundred stallions, her Turbo just a red blur on the high-up roadway.

In her mirror, Brigid saw the tanklike pursuit vehicles take the ramp at speed as they struggled to keep pace with her. Then, as she watched, the foremost of the pursuit vehicles popped something out of its roof, a blister bubble with two dark protrusions emanating from its midpoint— a gun turret. Brigid yanked on the steering wheel as the first shot was fired, a ruby-red laser blast that cut a great swathe in the blacktop in a sizzle of burning tarmac.

"Crap!" Brigid shouted as she pulled the steering wheel hard to the left, driving the Turbo so close to the crash barrier that it scraped it in a rush of white-hot sparks.

Maybe stealing an unarmored car hadn't been such a great idea. Definitely stealing the encrypted data from right under the noses of the local authorities had been a lousy one. Lousy and dangerous.

KANE HAD BEEN TREKKING through Hope for over an hour, cutting a labyrinthine path through the hodgepodge of streets that made up the refugee-camp-cum-shantytown, making triple sure he wasn't being followed. Built of junk and salvage, the streets were tightly crammed and they stank of human detritus. Feces scarred the surface here and there, wild dogs, rats and other animals stalking the alleyways in search of the rich pickings that the hungry humans left behind, sometimes making a meal out of an unlucky person who had strayed too far from safety.

It was morning. Kane had gotten here a little before sunrise, trudging across the desert from the hidden parallax point that his interphaser unit had opened. The interphaser was a teleportation device based on ancient plans devised by an alien race. Kane's colleagues in the Cerberus organization had spent many man-hours figuring out how the units worked before they had been put into field operation.

Kane was on a mission for Cerberus even now. A tall man with broad shoulders and rangy limbs, Kane was said to have something of the wolf about him. He was both a loner and a pack leader as the opportunity arose. His short dark hair was cropped close to his skull, and his gray-blue eyes were the color of gunmetal. Kane had once been a magistrate in the barony of Cobaltville, a post he had abandoned after a run-in with the baron years ago. That had been before Baron Cobalt had been revealed as a hybrid in thrall to the Annunaki, a jealous race of space aliens. The Annunaki had once ruled the Earth in the days before the Bible, when they had been mistaken for gods. Then, as now, their power was circumscribed only by their own infighting.

Though the most recent threat from the Annunaki was past, the repercussions were still being felt. Indeed, this ramshackle refugee settlement that lurked outside the tiny fishing ville of Hope on the West Coast of America was one example of the disruption that the Annunaki had caused, uprooting numerous people as nothing more than collateral damage in a war between would-be space gods.

And in a roundabout way, Kane was here because of the Annunaki, too. One of their number, Ullikummis, a prince of the royal family, had staged a devastating attack on the Cerberus headquarters, imprisoning its occupants and destroying much of the technology that they had come to rely upon. Eventually Kane and his allies had rallied and dealt with Ullikummis, dispatching him via interphaser into the heart of the sun, a death from which even the wily Annunaki prince could never escape. But the Cerberus redoubt remained in a state of flux, operating at 60 percent efficiency with just 40 percent of its tech online. Kane was here in Hope to change that. Rumor had it that a cache of prenukecaust military-grade technology was being employed by one of the lowlifes here to gouge their fellow refugees.

Kane had dressed in a battered denim jacket with frayed cuffs, dark pants and a pair of scuffed-up boots that looked as if they had seen better days. It was an act, of course—beneath the tired clothes, Kane wore something better: his shadow suit. The shadow suit was a highly advanced environmental suit that could regulate his body temperature no matter where he found himself, and it had a weave with armorlike properties that offered protection from environmental threats. Still, it didn't pay to look wealthy—or even comfortable—in a shantytown like this. Better to look as though you had nothing left to steal than to tempt the locals to come check.

Kane halted at the junction of four pathways, ramshackle two-story buildings lurking overhead in bent forms as if bowing in nightmarish salutation. Even at this time of the morning, with the sun just beginning to warm the Californian desert that loomed at the edge of the camp, the streets were busy with urchins and gaudies plying their trades. Unusual, underage, unfathomable—it was all freely available in places like this, and it didn't take much effort to find it. As an ex-magistrate, the place sickened Kane. People deserved better than this. The Program of Unification had brought humankind back from the brink of barbarism; to see those efforts turned to naught in places like this left Kane angry and frustrated. The problems were too big here. Cerberus could rally against a space-alien attack, but it struggled to cope with the thousands of uprooted refugees with nowhere left to go and a burgeoning crime fraternity that was more than happy to prey on easy marks.

The place was up ahead, a twin-story joint, clad in mismatched sheets of corrugated steel with narrow windows that were little more than slits. There was a symbol painted across the only door—a heavy slab of steel-plated concrete with a tiny eye slit that could be pulled back to check who was outside. Painted in a vibrant yellow, the symbol showed a stylized cloud with two circles arranged beneath it, one above the other. Imagination.

From his spot at the junction, Kane looked at the door for a moment, guessed it was at least six inches thick. The whole thing probably had to be worked on cantilevers just to get it to move; there was no way of passing through it unannounced.

But then Kane wasn't going in the front door.

THE STEERING WHEEL felt like a living thing as Brigid wrestled with its faux-leather grip, pulling the Turbo around in a hard right as another laser blast cut the road just a few yards behind her. Her eyes flicked to the mirror, back to the road, then to the mirror again.

The skyway was forty feet above ground level with solid concrete barriers on either side and nothing but ocean beneath her. There was nowhere for her to jump out and no option to turn off until she reached the next exit, and that was another mile and a half away.

120 miles per hour.

At the speed she was doing right now, she'd hit that exit in under a minute, but she could sense that wouldn't be soon enough. Her eyes flicked to the rearview mirror once more. Behind her, another gun turret had appeared on the rooftop of one of the pursuing vehicles with a third just materializing atop the last. She winced as the lasers came to life, twin beams burning through the air in bloodred streaks.

How had she got herself into this situation? Something about stealing plans to some piece of tech for Cerberus, she couldn't remember what it was. No, wait. That was wrong. Brigid had an eidetic memory, didn't she? Which meant...

"Shit!" Brigid cursed as another streak of laser light burned through the air just six inches from her side window, disintegrating her wing mirror. They were closing in on her.

Brigid wrenched the wheel again, switching her foot to the brake at the same time and bringing the Turbo 190 into a skid at breakneck speed. The car hurtled sideways for two dozen feet as the laser beams streaked past it, before Brigid gunned the engine once more and brought its nose back in line with the road. A triple laser burst burned the tarmac where she had been, but her stuttered speed caught her pursuers out and they overestimated where she would be.

The roadway bumped along beneath her squealing tires

as Brigid jostled along the street, speeding toward the off-ramp. The city map just wouldn't come back to her.

"Come on," she muttered to herself. "Remember where you are."

KANE TOOK ANOTHER ALLEYWAY parallel to the building, stepping over a pool of something unguessable. The pool was colored a putrid green and had a film of grease over it.

As he turned the corner, he came face-to-face with a tall man dressed head to toe in rags with a bandanna pulled low and a neckerchief pulled high, leaving just his dark eyes on show. Kane tried to step aside but the man stopped him.

"Private party," the figure in rags said in a growl, and Kane saw that a blaster had materialized in his hand from somewhere beneath his ragged robes. "Turn back, *muchacho.*"

Kane took a step back and turned as if to leave. Then, in a blur of motion, his right fist swung around and he socked the man in the face, striking his nose in a hard thump. "No can do, *'muchacho.'*"

The surprised guardsman stumbled backward, crunching against the wall as his broken nose caved in, blood streaming down his face behind the neckerchief.

Kane didn't let up. Already he was stepping close to the man, sweeping his left arm in a rapid arc that knocked the man's pistol out of his hand. The blaster sailed through the air before coming to an abrupt halt against the far wall.

"By dose," the gunman was muttering. "You broke by dose."

"Yeah," Kane agreed as he delivered another brutal punch into the man's face. The man's neck snapped back with the blow and he slumped to the ground, his head lolling back against the wall.

There wasn't a lot of time, Kane knew. He checked the guardsman, lifting his eyelids to make certain he was unconscious. He was.

Then Kane grabbed the man by his legs and dragged him into the nearest doorway, leaving him hidden there in the shadows as best he could. It was all about speed now. Smart guy back there was out for the count, giving Kane maybe five or ten minutes to get in, check what he was looking for and get out.

Kane wound his way down the narrow alleyway until he reached the door he was after. The building backed onto the one he had observed with the corrugated steel walls, but this one was a single story. The door was similar to the big steel-and-concrete one he'd seen at the front of the building, six thick inches of protection for whatever was inside and no handle showing on the exterior.

With a swift glance behind him to make sure he was still alone, Kane reached into an inside pocket of his jacket and pulled loose a tiny charge no bigger than a ball bearing. The charge had an adhesive strip on the back, and Kane pulled off the backing and slapped it in place against the door, about where he figured the lock to be.

He stepped back then, turning his head and placing his fingers in his ears as the charge went off. There came a boom like a bass drum and the bright flash of propellant as the explosive went off. Hope was the kind of place where shit happened, which meant no one took much notice of explosions or blasterfire or the screams of women.

"Gotta love hell on Earth," Kane muttered when no one came to investigate the noise. He turned back to the door and strode through the cloud of black smoke that was churning through the tight alley. Then he was at the door. It was still standing, though a gaping hole now rested where the lock had been, cutting all the way through the door and into the interior. Kane reached for it, felt the heat simmering from the hole and thought better of it. He drew back and kicked at the door where his charge had hit, kicking away the red-hot debris with a few swift blows. Then he reached his whole arm through the door, using his jacket sleeve to protect him from the worst of the hot metal and concrete, and pulled the door toward him from the inside.

It was dark within and it took a moment for Kane to adjust his eyes. The only lighting came from red-orange strips laid almost at ground level, casting the room in a vermillion gloom. The pungent scent of the explosive was dissipating already, leaving another scent behind it, one that hung heavy in the air. It was the smell of glist—that oddly familiar scent of children's candy; only, not the candy itself but the scent that lingered in your nostrils like an aftertaste when you ate too much, that smell that came when you tried to stifle a candy burp.

There was noise, too, a kind of whimpering as if someone—no, lots of someones—were afraid. It was the sound of fear and it sent a shiver up and down Kane's spine. He recognized it all too well from his days as a hard-contact magistrate.

Kane's vision was adjusting now, and he could make out the room better. It was a box of a room, windowless with stacked crates that made it feel smaller than it really was.

Warily, Kane took another step down the center aisle, pulling the ruined door closed behind him. They weren't crates, he saw now, but cages, with wire grills across their fronts and sides, stacked one atop the other like at a vet's or a research lab. Each crate contained a human-looking mutie.

"Help me," one pleaded from a wire crate too close to Kane's left.

"Free us," another called from a few feet overhead.

Yeah, gotta love hell on Earth, Kane thought bitterly.

Chapter 3

"How can you resist a sight as beautiful as that?" Grant asked, his thunder-deep voice echoing inside the helmet he wore.

Sitting behind him, Shizuka—samurai warrior and Grant's lover for the past few years—craned her neck to peer past his shoulder and through the cockpit displays of the Manta craft that he was piloting toward their destination. The sun was just appearing through the peaks of the Panamint range on the west side of Death Valley, a glowing ball of yellow-whiteness in the clear blue sky. Shizuka looked for a moment before *tsking* loudly and settling back into her seat.

"What?" Grant asked through the muffling visor of his command helmet. "Are you seriously trying to tell me that's *not* an impressive sight? Seeing something like that is what keeps me going when we're struggling to repel the latest alien invasion from Enlil and his cronies."

Shizuka thrust out her bottom lip and sighed again. She was a beautiful woman, petite framed with skin a luscious golden hue accented with peaches and milk. Her casual clothes of light cotton blouse and pants were colored pale to better offset her golden skin. Her luxuriant blue-black hair brushed the tops of her shoulders and framed her oval face with the precision of a razorblade, and she had full, petaled lips beneath a snub of nose while her eyes held the pleasing upturned lilt of her

Asian ancestry. Shizuka was not a member of Cerberus like Grant, but rather she led their frequent allies, the Tigers of Heaven, from their base in New Edo. A small woman, Shizuka looked comfortable in the rear seat of the Manta where another might seem crushed in. "Yes, it is most satisfying," she allowed, her voice drained of all emotion, "but it does little to make up for the duplicity with which you brought me here."

Grant turned his head as if to look at her from his position in the pilot seat before her. He could not meet her eyes, however, because right now his whole head was encased in the bulbous bronze-hued tactical helmet that entirely encompassed a pilot's skull during operation of the Manta.

Like the pilot's helmet, the Manta aircraft was a metallic bronze in color with the shape and general configuration of seagoing manta rays. Flattened wedges with graceful wings curving out from its body, while an elongated hump in the center of the craft provided the only evidence of a cockpit. The craft's wingspan was twenty yards with a body length of only fifteen feet, and the beauty of their design was breathtaking, an effortless combination of every principle of aerodynamics wrapped up in their gleaming burnt-gold finish. The entire surface of the craft was decorated with curious geometric designs; elaborate cuneiform markings, swirling glyphs and cup-and-spiral symbols. The Manta was alien in design, a transatmospheric and subspace vehicle that had been acquired by the Cerberus team for long-range missions after being discovered by Kane and Grant during one of their exploratory missions. The adaptable vehicles were used mostly for long-range and atmospheric work, but they could also be employed for stealth operations where a significant amount of rapid movement was foreseen.

"I promised we'd spend dawn watching the sunrise over the mountains," Grant reminded defensively. "Far as I can see…"

"Ah, but while those indeed were your words," Shizuka said, cutting Grant off with the same precision with which she handled her sword, "your meaning was deliberately hidden amid suggestions of romance. Instead, we're here to look at a bomb site."

"*Bombs* site," Grant corrected in his rumbling basso. "Plural. Kane, Brigid and I set off quite a few."

Behind him, Shizuka crossed her arms in irritation as Grant guided the sleek aircraft toward a valley between the mountain peaks. A dark smear could be seen down there in the lee of the mountains, three hundred feet long and still smoldering with dark smoke that wisped from the debris.

"Which is hardly my—or anyone's—idea of romance," Shizuka hissed. "Searching through the rubble of a bomb site. Really."

"We trashed an armaments factory here a couple of weeks back," Grant explained, ignoring his girlfriend's complaints, "and Lakesh asked that someone double-check on the wreckage to make sure no one's come back to try to get things up and running again. These people had blueprints not just for blasters but also some anti-tank weapons and a nuke. Don't kid me that you actually want a new batch of illegal weapons out there on the streets, Shizuka. You're not that hard. Besides, Lakesh volunteered me to check it out and you're the best person I could think of to cover my back."

"Since Kane and Brigid are busy on another mission," Shizuka pointed out, but she had a smile on her face.

"Could have asked Edwards," Grant muttered, his

voice lost beneath the noise of the engines. "Coulda, shoulda."

Grant brought the Manta down in a vertical landing, cutting the engines with the familiar whir of the air-spike propulsion units powering down. As the Manta settled, Grant pushed back his flight helmet and peered back at Shizuka, catching the smile on her pretty face. "What?" he asked, his dark brow furrowing in confusion.

"It is admittedly kind of sweet, you asking me to come along," Shizuka told him, "even if it's just a recon mission. We get barely enough time together as it is, and how could I not be flattered to know I'm your number-one choice for backup. Besides, the sunrise was pretty magical."

Grant smiled back, his white teeth bright in his ebony-hued face. "Yeah, it was, wasn't it?" He was a huge man in his mid-thirties, with an impressive bulk that mimicked the mountains that surrounded them right now. The hair on his head had been shaved to stubble and he sported a black goatee-style beard. While he may look intimidating, there was something undeniably soft about Grant; his chocolate-colored eyes contained a wealth of understanding and patience in each fleeting glance.

Grant slid back the cockpit cover and pulled himself out of the pilot's seat and onto one of the wings. Out of his seat, he looked even bigger, with the broad shoulders and long reach of a champion heavyweight. His body was encased in a formfitting shadow suit over which he had added pants and his old magistrate boots. Grant had been a magistrate once like his partner Kane, the two of them working the beat together in Cobaltville until the day they became caught up in a conspiracy whose tentacles reached into every aspect of human history. On that day, Grant had relinquished his position and joined Kane as an outlander, a man with no ville allegiance. Together, the two men had joined the nascent Cerberus organization in their quest to set right the wrongs that were being done to humankind. Alongside their colleague Brigid Baptiste, they had proved unconquerable to any number of foes intent on enslaving the human race.

Crouched on the wing, Grant reached back into the cockpit for Shizuka, helping the dainty samurai woman from her seat before delving into the cockpit once again to retrieve his coat. Grant favored a black leather-style duster coat that reached almost to his ankles. While the coat appeared to be made from leather, it was in fact woven from Kevlar, making it heavier than normal and able to dull the impact of a bullet. In Grant's line of work one could never be too sure when stopping a bullet might become necessary, and the coat had helped save his life more than once.

Grant had settled the Manta on a flat expanse of ground and, together, he and Shizuka made their way down its sloping wing and onto the rough ground below that stood at the edge of the smoldering remains of the armaments factory. The factory was a blackened mess now. A big section was caved in down to the foundations, while other parts remained standing but merely as blackened shells, the walls torn and ragged, struts protruding at odd angles where once they had marked production lines, storage rooms and conveyor-belt units. To the far side, a whole section remained largely intact, its walls charred black from where the fire had raged. And naturally the entire place stank of burning, so much so that Grant put his hand over his nose as he stifled a cough. Grant had been here less than two weeks before, when he and his teammates had put paid to the schemes of one

Jerod Pellerito, an arms dealer who was profiting from the turmoil wrought by the recent chaos in the villes.

Located out here between the mountain peaks, the factory had been inaccessible to all but the most determined. That was the way Pellerito had wanted it, ensuring none of his competitors in the illegal arms trade could sneak up on him and make a smash-and-grab. Almost every transaction had been conducted by helicopter, creating a kind of natural buffer zone from sneaky approaches. It had also meant that when the place had burned, no one had much wanted to stick around to wait for the fires to go out.

The place must have burned for days. For days and days and days, the heat so fierce that none could approach. Even now, the ruins smoldered, dark patches of smoke clinging close to the ground, fluttering away like birds on the wing.

It was little surprise that the factory had crumbled like a house of cards. The place had been built hastily to cheap specifications. Grant's field team had done a swift and effective job of exploding the bomb store within before they departed, leaving Pellerito and his crew high and dry, alive but out of the illegal arms trade—at least until they could secure a new source of product.

There had been a lot of little battles like this lately. In fact, they had been part and parcel of the Cerberus op for as long as Grant could remember, bringing an end to profiteers in misery, be it Billy-boy Porpoise down on the Florida coast or Papa Hurbon and his psychotic voodoo madness out in the Louisiana marshlands. Whatever alien plots might arise from outside the atmosphere, it seemed man remained quite capable of devising new and devilish ways to hurt his brethren.

The wind channeled up the valley with a banshee

howl, churning up flecks of ash and making them dance on the air in elaborate swirling patterns. It resembled a swarm of insects hovering just a few feet above the ground, as if pollinating the bomb site; the macabre pollinators of destruction.

Grant led the way toward one of the standing structures, remaining alert to the possible presence of others.

"You really did a number on this place, huh, Grant-san?" Shizuka said as she waded through the ankle-deep ashes of the north edge of the factory.

"Blame Kane," Grant told her. "It was his idea."

Shizuka looked around, making a show of admiring the wanton destruction that had leveled a vast chunk of the factory and left the rest uninhabitable. "Yup, that's what the evidence indicates," she teased. "Kane sure does like to be subtle, doesn't he?"

Grant didn't respond. He was busy thinking about Kane, wondering how his brother-in-arms was getting along in Hope without him.

The thing about setting off a bomb in a munitions factory is that it sets off everything it touches, which in turn sets off everything that *that* touches, and so on. Before you know it, you have a raging fire with explosions going off left, right and center. Looking around, Grant figured that at its peak the fire had probably topped one thousand degrees Fahrenheit. As such, it was a surprise to see that a good third of the factory appeared to have survived, though there was smoke damage running up its walls.

Grant slogged through the knee-deep ash, making his way toward the remaining section. Behind him, Shizuka was kicking her way through the mounds of ash, searching for evidence of anything that hadn't been damaged, anything worth taking. There were a few shards of metal, the metal skeleton of a swivel chair, a couple of handblasters that had survived the explosions intact, albeit with their tooling melted to an amorphous mess across their surfaces. It was reassuring, finding the blasters here like that—it suggested that no one had been back to check the place over for whatever they could scavenge.

Kicking soot over one of the pistols, Shizuka looked up, admiring Grant's impressive form as he strode into the section of the factory that was still standing. Despite his size, Grant moved like a jungle cat, silent, his muscles in a sleek, almost liquid flow. He stepped through the charred remains of a doorway, and she watched him go before following moments later.

The remaining area was made up of a few walled sections, and a cursory glance suggested to Grant that it was largely a storage area for the various products that the factory had been producing. The rooms were arranged a little like a honeycomb, small containment areas each holding their own product type. Grant stepped into one at random, picking up a box containing newly minted pistols, flipping through the box's contents with swift disinterest. It was strictly professional, his being here, just like his days as a magistrate. The explosions had done too much damage to leave anything worth the effort of recovering for Cerberus— even guns like these were valueless without ammunition.

Grant tossed the box back on its shelf and stepped back out of the room. Shizuka was waiting a little way down what remained of the smoke-damaged corridor, a sooty streak across her nose, a smile on her lips.

"Find anything?" she asked.

"Blasters, a stash of knives, some other crap," Grant told her. "Nothing we need. But maybe someone else does, so I'm tending toward the opinion that we should set a new round of charges here before we leave."

"Could have just bombed it from the air," Shizuka reasoned.

"And hit some family hiding out here for shelter from the cold desert nights? Leave some kid an orphan?" Grant shook his head. "No. It's a pain in the ass, but we have to check these things."

Shizuka nodded, and she skipped the remaining steps to meet him, reaching for Grant as he turned to check what the next area held. Grant turned back and found Shizuka looking up into his eyes, admiration in her eyes. "That's why I love you, Grant-san," she said. "That's why I love you."

ONE FLOOR ABOVE, three people were standing around a computer terminal, illuminated by its jury-rigged screen. The computer was blackened with smoke damage and the terminal had melted along one side, leaving the plastic in a smear. From the way the melting droplets had solidified, at a glance they appeared to be still dripping.

The man and two women were dressed in strange clothes, completely at odds with the twenty-third century that they had emerged into. The man wore a long swallow-tailed coat in rich wine-red; the women, sumptuous dresses whose skirts flared out from their waists, reaching down to hide their ankles and brush the floor with a shushing sound like autumn leaves in the wind.

The man, the same dark-haired individual whom Jake and Milo had spotted toying with a puppet, worked at the melted keyboard of the computer terminal with two fingers, gliding across its surface in a series of seemingly effortless gestures.

Antonia, with dark hair trailing halfway down her back and wearing a cream-colored dress, which had a daring cut that drew a man's attention to her ample décolletage, used one cream-colored silk glove to wipe the charcoal smear from the exterior window and peer outside. "I am undoubtedly certain that that wasn't there before," she said, eyeing the edge of the Manta where one bronze wing could be seen peeking past the side of the ruined factory.

Beside her, the other woman, whose golden locks were a match in length to Antonia's and who wore a dress of shot-silk pink and blue whose color changed as she turned her body, shook her head. "But what could it be, Antonia? I have never seen such a thing before."

Antonia looked at the blonde woman and smiled mischievously. "Perhaps it emerged out of the ground, like us, Cecily?" she proposed. "Perhaps it wishes to be our friend?"

Cecily's clear blue eyes searched around the smoke-damaged surfaces as though looking for something. "Well, I'm hardly dressed for company," she remarked. "I didn't even bring a hat."

Antonia shook her head in despair. "Any visitor who is offended by the sight of one's unclad head is never worth accepting as one's friend."

The two women began to make their way to the door, which hung from its hinges, the frame splintered and blackened from the fire.

The man at the terminal peered over his shoulder and called them back. "Antonia? Let Silly go exploring. I've discovered something here that may require your skills."

Antonia placed one creamy glove to her breast as if her heart fluttered beneath it. "Oh! To hear such words from you, a man so capable as to shame Great Alexander himself."

"How you mock me, Antonia," the dark-haired man said, a twinkle in his eye, "with your rapier tongue and turn of hip. And yet, I find myself bemused by this information machine. You were always so good with the WarCreche, and this slow-thinking device seems of similar pedigree."

The dark-haired man gave Cecily a firm look. "Silly—find Algie before you go exploring. He's downstairs somewhere, fiddling with something—I forget what."

Cecily nodded. "Of course, dear Hugh. It wouldn't do for a lady to be found exploring unescorted."

So while Cecily went to find Algernon and investigate the Manta, Antonia remained with dark-haired Hugh, teasing the damaged terminal back to life. They were geniuses all, and doing the near-impossible came as easily as taking a breath.

On screen, a blueprint flashed to life, showing the cylindrical shape of a bomb with fins jutting from the rear and a nose cone sharp as a tack. The design showed how the bomb was constructed, how it could be powered and where the nuclear payload was to be placed. It was a design that fascinated Hugh Danner, first superman of the British Empire, as it materialized before his eyes.

Chapter 4

Muties.

Kane stood in the claustrophobic room and stared at the stacked cages, doing a swift count in his head. Two rows of three-by-three cages, plus six more by the far door—twenty-four cells in all, all but two of them occupied.

Stripped naked and locked in tiny cages so small that they had to crouch because there was no room either to stand or to lie down, each figure was the size and shape of a human. Hell, they were human, only not quite; something in their genetic makeup had gone awry. Their skin was pink, the same dark shade of pink that Kane went if he caught too much sun, and it glistened with sweat, thick beads of it like saliva on their arms and legs and chests, the way a horse sweats. Some had hair on their heads or protruding from their bodies, but it was straggly, a few long strands budding from their skulls like those of an old man or someone after chemo. Kane had no doubt that there were males and females here, but it was hard to tell the difference, even stripped naked as they were. Under the orange glow of the lights, their naked bodies looked stark, the shadows sharp and abrupt, nowhere to hide, no way to cover themselves up.

Their eyes were wide as they stared at Kane, and they were human eyes with irises of green or blue or brown, whites around them just like a person's. Only humans had eyes like that; no animals had white that way.

But they had no eyebrows, and their lips were cracked and dry. They called to Kane from those lips, crying out from throats turned raw from mistreatment or simply from lack of use. There were many different strains of muties, but these were all the same, Kane recognized—they were called "Betties" on the streets, among people who knew about muties and what they could do.

The cages featured big bottles on the sides, locked to the outside and upturned with a hard plastic straw that bent inside the cage so that the sweating muties could drink. The straw worked by a simple valve to ensure that the prisoner had to suck at it to get any water—or more likely a glucose solution to keep them healthy, Kane suspected. He'd seen this kind of setup before.

Around him, the muties shrieked for attention, their raised voices sounding like wild animals fearing for their lives. In a way, Kane guessed, they were.

A lot of people thought muties were dead by the twenty-third century. Most, even. The world had been transformed by the Program of Unification by then, people resettled within the mighty towering villes that divided the old territories of the United States of America. As such, they had lost touch with what the nukecaust had wrought two hundred years before—with its brood of radioactive children, each turned from man to beast or beast to something worse in the era that had become known colloquially as the Deathlands.

Mutants—or "muties"—had been the consequence of the nuclear fallout that had swept across the globe, new products of the old weave of DNA. But while the muties had been hunted down and culled, they yet survived as loners or in small enclaves of hideous, godless things with extra eyes or scaled flesh, rogue limbs and razor teeth. Some mutations had helped them to survive.

In his role as a magistrate, Kane had crossed paths with a few muties. Not many. They kept to themselves these days, hiding in the shadows, well away from man. Seeing a load of muties here like this, twenty-two of them in all, was likely the result of a raid on a single settlement out in the desert, well away from human eyes where the muties had felt they were safe.

There were sodium-orange strip lights arranged in double rows close to the floor. No, not lights, Kane realized as he took a closer step—they were portable heaters. There were a dozen or more of the heaters arrayed in close succession, warming the cages and their occupants, forcing them to sweat and to keep sweating. It was sweltering hot in here, like noon in the desert, but Kane's shadow suit had automatically compensated, cooling his body without preamble.

The people who had put the muties here wanted them to sweat.

Little wonder, since it was that sweat that created the glist, a potent hallucinogen that could trigger powerful visions in anyone who imbibed it. Anyone human, that was. The drug naturally had no effect on the muties themselves, although it had inspired one of their crueller nicknames in the outlander communities—Sweaties. They were known by a few names, some more respectful than others. Sweaty Betties, or more simply Betties, was most popular, especially among the drug-using community. Kane was an ex-magistrate, so he didn't dabble in things like that, but he had had experiences with the kind of lowlifes who did, knew the way they spoke, the slang they used. You couldn't be an effective mag without knowing your enemy—a truism of all law-enforcement was that the law's enforcers and the people who broke laws were always trying to stay one step ahead of each other.

The room stank of the sweat, that thick, viscous sweat that poured from their bodies in great rivers to be collected by drain channels that ran across the bottom of each cage, gathering the liquid and sending it to a collection tank that stood poised by the wall closest to the door through which Kane had entered. There were two collection tanks there, in fact, wide as barrels, taller than a man and covered over without being properly sealed. Each had a gauge on its side, a little needle residing on a white crescent behind a tiny pane of clear glass or plastic, indicating the volume contained in the tank.

Kane strode over to the two barrels, stood on tiptoe and lifted the cover of the nearest to peek inside. A pungent stink assaulted his nostrils, so strong it made him flutter-blink for a couple of seconds. It smelled of candy or rotting fruit, the sweetness almost too much to process in one hit, the way gasoline can smell fruit-sweet. It was glist. Kane recognized it, wasn't surprised in the slightest. This room was a glist farm; that much was obvious. Dealers would take the muties, incarcerate them and then subject them to high temperatures, not enough to really hurt them but just enough to make them continually sweat.

The room was a collection center for the operation next door, the building that Kane had viewed with the cloud symbol on its door. That place was a dream factory, outlawed by all baronies, but the sort of thing that was hard to keep tabs on. Dream factories created and sold dreams, either as group experiences or, as with the more high-scale ones, on a case-by-case basis. The dreams were tailor-made to generate a mental thrill in the dreamer, who would plug him- or herself into some kind of virtual-reality tech that had been spliced by a tech genius so it could be pumped directly into the brain. The trouble with the setup was that the human brain doesn't fool easily and can usually tell when something isn't real. Which was where glist came in.

Glist was the by-product of a particular sweat reaction in a subspecies of muties who had, for reasons of survival, developed the ability to produce toxin-filled sweat when scared, presumably either to scare away or, in extreme circumstances, poison any predator who came near. The effect of these toxins on the human bloodstream in carefully administered dosages, however, was to fuel elaborate hallucinations.

Coupling glist with the VR tech in a dream factory helped solidify the illusion of the dream being real. In fact, the effect was so absolute that it was not unheard-of for a user to become lost in his or her dream and never reawaken.

Long-term glist abusers had other problems, too. Frequently, their desire centers would get unraveled and they'd begin to show strange sexual tendencies, or to hunger for poisonous foodstuffs. In short, for the users, sometimes the dreams became real.

It burned Kane, seeing people—even muties like these—imprisoned this way. In his role as a Cerberus agent, he fought against such things on a daily basis and on a far grander scale. But right now, he couldn't take the risk of freeing the prisoners. He needed to keep moving; speed was his only advantage.

Kane moved toward the interior door, tensing his wrist tendons in a practised flinch. In less than a second, a weapon had dropped into the palm of his right hand, a compact handblaster that unfurled to a barrel length of approximately fourteen inches as it met with his hand. This was the Sin Eater, a 9 mm semiautomatic that had once served as the official sidearm of the magistrate division. The trigger did not have a guard. Its necessity had never been foreseen, since the magistrates were believed to be above question or error. As such, if the user's index finger was crooked at the time the weapon reached his hand, the pistol would begin firing automatically. Though no longer a magistrate, Kane had retained his weapon from his days in service at Cobaltville, and he felt most comfortable with the weapon in hand. It was a natural weight to him, like an extension of his body, the way a wristwatch seems natural to the wearer.

"Free us," one of the muties pleaded from behind Kane as he strode past. There was desperation in his hoarse voice, a desperation that was hard to ignore.

Kane turned back, perhaps to apologize or explain to the mutie who had requested his help. As he did so, the interior door swung open and a startled figure stood there, staring into Kane's face. "What the—?"

"REMEMBER WHERE YOU ARE," Brigid told herself again as she gunned the Turbo's engine. "Keep heading north."

She was tearing across the skyway at 130 miles per hour, and the car showed no signs of flagging. Behind her, the pursuit vehicles were losing ground as they worked up the elevated street's incline, their laser turrets cycling through their power-up sequences before unleashing another storm of bloodred heat across the blacktop. Brigid bumped over a ruined bit of road as a laser beam split it in two. Sure, she could outrun her pursuers in time, but only if she had a road to drive on.

Brigid wrenched the steering wheel to the right, bumping over another slab of ruined roadway and hurtling past a stalled hatchback so close that they exchanged paint in a shower of sparks.

"Come on," Brigid urged herself. "Forget the escape route—what was your reason for nabbing the codes in the first place?"

Brigid noticed in her rearview that her pursuers were holding back a little, driving three abreast to block the raised street in its entirety. They've called for backup, she realized. They're hemming me in toward it, making sure I can't turn back.

The Turbo 190 roared like an unchained beast as Brigid weaved through the skyway traffic, horns blaring all about her as she cut off the other users of the road. A moment later, the three tanklike pursuit vehicles followed, bumping out of their way anyone who didn't move aside quickly enough, lasers flashing to literally cut a path through the traffic.

Then, up ahead, Brigid saw what they were forcing her toward. It was bigger than her other pursuers, covered in thick armor plate, and it hovered just above the elevated road, great rotor blades cutting the air with a heavy thrum. Painted a glossy black, the Deathbird had two great laser turrets on its underside, front and back, as well as a plethora of bullet-fed chain guns along its sides. Both lasers and chain guns worked on swiveling pivots, sufficient to cover all fields of fire between them.

Twelve seconds to impact, the lasers were cycling around to pinpoint her. *Eleven seconds. Ten.* Brigid eyed the Deathbird, estimating the clearing distance beneath its skids. There wasn't enough. Even if she managed to somehow outlast the lasers and all that other hardware the thing was packing, she simply couldn't make the route.

Nine seconds.

Frantically, Brigid scoured up ahead, searching for all

options. The road curved back toward the main body of the island just behind the chopper, an off-ramp located tantalizingly close, less than fifty yards beyond. Brigid's eyes flicked back to the Deathbird, then beyond, spotting the reason that the road veered back landward. There was a building there, some kind of shipyard admin building by the look of it, a great towering thing like a glass knife thrust into the earth by some almighty god.

Eight. The lasers were starting to glow as the power began firing through them, a ruby slash cleaving through the air toward her.

There was a trick she was beginning to recall, a trick she had learned when she was just a little girl, and one she had never stopped using. It was coming back to her now. All of it.

Brigid powered the automobile toward the barrier, pulling at the steering wheel as if she was wrestling with a bear. Beneath her, the tires screamed and she felt the car begin to roll.

IN THE RED ROOM of caged muties, Kane reacted without conscious thought. His hand came up, bringing the Sin Eater blaster in an arc that ended in the stranger's face.

The stranger reacted almost as quickly. Indeed, Kane could only marvel at the speed of the man's reactions. The figure was dressed in light clothes, cotton pants and shirt, the latter open to midway down his chest, revealing a tanned and muscular torso. The man's dark hair was gelled back and he wore a long knife on a low-slung holster at his waist. Kane guessed the man was in his early twenties, hired for muscle and grunt work.

As Kane's blaster came up, the other man threw whatever he had been balancing in both hands at him. Kane stepped aside as a box full of spare parts came flying at him. The throw was off, but it didn't matter, it had given his opponent that precious split second to step back from the line of fire before Kane could deliver a bullet to his skull.

"Damn!" Kane cursed as the man ducked back into the next room, pulling the door back. With his free hand, Kane snatched the door's edge before it could slam shut, automatically raising his blaster to cover the gap.

Cotton Shirt-and-Pants was already down the end of a short corridor that was little more than a cupboard, yanking at the far door and raising the alarm. "Intruder!" he called. "Back inna storeroom."

The storeroom. Yeah, that's all these muties' lives were to these people, just another "product" they stored until a customer arrived to purchase it, their lives nothing more than figures on a profit tally. Kane hated them then, hated the whole operation that existed here in the heart of the refugee camp, preying on people who had nothing left but dreams, giving them nothing but fake lives and false hope.

It was bright here. Sin Eater raised, Kane took a long two steps through the cupboardlike connecting space between the two buildings, pulling up short as he reached the door. The corridor here, what little of it there was, was covered in molded transparent plastic, its dirty roof letting daylight in. It was a shock after the darkness of the mutie pen, and Kane took the extra few seconds to let his eyes adjust before he tried the far door.

It was dark again in the next room and the place had a definite aroma of sweat—not mutie sweat, but human sweat, the smell of a lot of people in a confined and poorly ventilated space. There was mist, too, obscuring Kane's vision, and what light sources he could see were blurred by the smoke. There were a few light sources arrayed before him, a whole bank of them at waist height, a circlet of them higher up as though attached to the room's low ceiling.

Someone shouted from up ahead of Kane and to his left; a man's voice. "He's coming. Deren—Alana—take him."

There was the familiar *click-clack* of automatic weapons, of safeties being unlocked. Kane ducked back before the blasters fired, and a volley of bullets slapped against the door as he pulled it toward him for cover. Kane knew the pattern—they would fire, then they would wait to see if he shot back, and if he did they would fire again until somebody died.

"Time to change the tune," Kane murmured to himself.

Then he wrenched the door toward him and dived through the opening. Behind him, another burst of fire echoed through the mist-enshrouded room, the bullets smacking against the open door and the narrow corridor beyond. But Kane was moving swiftly now, his mind in the zone, his body acting almost on instinct. He scrambled across the room in a running crouch, his head tucked low to his body, the Sin Eater's barrel stretched out before him like a warning.

The room was large and ill lit, and Kane would estimate it took up almost all of the ground floor of the building that he had spied from the outside. He had entered by the back, but immediately his professional gaze took in the other exits—two in all, one at the front of the building, directly opposing his entryway, where what looked to be a curtained-off lobby area had been constructed. A second exit was over to the far right of the room, the door ajar and bright light nudging out from within.

The bulk of the room, however, was taken up by the

two dream engines that served as the heart of the operation. They looked like giant water lilies, residing close to the hard stone floor with six sloping petals emerging from the central hub. Each petal was as large as a single bed and it contained a person lying supine— a dreamer. The dream engines featured a strip of pale blue lights along their bottom edge, which ran around the base of the flowerlike creation, coloring the room a kind of midnight-blue, like an old day-for-night shot from a cheap horror flick. Above them, a second strip of circular lights could be seen, emerald-green and forming a much tighter circle where the dream unit fed the sleepers their neoreality visions. Great pipe work connected the two sections, with plantlike growths depending from the ceiling unit, hanging in the air the way that jungle vines will curl down from the trees.

The engine was really what Kane was here for. Sure, closing down an operation like this one, which preyed on the unwary and battery-farmed mutie subhumans, sat well with Kane's conscience. But it was Cerberus that he was here for—with their recent upset at the hands of the Annunaki prince Ullikummis, replacing their destroyed technology was becoming a very necessary and urgent requirement. Cerberus could function sufficiently, but the need for replacement equipment had become pressing. This operation, built around prenukecaust military-grade computer simulations, had a load of gear that could be better employed upgrading Cerberus and bringing Kane's people back up to full functionality. That was, of course, assuming he could survive this little spat.

Another bullet came whizzing across the room, cutting the air in front of Kane's face as it raced past. They had lost track of him as he ducked behind the closest of the dream engines, and the low light here gave Kane a minor degree of camouflage in his dark clothes. He checked around the room from his hiding spot, counting off his opponents as he located their positions.

There was a woman ducked behind a counter, wielding some kind of handblaster. The counter was well lit by a low desk lamp, and while Kane couldn't see the shade, the illumination cast stark shadows behind the wall, drawing in the woman's curves and her pistol with remarkable clarity.

Then there were at least two more people over the other side of the room and one of them was using the other dream engine for cover. Kane pegged that for Deren, the slick-haired man who had bumped into him in the sweatbox. He was reaching to retrieve something from a containment unit close to the dream engine, and Kane saw his bare arms unlatch its door. He could maybe shoot the guy in the arm, but there was too much cover between them, not to mention the risk of hitting the dreamers with a stray shot or a ricochet. Kane watched the man pull a bulky black metal tube from the cupboard, the familiar length of a shotgun, before he continued sweeping the room with his gaze. While he scanned with furtive eyes, Kane's ears kept track of the man's actions, identifying the sound of the breech of the shotgun being opened, shaky hands trying to load it.

Kane's eyes swept the room, spotting the third figure moving close to the lobby, along with two other figures who were just waiting there, oblivious to the firefight that was building just a few feet from them. Dream addicts, Kane figured, their minds so blown out by their abuse of the dream engines that they could no longer delineate clearly between reality and hallucination. The other figure, however, was moving with purpose. Dressed in a long dress or skirt—it was hard to tell in the low light—the thin figure took heavy steps as it moved about the room.

Three then, plus the guard outside that he'd already taken care of. Fair odds for an ex-mag.

As well as his training, Kane had an added advantage. Back when he had been a magistrate, he had been renowned for something his associates called his "pointman sense," an almost preternatural ability to sniff out danger before it happened. While the talent had often amazed his colleagues, in actuality there was nothing particularly superhuman about it—the danger sense stemmed simply from Kane's ability to use his other senses in conjunction with a near Zen-like awareness. The fact that Kane was adept at using this ability in even the most tense of combat situations had saved his life more than once.

Crouching beside the sleepers in the dream engine, Kane targeted the counter girl with his Sin Eater, snapping off a quick burst. The bullets struck the counter, drumming across its facade in a warning. Behind the counter, the girl's silhouette ducked lower and Kane saw the blaster shaking in her grip.

"Nice try, big man," she taunted. "There's no way out of here, you know. Not alive." She was trying to sound tough, but could not disguise the tremor in her voice.

Kane figured that fear would keep her where she was for now, reducing the risk of her shooting him in the back.

Kane moved, gracefully pulling himself up from his crouch and drawing a bead on the shotgun wielder. Kane didn't like shotguns; they were messy and dangerous, and even in an amateur's hands they had the potential of creating a lot of damage. The figure behind the second dream engine was still resting on his backside, frantically loading his weapon. He came up, bringing the blaster around to fire just as Kane rounded the edge of the dream engine.

Kane shot first, a single shot striking the long barrel of the shotgun with the ringing clang of metal against metal. Deren—if that was his name—dropped the blaster with a startled curse, but he reacted swiftly for all that. As Kane leaped at him, the man revealed a second blaster from his left hand, a little hold-out pistol just a couple of inches in length, the kind of weapon a professional gunman would have as backup strapped to his ankle.

Kane's leg kicked out, striking the gunman in the wrist even as he raised the weapon. The gunman held on to the blaster but he was surprised by the blow, and it took him a moment to recover. Kane delivered the follow-through by then, striking down with the leg he'd used to kick the man and using the momentum to spring up into the air in a running leap before bringing his other leg around in a brutal kick to the man's breastbone. Kane's opponent let out his breath in a *whoof* that sounded like gas catching light, falling backward against the dream engine that loomed behind him.

From across the room, a man's voice was calling shrilly, "Careful! Don't damage the dreameries!"

Kane landed and turned, all as one slick, athletic movement, bringing the Sin Eater's muzzle around as he targeted the voice by sound alone. His finger stroked the trigger, sending a triple burst across the gloomy room, kicking up flash-sparks as they struck the walls and floor. But his target was gone, hurrying across the room with the swoop of a long dress.

It was getting messy, Kane knew. There was too much risk now, and damaging the tech wasn't an option. He had to finish this—fast.

Kane ran, leaping over the outcropping of the nearest dreamer's crib, his blaster stretched out before him, searching for a target in the darkness.

Crack!

Something struck Kane from the left, slamming against his side with the force of a charging bull. Despite himself, he felt his legs give and suddenly he was crashing to the floor. Kane struck the floor with a crunch, his jaws clacking shut as his lower jaw smacked against stone.

He had written off the woman too easily. She was scared, but she'd managed to stop shaking long enough to wing him.

For a moment he saw the room spin, the dull, bluish light making it seem like the ocean, as if he had been dumped at sea. Kane's mind reeled, trying to cling to consciousness. His eyelids wouldn't stay open.

"Look, do you see?" The woman's voice was close, tremulous with adrenaline. "His blaster. He's a magistrate."

Something struck Kane hard in the side of his ribs; it felt like the toe of a shoe and it was directed with savage expertise.

"That's not a mag." This time it was a man's voice. "They don't come to this part of Hope."

The woman spoke again. "But he's using a Sin Eater. I recognize it." She sounded young.

"Well," the man replied, "we'll find out soon enough. Go see to Deren, Alana, while I figure out what we're going to do with our visitor here."

Kane felt the foot again as it kicked him in the side, in the exact same spot as before. Then something heavy crashed against his skull and after that he didn't know what.

Chapter 5

Accelerator pressed to the Turbo's floor, Brigid Baptiste held the wheel locked as far as it could turn even as the first of the Deathbird's laser beams sliced through the street in a bloodred streak. Light and nippy though the car was, the Turbo had a heavy engine. Brigid was counting on that— once it began to roll, it would keep going.

Another crimson beam of energy cut the air before her, blasting just six inches in front of the windshield and casting the whole interior of the car in a bloody red glow. She clung on for dear life as the vehicle slammed against the crash barrier and flipped, leaving the road entirely as it twirled through the air. Amid the shrieks of lasers and the rat-a-tat of the conventional guns, the barrier strike seemed soundless.

Then she was upside down with the car still flipping, its heavy engine drawing it slowly along its x-axis even as it flipped again 420 degrees along its lengthwise y-axis.

She couldn't picture the map to the city because there was no map, Brigid recalled now. There was no map, no history. An hour ago she had entered a dingy little shack in the back street squats of Hope and paid a man to pump her with glist and send her on a journey into the *traum wirklichkeit*. If she worked at it, thought about it, she could still taste the glist on her breath, smell the room with its months-of-sweat stink, like a locker room.

Her false reality played on all around her, feeling no

different to any other experience she had ever had. The Turbo 190 flipped again as it left the road entirely. Another blast from the chopper sawed clean through the hood with a scream. The view through the windshield spun with such speed that Brigid could hardly make sense of it, tossed as she was against the restraint of the seat belt. The shipyard building was ahead of her, rushing toward her as she sailed through the air, a great glass knife thrusting up from the street below.

Hovering over the roadway, the Deathbird turned on the spot, bringing its guns around to keep firing at Brigid's cherry-red car. The vehicle was clear of the skyway road now, fifteen feet past the raised crash barriers and beginning to drop as acceleration gave way to gravity. Even as the vehicle spiraled through the air, pulled toward the ground, the front end fell away and plummeted over the edge of the docks toward the ocean, the glow of superheated metal shining like lightning where the laser had cut through it.

The Deathbird fired again, sending bullets in a steady stream at the careening vehicle. Inside, Brigid pulled herself in a ball as best as she could, wincing as the bullets struck the side of the car with the loud report of hail on a tin roof. A moment later the car—or what was left of it—struck the side of the shipyard building in a crash of plate glass, breaking through on the second story and sending a dozen workers running. It skidded across the tiled floor on its right wing for twenty feet before striking a wall and coming to a halt.

Noise was replaced by silence, like an emptiness had come in the wake of the crashing car. Outside, the Deathbird spun in place above the elevated roadway, searching for its target, unable to get low enough or close enough to see where Brigid had landed. The car had left a streak of scuffed paint across the pale floor tiles where it had come through the windows. It looked like a trail of blood, leading to a wounded animal. Office workers were poised around the red wreck, stunned and helpless as they wondered what had just happened.

Inside, Brigid felt one hundred new aches in places she didn't know could hurt. Even if this was a dream, it still hurt like hell. And there was no way of waking up, not with the glist buzzing around her system and the whole VR dream engine feeding information to her brain. She had to play it out or shut it down. There weren't any other options. But then, that's why she was here, wasn't it?

She shifted against the seat restraint, reaching up to the driver's side door where it now sat to her left but also above her. She tried the handle, pushed at the door. The door was heavy, and its springs seemed determined to get it closed again as soon as she had it open more than an inch. She cursed, an incomprehensible shriek of annoyance, then leaned across until she could shove at the door with both hands. After a moment, the door swung open and teetered there, scraping against the ceiling of the room.

It was a lobby, Brigid saw when she climbed free of the wreck. In a moment she was on the floor, eyeing the office workers who watched her with incomprehension. She stood before them, dressed in formfitting black leather that accentuated her sinuous limbs, her long legs ending in heeled boots that came midway up her thighs. Her hair was in disarray from the crash and she shook it back—regretted it instantly when the impact of the crash left her dizzy.

"You need help, miss?" one of the office people asked, tentatively offering Brigid his hand.

Help? No. She just needed to remember everything so

she could run the op the way they'd planned it. Where she was just now, the so-called *traum wirklichkeit,* was a faked reality designed to confuse the senses. Users would enter the dream structures after they'd been primed with glist, the psychedelic drug distilled from mutie sweat, creating a seamless transition from real to dream, where a preset environment was waiting to greet them. The environments varied from dream factory to dream factory, but the principles were always the same—once the user was in the dream he or she should never have cause to question it, even though it was at its core a highly advanced computer simulation. The glist smoothed off the hard edges, making it seem more real, turning the *traum wirklichkeit* into the user's only reality.

In theory, there was no way to awaken from a *traum wirklichkeit* experience until the operators—generally black-market criminal gangs—stepped in to bring a user around. That gave the operators total control of how long a dreamer dreamed, allowing them to charge as much per session as the market could sustain. There wasn't a lot of money in Hope, but addicts always found a way.

However, the system had never been designed to handle an attack from within. No one could foresee a way for an insurrectionist to get into the *traum wirklichkeit* and still be aware that they were dreaming. For a while, Brigid had been lost in the *traum wirklichkeit.* But she had something that most users didn't have—a trick she'd learned back in her childhood and had employed ever since—her eidetic memory. With that, it was hard to fool Brigid for long; take away her memory of recent events and she cast back and recalled them, piecing things together with untold swiftness. She had been lost here for a time, caught up in the dream story she was being sold, the one she had paid credits to participate in, a new world painted on the canvas of computerized simulations developed for the military over two hundred years before. But she had come here with a mission, and recalling who she was and where she was was the first step in fulfilling that mission.

As the shadow of the Deathbird played across the ruined window by the skyway, Brigid stepped away from the car and addressed the gray-suited worker who had offered to help. "Roof access," she demanded breathlessly. "I need to get up to the roof."

Startled, the worker stuttered something, but Brigid grabbed him by both shoulders. "Now," she insisted.

PAIN.

That was the first thing Kane felt. A pain in his side, almost like a bite. It seemed to kick in before he had even woken up, like an alarm chron. He was sitting on a hard chair with his arms wrenched behind his back, hands tied at the wrists, the coolness of a breeze playing against the warm skin of his chest and arms and legs.

"We are the dreamers of the dream," a man was explaining, his voice close by.

With his eyes still closed, Kane surveyed his surroundings to the best of his abilities. It was a room, small room, the echoes of shoe heels against the hard stone floor told him that much. And there were two people here, one of them real close, looming over him and breathing into his face. The breath smelled sweet and strong, like four-day-old tangerine.

Kane opened his eyes, saw the man looking right at him, a desk lamp turned on its swivel arm to blaze at him with sun-bright intensity. The man had dark red skin, or maybe it was just a bad reaction to the sun.

"You have a magistrate's gun," the man began, his face close to Kane's. "Are you a magistrate?"

"Wh-what?" Kane muttered. His mouth felt raw, as if he'd been asleep with it wide-open. He realized why he could feel the breeze now, too—he'd been stripped naked before being tied to the chair, his jacket, pants, shadow suit and boots slung in one corner of the little room. There was a bruise on his left side where the bullet had struck a glancing blow, in line with his bottommost rib. The shadow suit had dulled the impact, deflecting the bullet before it penetrated, but it had still hit like a locomotive. Without the shadow suit, he'd be leaking blood right now.

The room looked like an office, and it was almost big enough to hold the half-length desk that had been crammed against its longest wall, although it was probably a bastard of a thing to get a chair in here to sit at it. The desk was smothered in paperwork, credits tossed casually amid it all like eclectic bookmarks, bags of powder that looked like sea salt. There were pictures over the desk, too. Pictures of ants and locusts with women's bodies—poor renderings done by hand, tacked to the wall.

"A mag's gun," the man repeated, lifting the weapon so that Kane could see it. "Tell me where you got it."

Kane fixed the man with his steely gray stare. "Get bent."

The man's black brows rose in surprise, and then he drew back and slapped Kane across the face. It was a poor slap, no power in it, like the man was scared of hurting him.

The red-skinned man wore a red dress, buttoned high to his throat, with great puffy sleeves and a three-quarter-length skirt. He had an afro haircut, bulging around his face like a great black halo, and a pencil-thin mustache over his top lip. He had a diamond embedded in one of his incisors and it caught the light every time he opened his mouth and breathed four-day-old tangerine in Kane's face.

"You're in no position to fuck with us here, little Chihuahua," the man with the diamond tooth said. "You know who I am?"

Kane looked the man up and down for a long moment, making a show out of it. "Some poor bastard's very disappointing blind date?" he suggested with a smirk.

The man struck Kane across the face again, the slap harder this time. Kane felt the warmth spread across his cheek.

"What? You think you're funny?" the man in the dress challenged. "You think this is all some great big gigglefest?"

There was another figure at the door behind the man, forced to stand almost outside the office because of the lack of space. It was a dark-skinned woman, young and with big breasts that made her T-shirt bulge as though she was smuggling two melons. Her hair was in ringlets, pulled back in a tail that hung from high on her crown. Kane tagged her for the woman behind the counter, figured her for maybe twenty years old.

Which meant there were two people missing: Deren, the guy with the shotgun, and the mook that Kane had coldcocked in the alleyway at the back of the premises. They'd had enough time to strip him, but maybe they hadn't found the mook in the alley yet—maybe Deren was looking for him even now.

As THEY EMBRACED amid the ruins of the smoldering arms factory, Grant felt something hard press against his leg. He pulled away from Shizuka, opening his eyes and peering down. It was the hilt of her sword, tucked as ever in its ornate sheath at her hip. The sword was a *katana,* the weapon of choice for samurai warriors for hundreds of years, dating all the way back to feudal Japan. The twenty-five inches of razor-keen steel were honed to an edge so fine that it sang as it cut the air.

"You ever go anywhere without that?" Grant asked.

"Take me somewhere truly romantic and maybe you'll find out," Shizuka teased, wrinkling her nose.

"*Maybe* I'll find out?" Grant challenged, but Shizuka ignored his implied complaint, pulling him closer to kiss once more.

JUST TWELVE FEET AWAY, a single eye was peering through the gap that had been created in a ruined wall that proudly displayed the mottled spitball evidence of a bomb blast across its surface like some unfathomable work of art. The eye was the blue of polished sapphire, stark and clear as crystal. The eye widened as it watched Grant and Shizuka kiss, before blinking twice, very rapidly, and turning away from the hole in the wall.

"Algie," a woman's voice whispered a moment later, "there are people here. Come quick, see. There are people. I told you there must be."

Behind the blackened wall, Algernon pushed the tails of his leaf-green frock coat aside and stepped up to the hole where his colleague Cecily had been just a moment before. His blond hair had streaks of soot in it and he had tied it back now with a thick black bow that rested low down on the nape of his neck, leaving much of his blond hair artistically loose. He had been working a few minutes before, but Cecily's demands had interrupted that.

"Do you see them, Algie?" Cecily trilled excitedly. "Tell me you see them. I do so fear I might be imagining such things, being stuck in this dreadful place for days like this!"

"Oh, must you make such a performance of everything, Cecily?" the woman called Antonia hissed from behind the two of them as Algernon peeped through the hole. She strode into the ruined room through a doorway that had seen better days. Stepping from the shadows, Antonia brushed at her luxurious mane of dark brown hair, which flowed down past her shoulders to the base of her spine. Those shoulders had been left bare by the daring cut of her cream-colored dress, which had long hems that showed black streaks now where they had dipped in the ash that littered the factory. "Do you not realize how tiresome it becomes?"

Annoyed, Cecily brought her gloved hand up, placing an outstretched finger to her lips. "Quiet, Antonia, there are people here now." The glove stretched past her elbow in the opera style and it was made of white silk that shimmered like moonlight when Cecily moved her arm.

"But we're not finished," Antonia said, paying little attention to the volume of her voice despite her companion's warning. "It would simply be in bad taste for someone to interrupt us now, and we have nothing to present to visitors should they demand it. No cake, no scones. We don't even have tea. Why, they surely would believe us to be barbarians if they found us here in such a lacking state of preparedness."

Cecily dabbed at her coif of blond hair self-consciously as Antonia continued.

"None of which alters the fact that we are neither stuck here nor have we been here so long that you need behave as if we are never to leave," Antonia chastised.

"But the people…?" Cecily began.

"There are people," Algernon confirmed, turning

away from the rude parting in the wall. "Foreigners, too, by the look of them."

"Foreigners?" Cecily's and Antonia's horrified response came in shocked unison.

A fourth figure appeared from the same room where Antonia had strode a minute or so previously, entering via the stairwell on silent tread. It was Hugh Danner, with his collar-length tresses of curling brown hair and a white shirt on the cuffs of which were two shining gold cuff links. "What is all the commotion?" he asked. His voice was honey rich, his tone nonjudgmental.

"Oh, Hugh, it's terrible," Cecily said while Antonia rolled her eyes at the performance. "There are foreigners here, just outside. Two of them. I told you that metal thing meant something. Oh, whatever should we do?"

A smile formed on the thin lips of the man, but it was a cunning smile, like the smile of a reptile. "Why, we should introduce ourselves," Hugh announced. "Without delay."

The clatter of heels on tiling, the swish of leather against her muscles as she ran. It was faultless, it felt so real.

Brigid Baptiste continued to run, driving herself to the staircase that would let her ascend that final floor to the roof. She had ridden the elevator up as far as she could, one story from the top of the dagger blade of a building. The elevators worked, even after she'd driven a ton and a half of sports car into the side of the building. They shouldn't, Brigid knew. The impact should have messed up the whole structure, and at the very least emergency protocols should have kicked in and shut down the system until it could be checked. But it was dream logic, dream physics; sometimes stuff kept working even after it should have stopped. She was counting on that. That, and the strength of her memory.

Boom! The heavy fire door slammed against the wall, the echo of wood against concrete resonating up and down the grim stairwell. There were windows running up one side of the stairwell wall, tall, narrow rectangles that swiveled open on a central spindle. One of them had been propped open and Brigid felt the wind in her hair as she ran past. Damn, but it was real.

"Remember, it's a dream," Brigid reminded herself as she reached for the door that waited at the top of the staircase. Outside, through the arrow-slit windows, Brigid could see the Deathbird waiting, moving through the air like a circling shark, hunting for her. There were more shapes in the distance, appearing over the line that marked out the sea. Where were they coming from? There was no land there, no island. The internal logic didn't work, the simulation and the dream drug were working at cross-purposes, trying to keep things moving forward, responding to her actions.

Brigid shoved against the door, scampered onto the rooftop, the familiar sound of gravel under her boots as perfectly realized as everything else. The Deathbird spotted her, turning its guns on her even as she ran. Was dying in a dream an option? she wondered. Was that something she had known before she took this assignment?

Laser blasts burned the air, carving toward the roof in sizzling lines of heat. Bullets joined them, spitting from the Deathbird's USMGs, kicking up loose gravel where they cut a path across the roof toward the fleeing woman in black. Brigid paid them no mind, focusing only on her destination. She ran, pelting across the rooftop to its edge where the building kneeled against the sea.

Jump! she told herself.

Another blast of laser light, another round of bullets. More Deathbirds swooping toward the building, their shadows stuttered as they crossed the ocean waves. Then Brigid was over the side of the building, arms spread out in a swan dive.

THE TANNED MAN in the red dress had picked up one of the bags of sea salt from the desk and rested it comfortably in his palm as he tore it open. Then he brought the bag up to his face and inhaled, squeezing at the sides of the bag to jostle the contents. It wasn't sea salt, Kane realized. It was glist, what remained after you'd evaporated the water content of the mutie sweat.

"Listen, buddy," said redskin after he'd taken a hit of glist. "My name's Red Mama O'Shumper—you heard of me?"

Kane shook his head once, back and forth. It felt kind of disorienting from where he'd been knocked out. "No. O'Shumper. What is that? Is that Irish? You don't look Irish."

"Ireland, Iceland, Atlantis? What the fuck does it matter with the way things are?" O'Shumper growled.

In a funny way, Kane could see his point. The world had been in a state of flux since the nuclear exchange back at the start of the twenty-first century, and even now the territories seemed to change size and shape quicker than those old African republics of yesteryear.

Smacking the bag of glist back on the desk, O'Shumper angrily slapped the Sin Eater beside it, making the strange insect girls flutter with the breeze. He was a dream addict, Kane realized, most likely in recovery but still running a pesthole like this. Sometimes addicts got too messed up by their time in *traum wirklichkeit,* found it hard to cling on to normality anymore. Their brains got kind of hardwired with the dreams, and their subconscious tried to take over.

"Just execute this mother," the girl in the doorway drawled.

Chapter 6

Arms outstretched, Brigid leaped from the edge of daggerlike glass building, the Deathbird's lasers searing red lines across its silvery facade.

The ocean was the edge of the map, she realized. Like in days of yore, when people had believed the Earth was flat and that the line of the horizon indicated the edge of the world. But there really was an edge to this world, a preconstructed dream environment, its structures bound by the processing power of the aging computer system that ran it.

As another thick red beam cut the air inches from Brigid's scalp, she remembered the car she had driven, picturing it in her mind. The recall was perfect, thanks to her eidetic memory; she could see every sleek line, every highlight, every detail on the dashboard.

And remembering something inside a dream made it real. Can't read a book in a dream without the story playing out before you, can't look at a photo without the photo expanding as far as you need to see. She remembered the car and suddenly it was there, forming around her as another laser beam slashed the air, breaking windows across the building's face.

Brigid's foot was on the accelerator, flooring it as the car materialized, as the Deathbird fired, as the windows shattered, as the ocean roared, as the sirens wailed, as the—

"WASTE OF TIME talking to him," the dark-skinned girl with the impressive chest emotionlessly added as she peered at Kane's naked and bound form from the open office door. "Besides, damn fool tried to shoot me."

O'Shumper fixed his gaze on Kane, the diamond chip in his tooth twinkling in the light as he spoke. "That true? Did you shoot sweet Miss Schnitzler here?"

"I shot *at* her," Kane allowed. "If I'd wanted to shoot her, I would have and we wouldn't be having this shit-bore excuse for a conversation."

"Oh, is that right?" Red Mama O'Shumper asked, leaning close to Kane and breathing that sickly sweet residue of glist in his face. "You know what? You've got ten seconds to tell me what in the name of the barons you were doing and who the hell you're working for."

"Cerberus," Kane said. "You haven't heard of them."

"Cerberus…? Cerberus…?" O'Shumper muttered, rolling the word around in his mind. As he did so, leaning back against his overloaded desk, a cry came from the door.

"Red Mama? We have a— What you call it?— I think we have a—a situation building out here." It was a man speaking, and Kane saw the figure peering past the girl—Deren of the shotgun.

"What kind of situation?" O'Shumper asked, a sharp edge of irritation to his voice.

"Engine A's going nuts," Deren explained. "I don't—"

"Alana?" O'Shumper said, looking at the dark-skinned girl. "You go check this thing over."

Alana Schnitzler lingered in the doorway for a moment, gazing over Kane where he sat naked in the chair. "Sure."

"You should go with her," Kane suggested as the girl withdrew from the doorway. "The situation's going to get very rapidly worse and you're going to want to be there to see it."

"What?" O'Shumper growled. "What are you talking about?"

"That thing that's going on," Kane told him gently, "that's my partner. She's about to, uh, put an end to your dreams. You'll want to see it happening. You won't get the chance again."

"That so?" O'Shumper snarled, leaning close to Kane as he reached for something on his desk. "'Cause you'll never see it."

Quickly, O'Shumper took the bag of glist clutched in his fingers and tossed the contents over his outstretched palm, raised it up and blew. Kane reared back as he realized what had just happened, but it was already too late—he had received a faceful of glist. The damage had already been done.

"Sweet dreams, *effendi*," O'Shumper taunted as he wiped the remaining glist from his hands and left the room.

Kane swayed back and forth in his seat, holding his breath. Refined and pure like this, glist could have a savage psychotropic effect on anyone who imbibed it, and while the preferred method of consumption was as a food supplement or mixed into a drink, breathing it in had just the same effect. Kane didn't know how much had hit him before he thought to hold his breath, but he could already feel his heart speeding up, thumping against his chest. He figured he had maybe thirty seconds, a minute at the outside, before he was fully in the glist's embrace.

Work fast, Kane told himself, a strict voice inside his head.

He pulled at the bonds that held his hands tied, felt them strain. He spent enough time in the Cerberus gym, as well as the proxy gym of his adventurous and often unbelievable life. He could do this.

One…

Two…

Three…

Snap!

The cord broke, unraveling in a second as Kane yanked his wrists free. He leaped out of the chair; they hadn't bothered to restrain his legs, just tied his hands with a cord that looped across his chest.

Kane barely glanced at the desk as he snatched up his Sin Eater where the cross-dressing O'Shumper had left it unguarded. "Amateurs," Kane sniffed, his eyes already on the open door, peering out to the main room, where the dream engines throbbed.

The glist was beginning to whir around his body now, he could feel its energy in his bloodstream. Without the connection of the dream engine, he wouldn't enter the shared state of *traum wirklichkeit,* but he would start to lose touch with reality, begin to hallucinate. Thirty seconds. Maybe twenty left.

Kane stepped out of the office, his head throbbing. The dimness of the room beyond seemed to pulse before his eyes, the blue-and-green illumination shimmering as if seen through a kaleidoscope. He brought the Sin Eater up automatically, his left hand slipping beneath the butt to steady his aim. Alana, O'Shumper and the other, younger man were crowded around a computer terminal in the lit area behind the counter, with Alana working the keyboard.

"Someone's overloading the system from inside," Alana was saying.

"Which one is it?" O'Shumper demanded.

"Bay seven," Alana read. "The redhead."

"Ring-fence it, cut her out of the loop."

"I...I can't," Alana stuttered. "She's too deeply involved. She's created an area beyond the *traum wirklichkeit* that's leeching our processing power. I can't..."

Kane strode past the dreamers, his head pounding as he selected his first target. The dreamers were shaking in place as Brigid interfered with the *traum wirklichkeit* program, their sleep restless now. For a moment the people at the computer terminal were unaware of Kane's presence, this naked figure striding across the room with a blaster poised in his hands. Deren, the young man who had so badly failed with the shotgun, looked up first, something catching in the corner of his vision.

"What the—?"

Kane's finger stroked the trigger, sending a 9 mm slug through the air to embed in the man's forehead.

O'Shumper swore as he jumped back, blood and brains splattering across the bodice of his dress. "He's loose," he growled. "How did—?"

Kane stroked the trigger again, sending another 9 mm bullet on its death race across the room. It drilled through O'Shumper's left cheek, exploding half his face in a mélange of muscle and bone.

Alana ducked down, snatching for the snub-nosed blaster she still had resting on the desk beside the computer rig. Kane shot again as the world began to blur all around him, his eyes following the bullet as it cut through the air and slammed into the girl's knuckle, turning her index finger into bloody mist. She cried out, called Kane a name.

Kane continued to drive on even as the world began to blow out around him. The girls on the wall were real, the ones with the locust heads. They were waiting in the shadows, waiting to devour him. Their eyes flashed as he tried to look away, keep focus on the dream peddlers.

He heard O'Shumper's voice from behind the distant counter. "Kill thim," he lisped through his ruined cheek. "Blefore he…"

Whatever else he said was lost to the cacophonous boom of the .38, too loud in Kane's ears now. He thought he saw the explosion of propellant, but it waited there like paint splashed on a wall. The glist was making it hard to see properly, to make sense of anything. Instinct was all he had left now, and still two targets to put out of commission.

Kane ran as though he was flying, concentrating hard on the feel of his bare feet on the floor, telling himself over and over that he was only running. Ahead, the illuminated strip that marked out the counter danced up and down like a broken vertical hold on an old-style television set. Something raced past Kane, a bullet maybe, but it felt as if it was waiting at his back, as if it was a creature moving around the back of his skull.

His hands worked the setting at the side of the Sin Eater, an act of muscle memory, something he had done countless times before. Around him, the room's dimensions were becoming uncertain, liquid filling a jar.

Kane closed one eye, narrowed the other, holding the Sin Eater out before him. Things were standing in the shadows; people. Only, they were without human faces, had bent-back limbs, metal parts, wooden.

Noises were loud but muffled, the sounds of shouting and the thrum of the dream engines and the boom of a discharging pistol.

"He'th loothing it," O'Shumper shouted. "Look at thim, thucker c'n barethy sthand."

Kane saw the silhouette wavering in the flickering

light of the counter, the light that kept edging up his vision like a rocket taking off. The girl's braids, bunched high on her head.

"Deren's dead," she said. "Oh, hell, he's dead. He ain't moving."

"Doethn't matter," O'Shumper screamed at her. "Kill thim. Kill... No, therget that. Giff me the blasht—"

Kane squeezed the trigger when the afro appeared over the countertop, sending a continuous burst of bullets at the target. Red Mama O'Shumper screamed, dropped back with a thump that sounded like a slab of meat hitting a butcher's board.

The other one was still behind there, he knew—the girl. Couldn't take risks now, not when he was like this, wired on glist, out of his mind. Something was beeping behind the counter, the computer display was flashing a warning as Brigid overloaded the dream structures. It was a distraction, one they'd planned before she came here, one that was timed to perfection. Brigid's eidetic memory could bewilder the dream program and create chaos for the other customers. Paying customers. Customers that O'Shumper and his team would do anything for to keep sweet. It was Kane's ace up the sleeve, just in case he needed it once he was inside the building. Of course, banging out of his mind on glist hadn't been a part of the plan.

Alana Schnitzler was scared now, scared enough to do something stupid. Her boss was dead, her colleague was dead, the dream engines were heightened to chaos mode and there was a naked man stalking her across a locked room in a locked building in the crime quarter of a shantytown. She was scared enough to peep out from behind the counter and try to take a shot.

She didn't make it. Kane blasted without remorse,

sending another burst of fire at the counter. Alana crashed back, burbling something through the blood that filled her mouth, and then died.

Kane sensed it was over. As the lights of the dream engines flickered and failed, Kane fell to his knees, flinching his wrist tendons in a futile effort to send his Sin Eater back to a wrist holster he no longer wore. Around him, the world seemed to spin like a wheel.

"This chaos is killing me," Kane muttered as he sagged to the floor. He was entirely in another world now. Thanks to the glist, he had entered an unstructured, unguided *traum wirklichkeit,* where what was real and what was false were no longer delineated.

What happened next he wouldn't know until much later.

INSIDE THE *TRAUM WIRKLICHKEIT,* the sky was flickering from night to day as Brigid slammed her foot on the accelerator of a vehicle that shouldn't exist. The Deathbirds were flickering, too, appearing in multiple places at once, blinking across the sky like a poorly tuned signal.

Beneath her, the ocean pixelated, righted itself, pixelated again, while the sound of the waves looped, running in reverse. The docks were behind her, visible in the rearview mirror of the Turbo 190, melting as if seen through a heat haze.

The ocean was the edge of the environment, she knew now; the dream structures stretched no farther. She had introduced an impossible element to the dream: the Turbo 190, driving across the ocean surface as if it was a road. The program didn't know what to do, as it had been designed to respond to a vast but limited range of possibilities, which meant that reintroducing something it registered as destroyed, manifesting the automobile in a place it categorically could not be, sent the dream engine into a frenzy. In trying to respond, it was overcompensating. A highway appeared for a moment, forming beneath the Turbo's tires, materializing in pieces like the slots of a child's model-train set.

The view in the rearview turned to mush, the fictitious Australasian city caving in on itself in a ruin of pixelated data. She could hear the turning rotors of the Deathbirds but they no longer existed in vision, only their echo remaining as a glitch in the dream engine.

The car kept threatening to decompose, but Brigid held it in place with memory, recalling its lines each time they became immaterial, demanding that the dream engine fill them in to satisfy her belief that they were there.

The other dreamers must be catching hell for this right now, Brigid guessed.

The *traum wirklichkeit* was an open environment that encompassed more than one dreamer once they had plugged into the feed. Dreamers might interact without even knowing it, shaping one another's dream experiences with their actions. But Brigid's action, overwhelming the processing units, would send shock waves right across the dream. The trauma could even be enough to wake them.

Which reminded her…

"Wake up," Brigid urged herself as the sky began losing coherence and the ocean fragmented into great glitching blocks of color and reverberating sound. "Wake up now."

The sky went dark one final time and Brigid peered through the windshield as a series of lit dots stuttered across the blank canvas.

+++ Data feed down +++

+++ Program aborted +++

AND THEN SHE was awake.

She lay on a cot in the dream factory, beneath the depending wires of the engine feed, the stink of sweat assaulting her nostrils as a wake-up call. Around her, the other five participants of the dream were coming around, trembling in place as their dreams broke down, legs kicking in myoclonic twitch. Sitting up, Brigid looked at them, left and right, as she brushed the gummed think-pads from her forehead. They didn't know what had happened, couldn't process it yet.

Brigid leaned over the side of the cot, placing her booted feet on the floor. It hurt. Her head was abuzz with glist, the trace of disorientation echoing through her mind as the dream reality—the *traum wirklichkeit*—faded.

Automatically, she checked for movement, alert for enemies, for the people who ran this joint. No one moved. Brigid peered about more slowly, her eyes struggling to take everything in, as if she had been violently awoken from a deep sleep. In a way, she had.

The room was dimly lit just like she recalled, a azure glow emanating from beneath the benches where the dreamers lay, the strip of jade flecks in a ring above her where the dream engine slinked into the ceiling. Beside her, the other dream engine remained intact, its half dozen users still fast asleep enjoying the interactive motion play they found themselves in, oblivious to the real world just an eyelid's width away.

Brigid wore a ragged poncho over her shadow suit, its frayed edges stained with dirt, a rip in one side coming down from around her right elbow. The rip looked haphazard, but it was deliberate, leaving her freedom of movement in her gun hand. She had no weapon, though. She could not have infiltrated this op posing as a refugee if she'd tried to walk in here armed. Besides the poncho, she wore skintight black gloves and boots whose heels hid tiny explosive charges behind a secret panel, similar to the one Kane had used against the back door to this facility.

She had been awake thirty seconds before she spotted Kane's naked body lying before the illuminated counter that glowed along one wall of the room.

"Kane," Brigid gasped, forcing herself to stand.

He was lying on the floor in a fetal position, resting on his right flank, a dark bruise showing down his left. He had a Sin Eater pistol resting in his hand, his palm open where he had held it.

Brigid scanned the area as she ran to him, making certain she wasn't about to be ambushed. There was no one else about, only the dreamers who were still locked into the two towering dream engines. Even the waiting patrons had left, no doubt alarmed by the firefight that had exploded through the room between Kane and the others.

A moment later Brigid was crouching at Kane's side, checking the dark patch beneath his rib cage. It was just a bruise where something had hit him with some force. But he was breathing, the rise and fall of his chest visible even in the poor light of the room.

They had history, these two, not just as field partners but something much deeper. It was called *anam-charas,* or "soul friends," a spiritual bond that existed between them outside the bounds of time, drawing them back together again and again with each turn of the cosmic wheel. Whatever incarnation they found themselves in, Brigid and Kane always came together, always watching out for one another, protecting one another and forming something greater than the sum of their parts. It was love of a sort, though they were not lovers. Their bond was deeper than that, a synergy of souls entwined. Whatever the bond was, however it manifested, it made them a formidable pairing in this incarnation, this roll of the cosmic dice.

Brigid heard a noise then, alerting her to a movement off to her right. She looked, saw a door there like the lid on a metal canister. The door creaked back and a figure came through, swaying woozily as if disoriented.

"Red Mama, I got clocked outside by some…" the man began before stopping and looking around the room in bewilderment. "Red?"

Brigid reached for Kane's blaster and rolled, scrambling for cover. The man in the doorway spotted the movement, called out.

"Hey, what the fuck happened in here? Where's Red?"

Brigid crouched down, her back to one of the dream engines, checking the Sin Eater. *Blast,* the thing was empty. Wasn't that just typical of Kane, to fall asleep before he could reload his pistol?

"Who is that?" the stranger was demanding as he strode into the room. His voice had a nasal quality and he sniffed wetly between each sentence. "What happened to Red? Alana, honey?"

The man was dressed in rags with a kerchief over his face that left only his eyes visible. The kerchief was stained with blood, dark and wet where Kane had broken his nose. Brigid saw him reach for something beneath his ragged cloak, pull loose a blaster with an eighteen-inch barrel.

"What?" the man asked, anger filling his voice. "You think I can't see you?"

An instant later the man shot, sending a bullet rocketing toward Brigid. It struck the dream engine, ricocheting from it in a burst of sparks. Beside her, one of the waking dreamers brought his hands up to protect his face. "Am I… Is this still the dream?" he asked.

Brigid ignored him, leaping to her feet and casting the Sin Eater aside. She had no chance of reloading the weapon here, couldn't begin to guess where Kane's belongings had wound up. Instead she ran, using the nearest dream engine for cover as the alleyway guard took potshots at her. The bullets cut through the blue-lit air in sapphire trails, glinting as they crossed through the light before embedding themselves in the far wall with determined thumps.

Brigid whipped across the low-lit room, her poncho billowing out behind her as she weaved between the dream engines to the rhythm of discharging bullets.

"Keep still, you bitch," the triggerman snarled as he tracked Brigid between the water-lily-like constructs.

There was just one dream engine between them now, the dreamers still fast asleep and locked in their private pleasures. Brigid raised her leg high and stepped up onto the nearest stretcherlike cot before vaulting into the air. She reached out as she sprang, grabbing the jutting base of the power unit above her, the thing that drove the dream engine. Her black-gloved hands held tight, lifting her through the air like a gymnast on the bars even as the startled gunman sent a barrage of bullets toward her.

Brigid swung, her lithe body whipping through the air like a thrown knife, legs stretched out, booted feet pointed. In a moment she had brought herself around the ceiling unit of the dream engine to face her attacker before letting go and racing toward him like an arrow, feetfirst.

The gunman blasted again, sending a bullet past Brigid's thigh and up into the rafters of the room as she struck him full force in the center of his chest. The gunman fell back with all the grace of a tossed stone, dropping down and back and striking both wall and floor at the same time, his legs bent under him. Brigid went, too, tucking and rolling off the body as they landed in a heap. She was on her feet again within a second, and she turned with arms poised in a fighting stance, facing her would-be killer. He lay in a heap against the wall, disoriented, his nose bleeding once more where the wound had reopened.

"Wha—? What happen—?" the gunman asked, his eyes wandering as he tried to focus.

Leaning down, Brigid palm-slapped the man's forehead, driving his head against the wall in a resounding thump. "Back to sleep for you, bugaboo," she told him. "And remember to dream nice."

Still catching her breath, Brigid made a swift circuit of the room and the building beyond, confirming there were no more surprises lurking the way the alleyway gunman had appeared from the back room. She found the three dead bodies of the people who ran the dream factory, and the room of muties in cages. The guard from the alleyway had come through this way, but he had had the good sense to pull the door closed behind him, which meant that while the lock had been ruined by Kane's explosive charge, at least the place looked secure from a cursory glance. The surprised dreamers remained disoriented, and Brigid assured them that medical attention would be arriving shortly.

Assured that she was safe, Brigid activated her Commtact and hailed Cerberus headquarters. "Cerberus, this is Brigid," she began. The Commtact was a radio communications device that was hidden beneath the skin of most Cerberus field personnel. Each subdermal device was a top-of-the-line communication unit, the designs for which had been discovered among the artifacts in

Redoubt Yankee several years before by the Cerberus exiles. Commtacts featured sensor circuitry incorporating an analog-to-digital voice encoder that was subcutaneously embedded in a subject's mastoid bone. Once the pintles made contact, transmissions were funneled directly to the wearer's auditory canals through the skull casing, vibrating the ear canal to create sound. In theory, even if a user went completely deaf he or she would still be able to hear, courtesy of the Commtact device.

The Commtact blurted to life beneath Brigid's skin, the familiar voice of Brewster Philboyd echoing through her ear canal. "Go ahead, Brigid."

"Operation Dream Thief is a success," Brigid said, "but the place is unsecured. Can you get our team over here ASAP?"

"Copy that, Brigid," Brewster assured her. "Will do."

"We'll also need a medical team here, if possible, Brew," Brigid added.

"You have casualties?" Brewster asked with concern in his voice.

"Some of the dreamers are a little shaken up," Brigid explained, "and Kane's tripping on something, probably a lungful of glist."

"He okay?"

Brigid's glance turned to the naked figure sprawled on the floor. "He'll live," she concluded. He would. There were no bullet holes and he was still breathing normally. He would be fine.

Close by, hidden in one of the tumbledown shacks that made up Hope's refugee village, a Cerberus mop-up team was waiting to go into action. Brigid guessed they would have just a few hours to clean this place of tech before other scavengers arrived, eager to take possession of the old military computers and acquire this location for their own outfit. It was dog-eat-dog out there right now, and the only way for Cerberus to survive was to be a smarter dog than all the others. Of course, according to myth, Cerberus was a dog with multiple heads—it seemed only fitting that its agents were celebrating a triumph here.

Chapter 7

Grant looked up as he heard the noise, his preternatural hearing honed from long years as a hard-contact mag, where such alertness meant the difference between life and death.

"Shizuka?" he hissed. "You hear something?"

The samurai woman Shizuka was working through a pile of blackened rubble, clambering over it with perfect balance despite its unsteady nature. She turned back to Grant and smiled ever so slightly. "Should I have, Grant-san?" she asked. "Did you prepare a candlelit dinner after all?"

But Grant shook his head briefly, cutting her words to silence. They were in a wide corridor that had once been used as a garage for storing the newly built choppers and armored wags that Jerod Pellerito and his team had been constructing here on an assembly line. The burned-out husks of several road vehicles remained, their windshields strewed across the stone-tiled floor in tiny shards of shattered glass.

Grant's right hand was already tensing with anticipation, threatening to draw out the Sin Eater pistol that he wore beneath the sleeve of his jacket. Shizuka saw the movement, placed her hand on the pommel of the sword she wore at her hip. Her eyes met Grant's, an unvoiced query clear in her expression.

Grant shook his head, still listening. He had heard

something just then, a high trilling like a woman's laughter. The laughter was quiet, as though it was distant… or from someone trying and failing to muffle the noise.

"Who's there?" Grant called, the Sin Eater powering into his hand.

Behind him, Shizuka drew the *katana* from its sheath, twenty-five inches of tooled steel like a mirrored scar in the air. She raced down the pile of rubble in a light-footed scamper to join Grant, the sword raised protectively. "I don't see anyone," she whispered as she took up a position beside him, standing back to back.

"Me, either," Grant told her. His body was tense now, muscles ready, and he had adopted a bent-legged stance, better to absorb any impact should they be attacked.

This factory had been built and run by an illicit arms-dealing cartel. If one of their number had come back, it wouldn't take much for them to recognize Grant and seek revenge on him.

"Come nearer, nearer yet." A woman's voice echoed through the ruined factory wing. "I have a story for your ear."

Grant spun on his heel, locating the source as the woman stepped through a blackened wall with a hole burned in its center. "So come and sit beside me," she sang.

Grant stared at her, not knowing what to make of this vision. The woman wore strange clothes, beautiful but ancient, like a debutante at a Victorian-era ball. She had blond hair that trailed down her back and she wore a long dress that seemed to switch between pink and blue with every step she took into the wide corridor. Grant held her determinedly in his sights, the Sin Eater poised in a two-handed grip. She was twenty feet from where he stood with Shizuka.

"You want to tell me who the fuck you are?" Grant demanded.

"...come and listen, mother dear," the blonde woman finished, before looking at Grant as if for the first time. Her eyebrows rose in surprise and she waggled one exquisitely gloved finger at him. "Such language," she said, "will never do." Her accent was cut-glass English, and the way she said things made it sound as though she was chastising a child.

"Hands where I can see them," Grant ordered, gesturing with the gun. "Up high, over your head."

Smiling, the woman raised her hands very slowly above her head. The way she did it felt more like a strip tease than a surrender; it was all Grant could do to stop his mind wandering.

"So tell me—" the woman began.

"I'll ask the questions here," Grant told her.

"Do you like girls or do you like boys?" the woman finished, ignoring him. "It's so confusing oftentimes."

Grant ignored her question, pacing warily forward and keeping the blaster aimed at her chest. "Have you been waiting here all this time? Watching us? Where did you come from?"

The woman smiled with all the warmth of a shark's grin. "I asked first," she stated. Grant stared at her, and when he didn't answer she went on. "Your skin's so dark—does it hurt?"

"What the—?" Grant began.

But Shizuka cut him off. "Grant-san—we have a second, at your six. Male, Caucasian, six foot plus, blond hair."

Grant continued to watch the woman. "How's...how's he dressed?"

"Oddly," Shizuka admitted. "Like something out of an old play."

"What is it?" Grant asked the blonde woman, raising his voice to address her. "A boyfriend-girlfriend thing? You come here and dress up to get your kicks?"

The blond-haired woman snorted and showed her perfect teeth once more. "Oh, Algie and I are not boyfriend and girlfriend. Lovers, frequently—but never boyfriend and girlfriend. How frightfully plebeian."

As the mesmerizing woman spoke, something caught Grant's eye from above them, and he glanced that way. There was a broken catwalk up there that had, at one time, led to some offices where the accounts and organizational side of the operation had been located. There was a figure up there now, a woman, wearing a dress like the blonde's. Only, hers was cream, her hair long and dark. She made no effort to hide, standing at the edge of the catwalk and peering over.

"Shizuka," Grant whispered. "We have another—high up at your nine."

Shizuka's hair swished around as she glanced where Grant had indicated, sword never wavering. "I see her."

"I like both," the blonde woman continued, and Grant's eyes flicked back to her. "Girls and boys, that is. There are so many combinations, aren't there?"

"What are you people doing here?" Grant demanded.

"Here?" It was a man's voice, and not the one whom Shizuka faced, no. This one came from over to Grant's left, striding through the ruined archway of the garage door in a swirl of wine-red coat that fell about him almost like a cape. "Why, do you own this place? Are we intruders?" he asked. The accent was polished English again. Just where the hell did these people come from?

Grant eyed the man warily. In less than two minutes,

he and Shizuka had been surrounded, boxed in within the wide garage space of the abandoned factory. He shifted his aim for a moment, bringing the gun over to cover the man in the red coat.

"Hands up in the air," Grant ordered.

"And why would I do that?" the man asked, raising his hands only high enough to gesture, waving them before him as if brushing something aside. He was tall, Grant saw, with wavy dark hair that trailed down past the collar of the high-buttoned white shirt he wore beneath the satinlike coat.

"Because I'll put a bullet in your head if you don't," Grant told him. "Final warning."

"I'm Cecily," the blonde woman announced, her voice loud in the enclosed space.

"Yes." The dark-maned man nodded. "We have rather been overlooking our manners. I'm Hugh. My friends— Algernon, Antonia and Cecily—you know." He still had not put his hands over his head, but they remained on show at least.

"Grant," Grant said, "and Shizuka. Now, this here is off-limits. Used to be a munitions factory until it got shut down a coupla weeks ago." He made no mention of his part in that termination; until he knew what these people were doing here, he would rather keep that aspect secret. "Place got blown up but there's still a lot of dangerous junk hanging around. You need to watch your step."

"You make it sound frightfully more interesting than it is," the man called Hugh stated. "Would you perhaps have a role to play here?"

"No role," Grant said. "Just don't like seeing people get hurt."

"Ah." Hugh sighed, raising one hand to his brow and brushing away a rogue lock of hair. "But, you see, there must always be suffering to create art. Isn't that so, Antonia?"

From up above, the dark-haired woman voiced agreement. "Suffering is the fuel of the great artist," she said. "The greater the suffering, the greater the art."

Grant didn't like where this was going. These people showed no fear of his blaster, and the way they spoke was strange, supercilious, as if they were mocking him. "I'm going to ask you all to leave," he said. "There may still be radioactive material around...."

"Really?" Hugh interrupted, clearly intrigued now, where he had been barely enduring the conversation before. "And would you happen to know where such material might be? It seems we require such for a little project I'm...considering."

Grant held his gun steady, watching the dandy through narrowed eyes. "I'm politely asking you and your friends here to leave, *Hugh,*" he said, emphasizing the name almost as if it was a curse. "I didn't see any vehicles out there, so I don't know if you had some way of getting here, but trust me, it's in your interests to leave. This place is marked for demolition—today."

"Oh," Cecily groaned, "how tedious. I thought new people would be interesting, but this one's so tense he's no fun."

"No fun at all," Antonia agreed from the catwalk.

"Silly's right, Hugh," the blond-haired man opined, his voice echoing from the far end of the high-ceilinged room. "We've been out for far too long to just stand around and converse with simpletons."

Shizuka bristled. "Simpletons? Did he just call us...?"

Hugh began laughing loudly at that. "You speak English," he said between loud guffaws. "Oh, how very splendid. That makes it all so much easier."

It was as if that was a cue. The four oddly dressed strangers were suddenly moving, closing in toward Grant and Shizuka, the woman who had been on the catwalk leaping down with pantherlike grace. Grant estimated that the drop was twelve feet or more, yet the woman landed with uncommon ease, barely bending her legs beneath the billowing skirts of her dress. Such a move spoke of exceptional muscular discipline and power.

"I don't like how this is developing," Grant said in a warning tone, "so I'm going to ask you all to back off and keep your hands where I can see them."

"Why?" Cecily asked as she paced toward him. "So that you may shoot us?"

"I'd just as soon not," Grant began, but the beautiful figure of Cecily took another step, her allies doing likewise.

The four wended toward Grant and Shizuka, walking not straight but in a circling pattern, hemming them in where they stood. Grant watched as the dark-haired man called Hugh reached for something inside his jacket pocket.

"Don't do that," Grant warned.

But Hugh Danner did it anyway. A moment later he had produced a gun from his pocket, a gun like nothing Grant had ever seen before. It was the length of a pistol, but it was shaped in a crescent, designed so that the wielder's hand held it at one end, a little like a banana. The weapon was constructed of metal with a single wide barrel. The sides, however, were not sleek—rather, they featured vents and pipe work that seemed to be employed in the weapon's discharge, presumably to filter the heat that it generated away from the user. "Let us do the dance of war and beauty, shall we?" the man asked in his accent.

Grant was a crack shot, and he aimed his own blaster on the weapon, snapping off a quick shot. His bullet pinged from the weapon's frame as Hugh raised it, almost as if he was using the weapon as a shield. Grant saw something shimmer in the air as the bullet struck, a circle of shimmering sparks like the explosion of a distant firework.

There was no time to process what he had seen, however. An instant after the bullet was flicked out of the air, the two women came upon Grant, their skirts fluttering around them in a sea of silks.

That was it, Grant reasoned—he had given more than enough warnings and offered more than enough chances for these people to retreat. In a split second, Grant squeezed the trigger of his Sin Eater, sending a second 9 mm bullet whipping through the air and striking the charging blonde woman just below her left kneecap.

The woman called Cecily tumbled to the ground with the impact, and her companions froze like children playing a game of statues. Cecily lay there, facedown on the ground, her layers of petticoats and skirts arrayed around her like an explosion.

"Sorry 'bout that," Grant said aloud. "That'll be a flesh wound, nothing she won't recover from. Now, maybe when I ask you to leave…"

Behind him, Algernon began to laugh, and the other two joined in. The laughter had a false ring to it, as if done as performance, something produced on cue out of politeness.

"Come now, Cecily," the other woman—Antonia— said as she strode toward her fallen colleague, "stop play-acting."

Grant felt something cold and hard in the pit of his

stomach as he watched the blonde girl roll over and begin to laugh.

"Did you see?" the blonde asked, clearly delighted. "Did I appear hurt? Were you convinced? Oh, tell me you were, Antonia. I don't think I could bear another failed performance after flubbing my lines in Hugh's darling *Night Versus Day*."

The two men, Hugh and Algernon, began to applaud, Hugh still clutching the weird blaster he had produced. The sound of their clapping was loud and eerie in the abandoned factory.

"Bravo," Hugh said. "A bravura performance, Cecily, dear."

From her spot on the ground, Cecily plucked something from the floor and held it aloft. "Look," she said, "the beastly man threw this at me." It was the bullet from Grant's gun.

Antonia shrugged, the flawless skin of her bare shoulders moving like ripples across cream. "Well, perhaps you should return it to the beastly man," she proposed.

"Oh, yes," Cecily agreed. "Yes, I shall. I so very shall."

Still standing his ground, Grant reared back a little as the woman called Cecily skewered him with her sapphire-blue eyes, a thin smile on her lips. Then she raised her gloved hand and flicked the bullet back to Grant with such velocity that he almost didn't see it, just a single glint of light catching the bullet's silver shell. The bullet raced past not much higher than Grant's ankle, at the exact same height that it had struck Cecily.

"You missed him," Antonia said with amused surprise. "He's a very large target—there's really no excuse."

"Then help me," Cecily said with a sort of casual disinterest.

Grant did not know what he and Shizuka had walked

into here. He couldn't really make any sense of these people and their strange clothes and their odd accents and mannerisms. The situation had spun out of his control in just a minute, going from odd to decidedly threatening. The woman in the pink-and-blue dress had been hit by the bullet, he felt sure. If she hadn't, she would not have been able to pick it up from the spot where she had fallen. Was she wearing armor maybe? Could the bullet have struck that before dropping to the floor? From her speech, it seemed there were theatrics involved. Grant just couldn't see where they came in—not yet anyway.

"Stand firm," Grant told Shizuka as the well-spoken strangers paced slowly toward them, cutting off all routes of escape.

Now he and Shizuka were forced to stand their ground, Grant knew, and he could only hope that these people didn't have reinforcements waiting in another part of the ruined factory. Enough bullets, less theatrics, and maybe they would get through this without too much trouble. But after what the blonde had done, that seemed suddenly like a very big maybe.

The two women were charging at Grant. Behind him, Grant heard Shizuka issue an irritated grunt as her own foe, the blond-haired Algernon, met with her.

Grant ducked as the first woman threw a straight-handed punch at his head. The woman's open palm cut through the air with a *whoosh,* blurring with the incredible speed of the movement.

Grant kicked out, driving his right foot sideward and into the blonde woman's left knee. It was not by chance that he had aimed his blow at the same spot where he had shot her, and he felt a grim satisfaction as she cried out and fell backward.

"He's strong, this one," Cecily announced proudly. "Is he one of us, after all? His skin is so dark."

Already the other woman, the brunette Antonia, had set upon Grant, her arms stretching out to either side before bringing the blades of her hands together on either side of his skull.

Grant staggered back with the blow, shook his head to force the pain away. Antonia's blow had been brutal, and it left his ears ringing.

Behind him, Shizuka found herself facing Algernon, whose leaf-green coat hid a polelike blade that extended in the manner of a car antenna.

"Are you seeking employment?" Algernon asked as he parried Shizuka's swishing blade with his own. "I imagine that with the right makeup you could be quite pretty. The theater, perhaps?"

Fencing his blade away, Shizuka whipped her elbow up and drove it into the man's smug face. "I already have a job," she told him as he toppled backward.

"That's delightful," Algernon told her as he brought his strange sticklike blade up in a ready position once more. He used it like an épée, his stance like that of an old-fashioned fencer. "One should always have an occupation. I hear that smoking is a popular occupation in London, but I myself could never quite get to grips with the pipe."

Shizuka ignored his words, batting aside his silver blade and forcing him back to the ashy pile of waste that lay behind him. Algernon stepped onto it, discovered it was rather less stable than he had expected.

"My own fault," Algernon continued as he balanced on the teetering trash. "The doctor always emphasized how I never did apply myself. Of course, he wouldn't say that now—not after I killed him."

Shizuka's *katana* cut through the air in a chest-high swoop, but her well-attired foe moved faster, leaning just clear of the blade's arc before stepping forward once more. Shizuka was on the unstable pile of ruins now, too, and she found it harder to get power into her blows as she struggled to keep her balance.

From behind her, shocking Shizuka, a thick beam of red light cut the air with the sound of an erupting volcano. The beam passed by just a foot from Shizuka's shoulder and she felt its crippling heat even then. Shizuka leaped and spun to find the source of the heat beam, saw the dark-haired Hugh holding his blaster at her with effete indifference. When she caught his eye, he smiled and nodded. "Just adding to the fun," he called to her over the sounds of battle.

The lance of the heat beam had momentarily distracted Shizuka. Algernon grabbed the advantage, lunging his épéelike blade at Shizuka's chest, striking a fierce blow against her ribs.

Shizuka's sense of balance was flawless, but even a warrior born needed something stable to push against to get power into their strikes. Algernon, by contrast, seemed to need no such stability with his more elastic weapon. His weapon flexed like a cord as he whipped it toward Shizuka's face, cutting the air with a high-pitched hum. Shizuka felt the flexible blade slap against her left cheek, flinched as a line of pain instantly began to throb there.

Her foe did not hesitate. Algernon brought the cord-like blade around again, whipping in a full circle until it struck Shizuka low in the legs. Its tensile strength was akin to a steel girder, and the strike snagged Shizuka's legs up into the air even as she toppled forward.

Shizuka reached out with her free hand, planting it

hard against the mound of ash and soot and rolling over into a ball with her *katana* close to her side. Algernon leaped from the mound, his strange blade-cum-whip drawing a circle in the air as he bounded toward Shizuka's fallen form. "I do so hope your profession does not involve swordplay, dear lady," he taunted, "for I fear you have been found lacking."

With those words, the heel of Algie's tooled shoe struck Shizuka's fallen form high in the chest, sinking his whole weight upon her and forcing the breath from her lungs.

Shizuka shrieked in agony, gnashing her teeth together as her cruel foe sprang away.

Close by, Grant was receiving similar treatment at the hands of the two women. Antonia struck multiple times and with such speed that Grant had no opportunity to recover, let alone fight back. From an observer's point of view, the engagement didn't even look like a fight. Instead it appeared more like a school bully attacking the class wimp, forcing the smaller boy to hit himself again and again in the face.

Grant felt himself go down, but in his dizziness he could not figure out how. The other woman was upon him now, while the man with the blaster paced closer to watch. Grant was hit from all sides, the Sin Eater useless in such close quarters. Grant was strong, but these people were relentless, and their speed, coupled with their strength, made it impossible for him to get a blow in. He sank into the ash amid a flurry of beautiful skirts, lay disoriented, gazing up at the sooty ceiling as the women watched him.

"Now, then," Hugh began, "what art shall we make of him?"

Grant saw the man's strange blaster enter his field of vision.

"What about inside-art?" Antonia proposed. "Red things, the color of life."

Hugh pressed his weapon to Grant's gut and pulled the trigger. With a hum, the odd-looking blaster emitted an orange beam of heat, which Grant could feel even through his shadow suit.

"Nyaaaaaaagggghhh!" Grant screamed as the pain racked through his body, vibrating his very atoms as he juddered in place, quivering on the floor like a jumping jack. The scream passed in a moment, and after that he just strained to cling to consciousness as the pain pressed against his chest. For a moment he lay there, feeling that heat against his belly until finally he passed out.

Grant was unconscious when it finally stopped as Hugh switched off the heat beam. "It doesn't work, Algie," Hugh declared. "Your heat brush doesn't work."

"It repelled his bullet, didn't it?" Algernon called from where he stood before the fallen figure of Shizuka. She was barely conscious, looking up at him from her position sprawled on the floor.

While Algernon examined Hugh's blaster, the two women peered at Shizuka.

"Oh, she's pretty," Cecily said.

"I like her eyes—they remind me of a cat's," Antonia observed. "A Siamese cat. The type that hiss."

Cecily closed her eyes as if in thought. Down on the floor, Shizuka felt something press against her thoughts, as if a blade had been sunk into the crown of her skull. "What…are y—?" she muttered, but the words wouldn't form properly and her thoughts seemed to jumble even as she tried to grasp them.

"I like her mind," Cecily said, opening her eyes once

more. "It's fresh and exotic. I like its flavor. You should taste it."

Antonia closed her eyes, too, and Shizuka felt the uncanny sensation again as something rummaged through her thoughts, sieving through her brain. Shizuka whimpered at the feeling of irritation. It felt like a cut in her gum, only the gum was inside her skull, and the cut was very, very large. Her teeth clenched as she tried to repel the mental intruder, and runnels of blood began to stream slowly from her ears. Shizuka felt the heat of the blood down her face, felt tears mixed with blood weep from her eyes, but still the pain would not stop. In a moment, she had blacked out, her face streaked with her own blood.

"Come now," Hugh instructed as he paced over to where the women stood amid the soot and rubble.

"Her mind is so sweet and different," Cecily said.

"Isn't it just," Antonia agreed, her eyes flicking open again as she disconnected from Shizuka's thoughts.

"Can I take it?" Cecily asked with girlish glee.

"No, leave the foreigner with it," Hugh advised. "She means nothing by her strange ways."

Cecily pouted. "But she thinks she's a warrior. They both do."

"Antonia once thought she was a poet, do you remember?" Algernon said archly.

"'My love, alack—alack, my love. Your kisses rain from heav'n above,'" Cecily recited, and they all laughed, while Antonia had the good grace to blush delightfully.

"Enough of this," Hugh said as the laughter faded. "This world is so broken, it shames me to be a part of it."

"We came here for a reason, old man," Algernon reminded him. "The craft is ready, finished it not an hour ago."

Hugh accepted this with a nod. "I found something,

too. Plans for a device that creates a mushroom of smoke."

"That sounds enchanting, Hugh, dear," Cecily squealed.

"Let's take your craft on a test flight," Hugh told Algernon, leading the way from the burned-out garage. "We have a new empire to build. A great empire, steeped in finery and frivolity, the only things that matter. We shall be an example to every country on Earth. Let them follow where we lead."

Together the foursome left, an empire just waiting to be constructed from their mind's eye.

Chapter 8

Kane had recovered both his clothes and his senses and he had returned with Brigid Baptiste to their base in the Bitterroot Mountains while the mop-up team came in and stripped the Hope dream factory of its assets.

"If I never see this place again, it'll be too soon," Kane told Baptiste as they took one last look at the refugee camp that had overtaken Hope.

"Seconded," Brigid agreed as she recovered the interphaser unit that would teleport them back home to the Cerberus redoubt.

The Cerberus installation was built into one of the mountains in the Montana range, hidden from view. It occupied an ancient military redoubt high in the Bitterroot Range, where it had remained forgotten or ignored in the two centuries since the nukecaust. In the years since that nuclear devastation, a peculiar mythology had grown up around the mountains with their dark foreboding forests and seemingly bottomless ravines. The wilderness surrounding the redoubt was virtually unpopulated; the nearest settlement could be found in the flatlands some miles away and consisted of a small band of Indians, Sioux and Cheyenne, led by a shaman named Sky Dog.

The redoubt was manned by a full complement of staff, the vast many of whom were cryogenic "freezies" from the twentieth century who had been discovered in suspended animation in the Manitius Moon Base, and many of whom were experts in their chosen field of study.

Tucked beneath camouflage netting, hidden away within the rocky clefts of the mountain range, concealed uplinks chattered continuously with two orbiting satellites that provided much of the data for the Cerberus personnel. Gaining access to the satellites had taken countless man-hours of intense trial-and-error work by many of the top scientists on hand at the mountain base. Now the Cerberus staff could, at any time of the day or night, draw on live feeds from the orbiting Vela-class reconnaissance satellite and the Keyhole Comsat. This arrangement supplied a near-limitless stream of feed data surveying the surface of the Earth, as well as providing near-instantaneous communication with field teams across the globe.

"Steady, Kane," Brigid warned as she and Kane materialized in the redoubt's mat-trans unit, which was a glass-walled structure in an antechamber to the Cerberus operations hub. "You look awfully green."

Although they had materialized in the mat-trans chamber, the two Cerberus field agents had traveled here via a similar but different system of matter transfer—utilizing a device called an interphaser. Standing twelve inches tall and pyramidical in shape with glossy, metallic sides, the interphaser utilized alien technology that could tap into naturally occurring energy pathways and move people through space to specific locations. While more amenable than the human-designed mat-trans, the esoteric technology of the interphaser was not fully understood. The full gamut of those limitations had yet to be cataloged, but what was known was that the interphaser was reliant on an ancient web of powerful hidden lines stretching across the globe and beyond, called parallax points. This network followed old ley lines and formed a powerful technology so far beyond ancient human comprehension as to appear magical. In some ways, the interphaser operated along the same principles as the mat-trans, but its logic was more ethereal to modern eyes. Though fixed, the interphaser's destination points were often located in temples, graveyards or similar sites of religious value. On Thunder Isle, the Cerberus personnel had discovered the Parallax Points Program, which documented these points around the globe. That data had been manually input into the interphaser unit, thus affording the Cerberus field teams access to points around the globe and even in outer space.

Cerberus personnel's access to an operational interphaser was the combined work of Brigid Baptiste and Cerberus scientist Brewster Philboyd, and had taken many months of trial and error to achieve.

Kane brushed away Brigid's concerns with a brisk movement of his hand. "I'm fine," he said. "Just still a little...out of it. I'll be okay."

The door to the hexagonal chamber opened with a hiss of released air. Like the walls of the chamber, the door featured a see-through armaglass panel colored a tan-brown. The antechamber opened immediately into the Cerberus operations room, busy as ever with staff who hurried about their business.

Well lit, the ops room featured twin rows of computer desks with a central walkway between them, at the back of which sat a supervisor's area where Dr. Mohandas Lakesh Singh was, even now, getting to his feet to greet them. Besides the double rows of computer desks and the mat-trans chamber, the room held one item that caught the eye—a vast Mercator map that dominated the back wall over the exit doors, traceries of colored lights dotted across its surface like the flight paths of a busy airline. These dots represented the locations of active mat-trans units, which the Cerberus redoubt had originally been tasked with monitoring back in the latter part of the twentieth century, before nuclear devastation had set humankind back hundreds of years.

Commonly known simply as "Lakesh," Cerberus's leader was a man of medium height and build with dusky skin and slicked-back black hair brushed through with a few lines of silvery gray. Lakesh's fine mouth and aquiline nose suggested a regal upbringing, while his eyes were an unusual vibrant blue. He appeared to be a man in his middle fifties but the reality was far more convoluted. Lakesh was, in fact, a transplant from the twentieth century when this facility had first been built. Indeed, as an accomplished cyberneticist and theoretical physicist, Lakesh had been a part of the research team that operated at this very base back in its first incarnation. A combination of cryogenics, organ transplant and alien technology had kept his body at roughly fifty-five years of age. And his prodigious mind remained razor-sharp. Like most of the personnel in the room, Lakesh was dressed in a white jumpsuit, down the center of which was a vertical blue zipper—the uniform of the Cerberus operation.

"My friends," Lakesh began as he strode through the desks toward the opening mat-trans door. "It is good to have you home. It has been lonely, especially with Domi off scouting a mission in Brazil." A smile crossed Lakesh's face at the thought of his lover, Domi, the reckless child of the Outlands and fearless Cerberus operative. "How are you two? Brewster informs me your mission was a success."

"It was," Brigid agreed, shrugging out of the dirty poncho she had worn as disguise to infiltrate O'Shumper's dream factory. "A field team is out there right now securing the equipment we require along with distributing medical supplies to those who need it."

"And in Hope, there's a lot of people who need it," Kane groused, rubbing his aching side with his hand.

Lakesh eyed the younger man with concern. "Kane, you look to be in pain. What happened?"

"Accidentally got myself shot," Kane admitted. "Shadow suit took care of it. Mostly."

"Of course, that was before he got pumped full of glist and wound up lying naked on the floor crying for his mother," Brigid added with a mischievous grin. "Your move," she added, staring at Kane, the pleasure clear on her face.

"Is this true, my friend?" Lakesh asked, clearly concerned for his top field agent.

Kane nodded. "Apart from the 'crying for my mother' part. Where do you pluck these things from, Baptiste?"

Lakesh fixed Kane with a no-nonsense look. "Kane, I want you to see Reba immediately to check out that bullet wound—"

"It's not a wound," Kane corrected with evident irritation.

"And I also want her to do a full check for any residue from the hallucinogens," Lakesh continued, ignoring Kane's complaint. The look he gave Kane made it clear he would not be talked down on this point and, after a moment, Kane nodded and made his way to the room's double doors, assuring both Lakesh and Brigid that he would be going straight to the infirmary, where the facility's physician, Reba DeFore, would check him over.

As he passed the communications desk, Kane rapped his fingers against the side of the computer terminal where Brewster Philboyd sat engrossed in his work.

"Good support out there, Brewster," Kane thanked the man. "Your timing was perfect—your team were there for us inside four minutes."

Brewster, a gangly man with receding blond hair and square-framed glasses over his acne-scarred cheeks, gave Kane an old-fashioned thumbs-up. "*De nada,* my friend."

As Kane strode from the room, Brigid joined Lakesh at his desk, passing familiar faces as she made her way there. Besides Brewster Philboyd at the comms rig, Donald Bry—Lakesh's ever-fretful shock-haired assistant—was sitting at one of the computer desks, taking the unit apart. Circuit boards, resistors and screws were spread all about him.

"Our technology is wearing out," Lakesh said when he saw Brigid peering at the debris-strewed table. "More and more we are feeling the pinch of its age and the devastation wrought by he who shall not be named."

Ullikummis was the person to whom Lakesh referred, the alien prince with delusions of grandeur who had managed to infiltrate the Cerberus redoubt, wreaking havoc and shutting down much of its technology. Only now were all systems operative again, and even then many of them were in a sorry state. It was this event that had forced Cerberus to seek replacement parts from places like the skanky dream factory operation on the West Coast.

"Well, for all it's worth," Brigid said with a weary sigh, "today's haul looked to be pretty impressive. I only got a peek at the processing core units that O'Shumper's people used to run the dream engines, but they worked to high-grade military specifications. I'm sure Donald can scrabble together enough parts to at least repair some of the damaged equipment we have here right now."

Lakesh looked thoughtful. "Quite a strange thing, this dream-factory business," he mused.

"You don't know the half of it," Brigid agreed. "The dream environment they put me in was called the Hoop, a kind of mythical city located somewhere in the Pacific region. It felt real but it was weird. The city functioned perfectly, clean and tidy with numerous road vehicles... and the roads to run them on. Strange, isn't it?"

"How so?" Lakesh asked.

"The things people crave," Brigid said. "We—humans, I mean—lost almost everything to the nukecaust and the hell on Earth that followed it. This dream ville was like something I read about from the beforedays, a kind of ideal civilization."

Lakesh stifled a laugh. He had lived in the twentieth century—the "beforedays," when the shadow of the nuclear holocaust was yet to be cast. It hadn't seemed such a utopian world then, with starvation and poverty and financial bubbles bursting every few decades. Back then, people had thought of fantasy as an unspoiled environment with rolling hills and dragons swooping the air, magicians casting spells. But the nuclear war and all that had followed had left a great scar on the psyche of humankind. Brigid was right, he realized. "It is funny," he agreed, "the things people crave that they can never have."

KANE TRUDGED DOWN the familiar corridor that formed the central artery of the Cerberus base toward the medical bay. The Cerberus redoubt had been carved directly into the heart of a mountain, and its main corridor had vanadium walls and a high, arched ceiling. The cool temperature still gave that sense of it being a mountain cave, and sometimes navigating the redoubt could feel more like spelunking.

Chief medical officer Reba DeFore was waiting for Kane when he arrived. A buxom woman in her early thirties, DeFore had bronzed skin and ash-blond hair that she wore in an elaborate braid to keep it from dangling onto her patients. She had known Kane a long time, and her concern for him was evident when he explained about getting blasted with a jolt of glist.

"How much glist?" DeFor asked as she gently checked Kane's eyes with a light.

"I don't know, Reba," Kane admitted. "Less than a handful. The guy blew it in my face."

"And what effects did you suffer?"·

Kane thought back. "It took about a minute to really hit me," he said. "At first I just felt woozy, and I made myself get up and finish things there...."

"Finish things?" DeFore asked.

"Execute the people who'd dosed me with it," Kane clarified.

It was a hard thing to explain to DeFore, who was dedicated to the protection of life. But DeFore understood—she had been the main medical facilitator with the Cerberus operation for a long time now, and she knew the realities of their field missions, how Kane and his companions frequently found themselves in kill-or-be-killed situations where the stakes were higher than simply their own lives. They were soldiers in a war for humanity; their enemy had many names and many limbs.

"After that," Kane continued, "I started to lose it. Saw stuff. Couldn't quite tell what was real and what was just in my head. There were people standing in the shadows, with big grins, like their whole heads were just teeth. It's hard to...remember."

"How did that feel?" DeFore asked as she took a sample of Kane's blood, pricking his arm with a needle.

"It felt…" Kane thought for a moment. "It felt real. Like it was a whole other world I was in. And I didn't question it. The farther I got away from that moment when I'd breathed in a mouthful of glist, the more I believed what I was seeing was real. Does that make sense?"

The medic nodded. "That's a typical hallucinogenic effect from a psychotropic drug. Your system metabolizes it and the effect on your brain is to go into a new state of awareness, open to its own subconscious. It's a lot like dreaming, but while you're still awake.

"It's nothing to worry about, Kane," she added gently after a moment. Kane was an ex-magistrate, she knew. Losing control was not something he endured well; it left him feeling vulnerable in a way that was hard to define. "Are you still seeing things?"

"No," Kane said firmly. "I pretty much passed out when its full-blown effects kicked in. Baptiste had to come revive me."

DeFore brought out a cotton bud and asked Kane to open his mouth before taking a swab from his tongue and, with another bud, his nostrils. "It's one dose," she reassured Kane, "and you're at the peak of physical fitness. You'd shrug off any aftereffects quickly—seems like you've already done just that."

Kane looked pensive as he nodded. "Threw me for a loop," he murmured. "No question about that. A whole other world made up from my subconscious."

"I'll check your blood and the cultures in your breathing passages," DeFore told him as she labeled the samples, "but my inclination is to say you're fine now. Take it easy for the next few hours and let me know if you feel anything you oughtn't to, okay?"

"Sure," Kane assented, pulling himself up off the couch where DeFore had been looking him over. "Rest for a few hours. Gotcha."

"Kane?" DeFore said as he walked toward her office door.

Kane stopped and turned back to look at her.

"I said *rest*," the medic explained, "and I mean it. No blasting targets at the firing range or kickboxing a mannequin into submission."

The corner of Kane's mouth rose in a sly grin. "What? Trust me."

DeFore smiled, shaking her head. "I know you too well for that, Kane. Someone stubs their toe on a desk and you'll go in, guns blazing, to make sure that desk never attacks anyone ever again."

Kane laughed, and DeFore watched him leave, closing the door behind him.

GRANT FELT RAW. His teeth were chattering.

He was freezing cold. He woke up without remembering falling asleep, and it felt as if there was an elephant resting on his rib cage. He was lying on his back, the weight pressing against his chest, and he could feel his heart pounding like an old water pump straining to draw the last drops of water from a dried-up well.

What hit me? he asked himself as he opened his eyes. The first thing he saw was the burned-out husk of a jeep, tires flat, the frame blackened to a charcoal skeleton. He was still in the garage area of the bombed armaments factory. His teeth kept biting together with the cold.

He moved his head, gazing down his body, bringing his shaking hands over to press tentatively against his chest. The black fabric of the shadow suit was visible where his coat had fallen open, and so he touched himself there with icy fingertips.

"Arrgh!" Grant shrieked, a sort of gasp and scream in one, his hands flinching back as if shocked.

He remembered the strangely dressed quartet as they had grouped around him like circling wolves. Whatever they had used on him, it had packed a hell of a wallop. A blaster, wasn't it? A strange-looking handgun that fired a beam of orange-red light. A heat beam.

They weren't here now. Maybe they were nearby, just waiting to pounce. Couldn't worry about that now, needed to keep moving, get himself up off the floor.

His hands trembled, not from shock but from the cold. Grant reached down again, touching his chest once more, wincing at the pain. It was like sunburn. Sunburn and cold. A strange combination.

With determination, Grant pushed himself up to a sitting position, searching around himself with a head so heavy it felt like it was carved from rock. "What…happened?" he muttered through chattering teeth.

Shizuka lay nearby, sprawled in a mound of ash, still clutching her *katana*. She looked asleep. Grant was relieved—her clothes were dirty, but otherwise she looked unmolested, and she was here. Her body was shaking slightly, trembling where she lay on the bed of soot. He pushed himself up, moved over to Shizuka on hands and knees, unable to make himself stand upright thanks to that pain in his chest.

"Shizuka?" Grant said quietly. "Babe? You okay?"

She didn't answer.

Swiftly, Grant checked her over, confirmed she was still breathing. When he drew back her eyelids, he could see the whites of her eyes and her dark, chocolate-colored iris was flickering back and forth like Jell-O on a plate. REM state maybe. Grant didn't know for certain.

He was still cold, and couldn't figure out why. The shadow suit was designed to regulate his personal environment, keeping his body at a comfortable temperature even in the harshest of conditions. Then he realized— he'd been struck with the heat beam, and it had evidently fried his shadow suit's workings, causing the miraculous weave to overcompensate. Probably saved my life, Grant realized. Without it, he'd be nothing but a sloppy pool of braised meat right now. No wonder he was so cold.

"Shizuka, I need you to wake up," Grant said, warily scanning the vast room as he spoke. "Those people could come back at any time. We need to get out of here right now."

Shizuka didn't hear him; instead she just lay there trembling slightly in her sleep.

"Okay," Grant told himself, "you can do this. Get Shizuka. Get to the Manta. Get back home. Come on."

He heard the words, but his body strained at the effort. Simply standing took Herculean willpower, his body ached so much. He pushed his shaking arms beneath Shizuka's frame, drew her toward him and lifted her from the rubble. Normally, Shizuka weighed almost nothing, so lithe was her frame. But now, with the pressure burning against his chest, with the feeling of icy numbness in his limbs, it seemed to Grant that she weighed as much as he did, maybe more. He walked slowly across the ruined garage area.

It took four minutes. Grant carried Shizuka's unconscious form through the abandoned factory ruin, wary of his foes being nearby, keeping his body tense, his mind on high alert. But nothing came for him. Wherever the dandified quartet had disappeared to, they didn't seem to be coming back here anytime soon.

Eventually, he made it to the Manta where it rested on the flat ground outside the factory's ruins. The aircraft looked just as he had left it—heaven knew what he would have done had it been destroyed or tampered with in some way.

Still shivering, Grant clambered over the sloping wing with Shizuka in his arms, brought her over to the cockpit and placed her gently inside. There was a small first-aid kit beside the pilot's seat, and Grant used it to clean the samurai woman's wounds and spray them with antiseptic. It didn't rouse her; it seemed as if nothing would.

Once he was done, Grant eased himself into the pilot's seat and drew the lid of the cockpit down over him, sealing its protective dome.

"Cerberus," Grant said, and his hidden Commtact automatically engaged, "this is Grant. Come in, Cerberus."

There was a pause while Grant waited for a response. The silence seemed to last forever, and Grant felt his stomach try to claw its way into his throat as he sat there waiting, shivering.

Finally, Brewster Philboyd's voice came loud and clear over the medium of the hidden radio receiver in Grant's skull. "Receiving you, Grant—how's it going?"

"Not good," Grant said through lips thick with cold. "We got ambushed."

"Pellerito?" Brewster asked.

"No," Grant said, "not this time. Shizuka's down. I'm bringing her in."

"Grant, is she…?" Brewster began.

Grant cut him off. "I don't know," he growled. "Just have the medical bay ready. Tell DeFore to be there when I arrive. I'll be home in—" he checked his wrist chron

"—forty minutes. Less, if I can navigate out of this valley quickly."

"Take care," Brewster advised. "Grant? What about you? Did they hurt you?"

Grant ignored the man, flipping the switches to start the launch sequence for the Manta. A moment later the bronze-hued wing was lifting off, casting debris in its wake as its air-pulse jets surged to life. Whatever Grant felt could wait until Shizuka was safe.

Chapter 9

An hour later, Grant found himself in one of the research laboratories in the Cerberus mountain redoubt as Lakesh and a ballistics expert called Roy Cataman checked over the damage to his coat and shadow suit. The Kevlar weave of the coat had melted across the front panels where it had been buttoned up, leaving a black coating on the fabric that looked like smeared butter.

"Touched by something very hot," Cataman said in a detached, emotionless tone. He was a pale man with salt-and-pepper hair brushed back from the sides of his head in two extravagant wings. It gave him the air of an addled professor, an impression his singed lab coat only served to enhance.

Grant had changed out of the coat and his shadow suit and sat now wearing camo pants and a gray shirt with sneakers. Still feeling the effects of the shadow suit's cold setting, he had buttoned the shirt up tight and kept his arms folded over his chest, rubbing them occasionally to stimulate warmth. A lab assistant called Gus brought Grant a mug of coffee as he sat shivering. Gus was a handsome young man barely into his twenties, with unruly locks of russet-brown hair. "Drink this," he said quietly as the lab jockeys continued examining the artifacts that Grant had brought back from the Panamint encounter.

Cataman was running a current through the shadow

suit, testing its status. "This-was hit by the weapon's beam, as well?" he queried.

Grant nodded. "Went cold while I was wearing it."

"Artificially so?" Cataman asked, and Grant nodded again. "Probably saved your life, then," he said. "Whatever that weapon was, it sent a jolt of heat at approximately five hundred degrees Celsius. It would need to be that high to create any degradation in Kevlar and, as you can see from your coat, some degradation has occurred."

"Five hundred degrees," Grant muttered, shaking his head.

"You're lucky it didn't flash-fry your face clean off the bone," Cataman explained.

As they spoke, Kane came striding into the laboratory. He had showered and changed and his hair was still damp, clinging to his head in unruly clumps. "Hey, I heard you were back," he said to Grant. "What happened?"

"Went to make sure Pellerito's op was dead and buried," Grant summarized. His eyes flicked to the melted front of the Kevlar duster where it hung from a hanger. "Ran into some trouble."

"Pellerito again?" Kane asked.

"No," Grant told him. "Someone new. Didn't know us."

Kane examined the coat, brushing idly at his damp hair. "What did I tell you?" he mocked. "This is what happens when you go out there without me to guard your back."

Grant nodded. "Well, I'll live. Shizuka's still with the doc, though."

Kane looked querulously at his friend but Grant shook his head just slightly. "She was unconscious when I brought her in. Don't know anything more just now."

Grant and Kane had a long history together, first as magistrates, where they had been partnered to protect the sanctity of Cobaltville, then later as Cerberus field agents after they left the magistrates and ville life behind them. They had an awareness that went deeper than words, a closeness akin to brothers. They relied on one another in combat and out of it, trusting their lives to each other without question. Kane had come to find Grant as soon as he had heard that he was back.

Cataman continued his report, bringing Kane up to speed as he outlined his findings to Grant. "Your ally here was lucky to escape with his life," he said with no sense of hyperbole. "The heat beam that struck him was enough to melt a man's flesh from his bones."

"That doesn't sound good," Kane deadpanned.

"Lucky for Grant, his shadow suit kicked in and provided a freezing environment for his skin—the upshot of which was to keep him at a survivable temperature. When he handed it to me, the suit was at an almost cryogenic level of coldness—long term, it would have slowed Grant's heartbeat and other bodily functions to such an extent that he would, effectively, have gone into hibernation."

Kane turned from Roy to Grant. "What was this weapon they used? Who were these people?"

Grant outlined to Kane everything he could remember about his encounter with the four strangely garbed individuals.

"The speed these guys moved at," Grant concluded, "they might not be human. Could be robots or something like that."

"Annunaki?" Kane asked, a warning in his tone.

"No," Grant confirmed with a shake of his head. "If

they're otherworldly, they are a new otherworldly to what we've faced before."

Peering up from the ballistics report, Lakesh shot Grant a warning glance. "You say that as if you expect to face them again," he said.

Grant nodded. "I do," he said, pushing himself up from his seat. Lakesh, Kane and Roy watched as the broad-shouldered ex-magistrate strode over to the doors of the laboratory and left without another word.

After the doors had closed, Kane looked at Lakesh accusingly. "Way to go, Lakesh."

"What?"

"Shizuka's hurt. You think Grant's just going to let that lie?"

"Making it personal won't help..." Lakesh began.

But Kane stopped him. "These people sound like trouble" was all he said before leaving the room to find Grant.

IT HAD NOT TAKEN a great detective's insight to locate Grant. Kane caught up with him in the patient observation room of the medical suite, where redoubt physician Reba DeFore had placed the sleeping Shizuka on a drip feed in a clinically clean bed. Shizuka had been stripped of her dirty clothes and placed into a simple cotton nightgown, a thin sheet draped over her resting body. DeFore was taking inventory in her office when Kane walked in, and he spied Grant and Shizuka through the glass pane that looked into the observation unit.

"He just got here," DeFore said without bothering to look up.

"Yeah, figures," Kane acknowledged. "How is Shizuka?"

DeFore looked up, her fierce eyes meeting with Kane's. "Between you and me—not good. From what

Grant told me, she took quite a physical beating out there. But that's not all of it. She's comatose right now, Kane. I don't mean unconscious or sleeping—her body's just shut down."

"How long for?" Kane asked.

"You mean, how long will it last?" DeFore clarified. "I can't say. She could wake up in an hour, or she might never wake up at all."

"It's that serious?" Kane asked, surprised.

DeFore nodded solemnly. "I don't know what she went through to trigger such an extreme reaction—it's certainly not from the physical assault. She's a strong woman, she wouldn't go like this from the wounds that are apparent."

"Grant told me a little about them, the people who attacked him and Shizuka," Kane explained. "One of them had a heat beam, handheld like a blaster. Its beam was strong enough to melt Kevlar."

"You think they used something like that on Shizuka? There's no evidence of that."

Kane looked thoughtful. "I think they used something," he said finally. "Don't know what it was, but there's a good chance it's like nothing we ever saw before."

With those words, Kane made his way to the connecting door that led into the observation room. DeFore caught his arm as he reached for the door. "Kane," she said, "be gentle. He's hurting."

"I know he is," Kane said. "He's my partner."

Kane pushed the door open and walked into the observation room, nudging the door closed with a dull click. Grant looked up from his vigil as Kane entered, and Kane saw the barely restrained fury in the bigger man's eyes.

Kane eyed the figure between them as she lay there,

her eyes closed, a pulse monitor taped to her finger, a drip running into her vein just above her left wrist. "She looks peaceful, lying there like that," he said. "You wouldn't take her for a deadly samurai warrior."

"She tried to fight them," Grant began warningly.

"I know," Kane said. "She would. She's Shizuka."

"Then what—?" Grant began.

"We'll motivate the forces, get things started," Kane said, "see what we can find out about these oddballs you tussled with. Lakesh will back us—don't you worry about that."

Kane saw the anger in Grant's expression.

"He didn't mean anything by it, you know," Kane told him. "Shizuka will be fine. She's a fighter. What she's doing right now is some samurai whamma jamma on whatever shit has got her lying down like this. You know that."

Grant snorted and smiled. "Yeah, I guess I do."

"We'll find these people," Kane told him. "All of us, all together. We'll deal with it."

Kane turned and left his friend to wait at his lover's bedside. Grant would be out in his own time, Kane knew. By that time Kane planned to have some idea about who it was that had done this to his partner and his girl.

Chapter 10

While he could wait on an enemy for hours or days, Kane was not known for his patience. As soon as he left the medical suites, he made his way straight to the operations room and called a hasty meeting to bring all staff up-to-date regarding what had happened to Grant and Shizuka. Brigid Baptiste joined Kane just as he began to outline the situation, and she was genuinely concerned. Like Kane, Brigid had partnered with Grant for most of their time with the Cerberus operation, and the thought of his being wounded while out there on what should have been a standard recon upset her greatly.

"Seems we're taking too many hits lately," she told Kane as he brought up a map of the Panamint range on the main screen.

"And we always recover," Kane stated in his no-nonsense way. He was here to buoy the spirits of Cerberus, not to dampen them; his natural leadership quality was once more coming automatically to the forefront.

"This is the area where Grant got slugged," Kane said as the map flashed up on screen. The staff of the operations room watched as Kane indicated the specific spot where the arms factory had been. "Grant estimated this would have been three to four hours ago. I want someone to backtrack through the satellite logs and see if we can identify the departure time of these mysterious people he met. I've been to that factory and it's an unforgiving journey at the best of times, not something people would choose to walk 'less they had to. My guess is they traveled through there via vehicle.

"Which means they also had to get there in the first place," Kane concluded. "Let's get a second team looking into that, see whether we can discover how and when they arrived and how long they've been waiting in those ruins. The window is thirteen days, people, that's how long it is since my team blew that place to rubble. Odds are that our mysterious quartet appeared after that. Track them, then track back from there—see if we can find out where they originated from. And, crucially, if there are more of them."

"That's a big ask, Kane," Brewster Philboyd said, peering over from the communications hub.

"We have a very close friend of ours lying in a coma in the infirmary," Kane said, addressing his point to the amassed operators in the room and not just to Brewster. "Shizuka came through for us when Cerberus was at its lowest ebb, when the world was turned against us and Ullikummis had come and ransacked and almost destroyed this place. Shizuka and her Tigers of Heaven stood by our side, not as benefactors, but as equals. We will turn over every rock on the planet if that's what it takes to find out who did this to her and why. Do I make myself clear?"

A rumble of assent bubbled through the room, surprise mixing with shame at Kane's passionate words.

"And what if they don't want to be found?" Donald Bry proposed, a worried look on his face.

"Then it'll be that much more satisfying when we do find them," Kane told him.

From the back of the room, Lakesh nodded in admiration. He had slipped into the room during Kane's rallying speech and remained standing by the doors throughout. To see Kane in action like this reminded him what an asset the man was. With Kane, it seemed, nothing was impossible.

THEIR FIRST LEAD came two days later. The Cerberus satellite teams had backtracked through countless hours of time-lapse footage, while Kane and the other field agents had put feelers out to whatever contacts they possessed beyond the hidden walls of the mountain base.

Forty-eight hours after Grant had first arrived back at Cerberus with the comatose Shizuka, a call came through via the comms desk asking to speak with Kane. The caller represented an old friend, a trader called Ohio Blue who operated out of what had once been the Louisiana-Tennessee region and was now known as the barony of Beausoleil. Blue was a black-market trader who had a hand in various schemes and scams across the Midwest. Quite how large her operation was Kane had never determined, but she was well connected enough to prove a useful contact, despite the questionable morality of her occupation.

As always, Blue elected to meet Kane in person, refusing to discuss anything over a radio network, no matter how secure. He met her in a tumbledown boathouse poised on a backwater stream off the Tennessee River. Constructed of aging wood, the boathouse looked rotted with a patina of green, seaweedlike mold clawing up the side that touched the waters. Kane had brought Brigid Baptiste with him, the two of them traveling together via interphaser to a convenient parallax point about a quarter hour's march from the boathouse itself.

"Kane, my sweet prince," Ohio Blue trilled as he

stepped through the rotted door and into the low-lit boat-house. "You look as handsome as ever."

Kane looked at the trader where she waited in a dark corner of the structure with guards standing to either side of her. Somehow, she had found a grand, velvet-backed armchair with gold gilding running across its beautifully tooled frame and legs. The chair was wildly out of place in the otherwise decayed shack, and Kane wondered if the rotted floorboards could take its weight. Evidently they could—or at least they were hanging in there for now.

The windows were fogged with mold, and candles lit the room with wispy trails of white smoke.

Blue herself was a striking figure. Languishing in the seat, she was a tall, slender woman in her mid-thirties with long, thick hair the color of molten gold that was styled to hide her right eye in a peekaboo cut. She wore a tight-fitting gown of midnight-blue that shimmered silver with each breath she took, cut low to reveal the tops of her breasts, with a hip-high slit that revealed one long, smooth leg. She sat with legs crossed, extending the grand length of bare flesh that was her exposed left leg.

"You're looking pretty healthy yourself," Kane said, passing into the room and striding toward her.

Brigid Baptiste followed a few steps behind him, her right hand open and poised close to the low-slung hip holster she wore openly. Ohio Blue had an understanding with Cerberus that stemmed mostly from a moment when Kane had saved her life during an intergang war. However, she was still a black marketer. It wouldn't take much for her to turn on Kane and Brigid, especially if there were profits to be made.

The glamorous trader laughed. "'Healthy'? 'Healthy'?

Oh, I do so hope that's a euphemism, Kane, my sweet prince."

"You said you had some information for us," Kane said, ignoring the woman's teasing. "Something that might help us on a case we're investigating."

"Oh, my poor, sweet Kane," Ohio replied, "always so serious. Don't you ever feel your talents are—" she stretched the word out for a moment, brushing some imaginary speck of dust from her décolletage "—wasted where you are?"

"My friend was hurt, Ohio, and his girlfriend's in the infirmary just now," Kane said, striding closer to the female trader, an imposing bearing to his swagger. "I don't have time to play games. Tell me what you know so we can get our asses out of this—" he gestured vaguely to the rotting walls "—rat hole and get on with cleaning the whole mess up."

Ohio raised the one perfectly arched eyebrow that could be seen, the whisper of a smile on her painted lips. "I find forcefulness a desirable quality in a man," she cooed. "Perhaps someday soon you'll take a position with me, be it for business or pleasure."

Kane held his tongue and waited. This was the game they played, Ohio Blue and himself; she waving her desire before him like raw meat before a lion, he resisting despite her obvious charms. Perhaps they would make a good team, were their circumstances different, if she could only see beyond her selfish profit margins.

"Two men came to me a month ago," Ohio said in her throaty, rich voice, "with an offer of some artwork and ancient treasures. They were known to me, these men—their names were Jake and Milo, and we had traded before. They were corpse turners, grave robbers, dress it up as you will. They were successful enough in their chosen profession. Jake had a knack for rooting out the right sites."

Kane nodded. "There are a lot of them about since the nukecaust redrew the maps."

"Jake had acquired a map to a site some way from here, out in the region once called Nevada and now known as Luilekkerville," Ohio continued. "It was a military place, I didn't get all the details."

"What did it hold?" Kane asked.

"Now, that, my prince," Ohio answered, "is a very insightful question. The short answer is, I don't honestly know. The map that my freelance associate had acquired was a copy of a copy of a copy—" She rolled her eyes as if to indicate the sentence could continue forever. "You get the picture. It contained the royal seal of the House of Hanover—British care of old Germany."

Kane glanced over to where Brigid was waiting in the shadows by the door, and he watched as she shook her head with uncertainty. "What does it mean?" he asked, turning back to the trader reclining in her gold-trimmed chair.

"Hard to say for certain, sweet prince," Ohio admitted. "One thing I can confirm is that Jake and Milo never came back. These were good operatives, adept at tracking down the kind of items clients will pay good credits for. They knew how to survive in the rough-and-tumble world of grave turning."

"You think they were killed?" Kane asked.

"By whatever they found down there," Ohio told him with a nod of her head.

Brigid spoke up from the doorway. "Couldn't they simply have been scared away?" she suggested. "What you— What they do is hardly the most reputable of occupations."

"It's a reasonable assumption," Blue accepted, "but if they had been scared away, I would have heard from them by now. Jake was getting a little edgy for financing. His income stream had dried up."

"There are other streams," Kane pointed out.

"Yes, but they're not open to dead men," Ohio said.

"You sound pretty sure they're dead," Kane said.

"One doesn't survive long in this business without developing something of an instinct for these things," the blond-haired trader told him, reaching into her bag. Kane watched as she pulled free a tiny paper scroll tied with a ribbon. The scroll was no wider than three inches. "I retained a copy of the map for safekeeping, a little insurance for part-funding their expedition."

Kane reached for the scroll. Ohio stroked the back of his hand before she handed it to him, squeezing his fingers with hers. Unfurled, the map was just six inches by three, and the ink was a muted gray where it had been reproduced too many times. Kane could make out some handwritten notes down the side that stretched across portions of the map, frustratingly obscuring details.

"This it?" he asked.

"That's all I have, yes," Ohio assured him.

Kane tilted the map to better catch the low light in the shack. "Out west, you say? Luilekkerville territory?"

Ohio admired him, saying nothing.

"Your friends could have just got bumped off by a competitor, you know," Kane said, striving to keep the irritation from his voice.

"They could," Ohio agreed.

"I'm not your errand boy, lady," Kane growled. "I don't go to places for your amusement."

"Kane," Ohio said gently, "my sweet, sweet prince. If it was for my entertainment, I would not be asking you to dig graves. I wouldn't have shown you if I didn't feel it might be important. There are no guarantees with this, no, but I don't think you expected any."

"So what you're asking me to do is check out a hunch," Kane confirmed.

"A very credible hunch, my sweet prince," the trader told him. "The kind worth flexing your muscles for."

Kane gritted his teeth in irritation, biting back a curse. "Yeah," he said finally. "I can play a hunch. You need this back?"

"The map? Oh, heavens, no." Ohio laughed. "Bring me whatever's inside that place and we'll call it even."

Kane shot her a fierce look. He was never quite sure if the alluring trader was kidding him or not. Together, he and Brigid left the tumbledown boathouse, knowing full well that they were being observed by at least a dozen of Ohio's scouts hiding in the foliage. Once they were out of sight, Blue would leave the shack and all trace of her existence there would be removed, leaving just a rotting boathouse sitting on a pondweed-covered tributary of the Tennessee once more.

Chapter 11

Twin Mantas cut the afternoon skies over Luilekkerville, their graceful bronze outlines like the marine creatures that they had been named after.

Luilekkerville's towers shimmered in the afternoon light, a walled city rebuilt just a few months ago. Once, it had been called Snakefishville, named after its ruler. But Baron Snakefish had long since disappeared, and the ville itself had been leveled by a subterranean attack, leaving it little more than a smoking crater. Religious zealots had constructed their new settlement on the ruins of the dead ville, bringing a new peace to the region. Now it was a bustling ville once more, home to an estimated three thousand people.

The thought of that transformation left Kane cold as his Manta overflew the ville's golden spires. He had been among the forces that opposed those religious fanatics, had seen firsthand how their indoctrination could warp and change people beyond recognition. One of their victims had been Brigid Baptiste, who sat behind him in the Manta's tight cockpit. During Cerberus's darkest hour, she had all but lost her mind to the intrusive teachings of the religion's figurehead, the vengeful Ullikummis.

"Quite amazing what they've done down there, isn't it?" Brigid commented as Kane brought the Manta around in a swooping arc.

"The stone-heads rebuilt a lot of things," Kane said noncommittally, "some better than others."

Brigid understood Kane's bitterness. While she had been in the thrall of the Ullikummis cult, it was Kane and his allies who had been striving to stop them in a conflict that had brought the two friends to blows. Brigid had shot Kane in an encounter not far from this site in an act that must have seemed like the ultimate betrayal.

Sitting up front, Kane continued to pilot the Manta, urging it toward the point indicated on the ancient map that Ohio Blue had given him.

The map showed a region of old California/Nevada roughly ninety miles from the Pacific coast. The reproduction was faint, and Cerberus operatives had run it through enhancement software to divine as much detail as they could from the aged parchment. The map was three hundred years old, and one problem that that created was in the way the landscape had changed between then and now. Landmarks that may have been obvious at the time it was drawn were now nothing more than distant memories, whole towns turned to dust by the onslaught of the nuclear war that had punctuated the start of the twenty-first century. Even the coast had changed, a great chunk of California shearing along the San Andreas fault, leaving whole regions submerged.

Cerberus was manned by some of the smartest scientific minds and they had pieced together the map's details, translating them into modern landmarks that might possibly represent the same area. It had taken three and a half days of comparing satellite footage and archived maps to triangulate the area in question; Ohio Blue's suggestion that it was somewhere in Luilekkerville had at least given Cerberus an indication of where to focus the search.

The trouble that they had gone to had made Kane wonder how Ohio's grave robbers had managed to locate the place, or indeed whether they really had. When he raised that question to Brigid, she had shrugged. "They're seasoned professionals," she told him. "I guess you get good at reading old maps when your next meal depends on it."

Now Kane, Baptiste and Grant were heading to a location close to Boundary Peak, Mount Montgomery on the forgotten border of California and Nevada.

Grant followed Kane in his own Manta, playing wingman to Kane's lead. His chest still burned from the heat blast he had taken a few days earlier, but the ache had turned to an itch which Reba DeFore had provided lotion to soothe. Grant sat alone in his Manta cockpit, the all-encompassing bronze flight helmet over his head. Shizuka was still at the Cerberus infirmary, where she remained in a coma. She was stable and had shown no signs of decline at least, but it was considered too risky to move her while she was in this state, much to the frustration of the Tigers of Heaven, who had wanted their leader returned. A compromise had been reached that saw a unit of twelve Tigers of Heaven guards keeping a round-the-clock vigil over their leader's bed, running in shifts, six on and six off. The Tigers had a fine relationship with Cerberus; they had even protected the Cerberus operatives during the religious purges that came with the rise of Ullikummis and his campaign against the Cerberus rebels. Even so, the situation left things tense, and more than once Grant had found himself almost coming to blows with one of the guardsmen as he went to check on Shizuka's progress.

Even now, Grant was tense and angry, his rage just barely restrained. Whatever they found out in Luilekkerville territory, he could only hope it would lead them to the strangers who had done this to his lover.

Though they originally hailed from Cobaltville, which bordered Luilekkerville and incorporated some of Nevada, neither Kane nor his companions knew this area especially well. Brigid had read up on the immediate area surrounding the location in question, concluding it had remained a sparsely populated region since the time that the map had been drawn.

Kane weaved the Manta through the cloud cover wafting over Mount Montgomery before beginning his descent. His instruments indicated the location that was shown on the map, a running heads-up display feeding Kane with additional information as he brought his aircraft lower. Behind him, Grant followed, acknowledging the maneuver with a brief exchange over their linked Commtacts.

They were six miles out from Mount Montgomery itself, in a kind of no-man's-land situated on the forgotten border of the states of California and Nevada. Kane scouted for a suitable location to land, settling on a gently undulating slope that was brushed with grass and a smattering of trees. The Mantas were enviably maneuverable and, with their VTOL design, could land on the proverbial dime. The engines of Kane's Manta were powering down as Grant brought his own craft in for a landing, turning the nose around in midair as he circled an unspoiled spot between the trees.

"We're a little exposed out here," Kane said as Grant threw back the hatch on the cockpit. "Let's try to make this quick, in and out."

Removing his own flight helmet, Grant raised his index finger to the side of his nose in the friends' private 1 percent salute. "Roger that," he said. The 1 percent salute was an acknowledgment that no matter how much one might plan for a mission, there was always that 1 percent factor of chaos that could throw things out of whack. Being prepared for that eventuality, however it manifested itself, could mean the difference between staying alive and taking a bullet.

Brigid followed as the two men began to scout the area, checking for hostiles. She scanned the space with emerald eyes, searching for landmarks that she might recognize from the satellite surveillance that Cerberus had put on this place once they had located it. To the west, the orange ball of the sun was drawing slowly toward the horizon, casting elongated shadows behind them as they strode across the grassy scrubland.

They found the trapdoor in a copse of trees, exactly where the Cerberus techs had triangulated it. Kane wasn't surprised. "Eggheads came through for us again," he said. While they weren't infallible, the Cerberus support staff had proved invaluable time and again in locating esoteric items across the globe.

Brigid brushed a stray red-gold lock of hair over her ear as she peered at the trapdoor. It looked like an manhole or the entry hatch to a submarine, the metal frame buried a few feet into the soil with an open door poised upward on its hinges like a flap. The door, like the hole, was circular, and it looked wide enough to allow more than one person to pass through it at once. "That's it," she said, a little overwhelmed.

"Looks old," Grant muttered, idly working the safety on his Copperhead assault subgun. He was dressed in a new duster coat, black like his old one and with a Kevlar and Nomex weave, making it both bulletproof and flame retardant. Beneath this, he wore a new shadow suit, fitted snugly to his body like a second skin.

The Copperhead was a favored field weapon of Grant's. It featured a two-foot-long barrel, with grip and trigger in front of the breech in the bullpup design, allowing the gun to be used single-handed. It also featured an optical, image-intensified scope coupled with a laser autotargeter mounted on top of the frame. The Copperhead possessed a 700-round-per-minute rate of fire and was equipped with an extended magazine holding thirty-five 4.85 mm steel-jacketed rounds. Besides his magistrate's Sin Eater, Grant would defer to the Copperhead, thanks to ease of use and the sheer level of destruction it could create.

Brigid crouched down beside the open manhole while Kane and Grant covered her, alert to danger. Kane had brought his Sin Eater with him in its wrist sleeve, and he popped it out from beneath the black denim jacket he had elected to wear over his own shadow suit.

Brigid, too, was armed—a TP-9 pistol strapped in the low-slung hip holster that clung to her right leg. "It's wet down there," she said as she ran the beam of her flashlight down into the hole. "A puddle or pool, by the look of it."

"From what Ohio said, the place could have been open for maybe four weeks now," Kane said. "Guess it caught a little rain."

Automatically, Brigid's thoughts turned to the average precipitation figures for this area, yet another jot of trivia stored in her capacious eidetic memory. Luilekkerville was a relatively dry area in a temperate zone, but it did have rainfall, sometimes torrential. Something glinted in the beam of Brigid's flashlight, bringing her focus back to the present. "There are handholds down there," she said, "secured to the wall like ladder rungs."

"Then that's how we're getting down," Kane said, his eyes still fixed on the Mantas where they stood at the foot of the slope. No one seemed to be about; the only movement came from birds swooping overhead and insects buzzing in the long grass.

Without argument, Brigid moved her agile form fluidly over the lip of the opening and dropped down onto one of the ladder rungs, descending to the pool of water in a few swift movements. It was twelve feet to the floor of the underground chamber, and when she reached it, Brigid discovered that the shallow puddle came barely over the sole of her boots. "It's empty down here," Brigid called up to her partners. "All clear."

Kane followed Brigid down the ladder, while Grant clambered down last of all. The area below was just a few feet square, and Grant had to wait halfway down the ladder rungs while they discussed what to do next. There was really only one option open to them—the square lobbylike area had just one opening, which led to an inclined tunnel that went deeper into the hillock. Kane and Brigid led the way while Grant followed a few paces behind them, waving the Copperhead in a sweep fore and aft to make sure nothing popped up to surprise them.

The initial tunnel was narrow, with sketches drawn on the walls in faint pencil, each one a perfect study of the naked female form. Brigid ran the beam of her flashlight over them and Kane smiled. "Looks like someone's been having a time of it," he said.

Brigid glared at him. "Men." She *tsked.*

But beside her, Grant's attention was held by the illustrations and he reached for Brigid's hand as she pulled the beam away. "I know this woman," he said, leaning in a little to get a closer look. "She was one of the ones who attacked me. Tossed a bullet at my kneecap."

Brigid and Kane took another look, examining the illustration that Grant indicated. It showed a curvaceous blonde woman in repose, nude, with her legs angled in such a way as to protect her modesty, her hair teased up in a coif.

"Cecily," Grant said, "that's what they called her." His eyes roved over the illustrations, searching the other figures who had been added onto the tiled wall until he found a study of another woman, just her head and torso, peering back at the viewer from over one naked shoulder. "And this one's called Antonia."

"Good," Kane said. "Then we're in the right place."

Together, the exploration party moved on, following the narrow tunnel until it opened into a broader one with a high arched ceiling and an elaborate painting dominating one curved wall, gas lamps lit and illuminating the whole thing. The painting showed beautiful sea nymphs emerging from the waters, and it was clear to all three Cerberus exiles that they were based in part on the same models as the two studies of Cecily and Antonia that Grant had pointed out.

"Seems that somebody had a lot of time on their hands," Brigid observed.

"How so?" Kane asked.

"The detail and artistry here are worthy of Michelangelo's work in the Sistine Chapel," Brigid told him. "Though appreciably a colossal undertaking, Michelangelo was an incredibly accomplished artist—it took him close to five years to decorate the whole chapel with artwork that went down in history as one of the greatest achievements of any man."

"You think this took five years?" Kane queried.

"I think someone was down here with nothing better to occupy them," Brigid rationalized. "How long it took depends on the individual artist, I guess."

They walked past the vast mural, striding three abreast down the wide tunnellike corridor. The gas lamps flickered slightly, creating a warmth to the light they cast.

"Any ideas what's powering the lights?" Grant asked.

Brigid shook her head. "Self-sustaining gas supply of some kind," she suggested. "Which means that there must be an efficient ventilation system to this bunker, perhaps hidden among the trees up there."

They moved into another corridor, this one running in a shallow curve that took it down deeper into the hill. There were several rooms branching from the corridor, some of which were filled with what appeared to be junk: yellowed manuscripts with handwritten alterations, paintings, sketches and statuary both large and small.

"Looks like an art dealer's paradise," Kane said as he glanced into the third of these storerooms.

"Yet there's a similar sensibility to all of it, do you notice?" Brigid pointed out. "It's all harking back to a specific time period—the Italian Renaissance as reinterpreted through Victoriana."

Kane looked at her with disdain. "Your knowledge never ceases to amaze—and bore—me, Baptiste."

"It may be important," she told him in response. "This whole…redoubt, perhaps we should call it…it's stuffed with art treasures from a certain era. What's more, I haven't seen anything I've recognized. Like the sketches we found at the entryway and the giant mural in the tunnel back there, a lot of this stuff seems to have been inspired by a particular set of models, implying that they may have been created by the same hand."

"You think an artist was stuck down here?" Grant asked, a little taken aback.

"I think art played a very great role in these people's lives," Brigid said thoughtfully. "If they were locked down here for a long time, that may in fact have been all they had to cling to."

"Deranged playwrights," Kane muttered, shaking his head. "What are they going to do? Baffle us with their witty ripostes?"

"One of them spoke of art," Grant recalled, bringing the tone of levity back down. "When they attacked us, he said something about a dance.... 'The dance of war and beauty.' That's what he called it."

Warily, the three Cerberus warriors backed out of the storeroom and continued along the brightly tiled tunnel. There was no noise coming from the underground facility other than the faint hiss of the gas lamps, spaced wide apart along the tunnel's length. The tunnel ended in a broad archway decorated with elaborate toolings in gold and bronze beyond which hung a heavy drape. Like the mural, the workmanship was exquisite, representations of what appeared to be Greek gods reaching down to touch man with fire.

"Prometheus bringing fire to mortals," Brigid observed. "A parable for knowledge."

Weapons raised, Kane pushed back the heavy drape and the three of them passed through into the next area of the underground complex. They found themselves in a small room with a balcony that left it open on three sides, with the drape hanging over the wall behind them. There were stylized columns to either side of the partitioned doorway, with decorative carvings akin to those they had found around the door. Four seats had been placed in the area, facing out toward the low balcony. Something was illuminated beyond the balcony, casting its ghostly light into this otherwise unlit space.

Warily, Grant padded forward, his Copperhead held out before him in readiness. Beyond the edge of the balcony stood a wooden theater stage with heavy curtains drawn back from its performance area. The balcony looked onto the stage where it lay ten feet below, providing a perfect view of any activity that happened there. Right now the stage contained just one thing—a figure, naked and kneeling in its center, uplit by the lights that rang along the foot of the platform. The figure was hugging itself, sobbing in great silent shudders of agony.

"What the hell?" Grant muttered as he peered over the balcony's edge. He brought his blaster to bear on the mysterious figure and shouted a command. "Hands where I can see them—right now!"

Grant had a clear shot. It would be the work of just an instant to dispatch the stranger. On stage, the naked figure didn't so much as react, though its shoulders continued to heave as though it was sobbing heavily. Grant recalled what had happened to Shizuka and to himself over in the Panamint factory, how quickly their attackers had moved. This time he wasn't going to take any chances. He slid his finger against the trigger of the Copperhead assault rifle and prepared to fire.

Chapter 12

They walked the streets of Hope, gods among men.

Antonia, Hugh, Algernon and Cecily walked four abreast through the slums, where the lost sold their wares or their morals or their lives, whatever they still had that people would buy.

The streets were like rabbit warrens, human waste and death littering every corner and every nook. But there, amid all that devastation, all that horror that had become normalized, there walked four godlike beings dressed in the finest silks and velvets, lace collars and cuffs on the men's shirts, lace trims on the women's dresses that swept the ground like the wings of a swan taking flight.

The people of Hope stopped and watched—how could they not? The gaudy slut whores sneered in inverted snobbery at the way the two women presented themselves, calling them cheap, calling them the very things that the whores were. The men elicited comments, too, some unkind, some appreciative. But they made an impression on everyone, these beautiful, transient beings walking amid the scum and the wretched evil to which the people of Hope had become desensitized.

"Look at them," Algie sneered, his golden locks bouncing with each step. "Poor, wretched creatures. They have been forgotten by their gods."

From the end of the line, Cecily inclined her head,

catching Hugh's attention. "Is that true? Have their gods really abandoned them?"

"Gods?" Hugh repeated. "These people never had gods. Places like this—no god would step in a place so morbidly defiled."

"Is the whole world like this now, do you think?" Antonia asked. Her dark hair had been propped beneath a hat whose crown appeared too small, its broad brim shading her eyes from the afternoon sun.

"So much has changed since we were…" Cecily stopped, seeing the warning in Hugh's eye. "Since the last time we looked," she corrected.

Hugh nodded once, accepting the blonde woman's point in the spirit in which it was meant.

"But people surely cannot live like this," Algernon insisted as he stepped over the rotting corpse of a dog. Flies buzzed around the corpse and bold rats scurried just a couple of feet out of the path of Algernon's patent leather shoes. "Surely this cannot be."

Hugh shook his head. "They can and they do," he insisted.

"But it isn't *moral*," Antonia insisted. "Algie's right."

"We should do something," Cecily chimed in, looking to the others for approval. "We should—oh, I don't know—fix things."

"Make the world a better place," Algernon clarified, his blue eyes roving the street where beggars and cripples lay in the shadows of hastily constructed shacks, waiting out their days until death took them. They would suffer first, he could envisage, suffer more than they already had. It wounded him in a distant, removed kind of way.

Antonia took three quick steps ahead of the others and turned around to face them, stopping them in their tracks. "We were born for better than this," she reminded them. "The empire was supposed to fall to our protection, the Dors who ran the world."

"That dream was boring," Algernon said, mocking her with an affected yawn.

"It got old very quickly," Cecily agreed. "That's why they chose to hide us away, isn't it?"

"Perhaps it was for safekeeping," Antonia challenged, "the way one keeps one's Sunday best hidden in the wardrobe, away from the light."

As she finished, Algernon's right arm snapped out and he pulled a street urchin from his feet. Ten years old, scrawny and malnourished, the urchin had a dirt-smeared face and he was just in the business of pocketing Algernon's fob watch—pure gold with diamonds in the fidget.

"Hey, let me down," the street thief shouted, calling Algernon and his friends a litany of vulgar names.

"You stole my ticker," Algernon berated the child.

"Get off me," the child replied, squirming in Algernon's grip.

"I'll tell you what," Algernon said, clutching the lad in a strong one-handed grip. "You may keep my ticker if I can have yours. Fair?"

The boy's face screwed up in consternation and he spat in Algernon's face. "Go fuck yourself, big nose!"

Algie looked the boy up and down, a thin smile curving his lip. "Quite," he dismissed, reaching forward with his free hand.

The boy watched as the dandy's hand came very slowly toward him, and all around Algernon's friends fell silent to watch. Fingers extended, Algernon pressed his fingertips against the lad's chest. The boy squirmed and began to scream, struggling against Algernon's strong grip. Then Algie's fingers penetrated his chest in what appeared to be an effortless move, tearing through the dirt-stained shirt the youngster wore, bending his ribs as he reached inside their cage.

A moment later Algernon's hand emerged from the boy's chest, red and bloody, and it clutched his still-pumping heart. "A ticker for a ticker," Algernon said as he let go of the boy's collar. Already dead, the boy crashed to the ground, his heart beating its last in Algernon's hand.

If anyone had seen this episode in the cruel back streets of Hope, they wisely chose to ignore it and go about their business, preferring not to get involved with immaculately dressed strangers who could pluck a child's heart from his chest with no more effort than one might pluck an apple from a branch.

"So what are we to do?" Algernon said, tossing the warm heart in the air as if he were casually flipping a coin. "Fix all this? The Sunday best come out of the wardrobe?"

Cecily sighed as she spoke. "A place like this...it's beyond redemption."

"No," Hugh told them. "A man must always strive to be better than the environment he inhabits. A place like this can be *adjusted*."

"What do you propose, Hugh, old man?" Algernon asked, the cooling child's heart forgotten in his hand.

"Art shall be the people's salvation," Hugh decided. "For no society can possibly flourish without great art. We shall encourage them, like the gods they are so sorely bereft from."

Antonia unleashed a braying laugh that echoed off the close-packed quarters of the street. "We'll be their gods," she said between loud guffaws. "Oh, how rich. How absurdly delicious."

Algernon turned his hand over and dropped the heart.

"We are gods to them already. They are weak where we are strong. We have invention—they have *this*."

"I like this idea of using art to spur them," Cecily announced. "We could make sure art from the smells and the hells and the...cells that make up their fragile little lives."

"A challenge, then," Hugh proposed, leading them from one alleyway to the next, past a stall selling char-grilled rat in chunks. "We shall, each of us, generate a new piece of art. A piece of art so magnificent that it can alter the world and its people's outlook. Art worthy of our new empire. Are we all agreed?"

Algernon applauded. "What is there to possibly disagree with?" he pointed out quite reasonably.

"Then we rise to bring mankind up from the swill of the gutter," Hugh said, "to show it the error of its ways, to see once again the magnificent stars."

Together, the four strangers made the pact, as the denizens of Hope fought and starved and rotted all around them.

Chapter 13

"Grant, wait," Brigid said, her hand reaching across and dipping the muzzle of Grant's blaster as he prepared to fire.

The dark-skinned ex-mag glanced at her angrily, eyes narrowed in rage. "What the fuck do you think you're…?"

"We don't know who this is," Brigid said, keeping her voice calm.

"He's one of them," Grant insisted, pulling the Copperhead up against the pressure that Brigid had placed upon it. "I'm not taking any chances, *archivist*." He spat the last as though it was an insult.

Kane had stepped up to the balcony now, as well, and he turned from the figure on stage to Grant, eyeing his partner with concern. "Baptiste is right," he said.

"The hell she is."

"Put the gun down—partner," Kane urged.

"We won't learn anything if he's dead," Brigid added.

Grant looked from Kane to Brigid, the need for revenge burning inside him. Logically he knew he was acting foolishly, that he needed to stay rational. Shizuka's condition had gotten him freaked; the way those strangers had taken him and the most capable woman he had ever met out without even breathing hard was preying on his mind. Finally, he lowered the weapon, though his expression remained dark. "If he moves, does anything—

I'm blasting and you can question whatever body parts remain," he told the others.

Kane patted Grant firmly on the shoulder. "Seems fair."

On stage, the mysterious figure had not moved.

"There has to be a way to get down there," Brigid reasoned, leaning out over the balcony and searching for a staircase.

Kane brushed past her and placed a firm hand on the crossbar of the balcony itself, testing its strength. "Up and over," he suggested.

Before Brigid could respond, Kane had done just that, vaulting over the side of the balcony and leaping the ten feet or so to the floor below.

Grant shrugged and followed, hefting one booted foot onto the balcony and using it to spring over the side, the Copperhead rifle held in one hand as he leaped.

Annoyed, Brigid followed the two men, edging herself over the side and dropping down with a little less gung-ho machismo on display.

Down on the stage, the naked figure remained hunched over himself, his legs pulled up and together, arms wrapped around his knees. He was definitely male, Kane noted. The musculature was that of a man—and a physically strong one at that. His head was hairless, though Kane could see he was still a young man.

"Hey, friend," Kane called as he walked across the tiny auditorium between twin rows of seats, a dozen in all. He had his Sin Eater still resting in his grip, but he held it to his side, disguising it somewhat with his leg. "Sorry if my buddy scared you back then—he's a little tense. You okay?"

The figure on stage didn't move, and as Kane got closer he could hear the sobbing like a low, whimpering trill.

"Hey," Kane said, climbing onto the raised stage. It was raised only a few feet off the ground, the step up just a little higher than a normal stair. "You okay? What's up? Why are you crying?"

The figure said nothing; he didn't even bother to look up at Kane. As he got closer, Kane saw something glinting on the figure's wrist, a chain with a little metal tag set in it like the face of a wrist chron.

Kane leaned down, still holding the blaster in his hand as he brought himself to roughly the same level as the crying man. Behind him, Kane knew that Grant would be covering them both with the Copperhead, and he suspected Baptiste was doing much the same, covering the tiny auditorium in case anyone else materialized from a shadowy corner or from behind a drape. Kane reached out and touched the figure's left arm, and the sobbing man flinched, ducking away from Kane's touch as if it had burned him. He looked up at Kane, eyes wide with fear. One eye was pale blue while the other was brown like tanned leather.

"It's okay," Kane assured him, "I'm not going to hurt you. I'm Kane. Care to tell me who you are?"

The figure continued to eye him warily, tears staining his cheeks, eyes wide and fearful.

Brigid was searching the auditorium in front of the stage. The seats looked well upholstered, although the stuffing seemed to have sunk with age, and they released the distinctive smell of dust when she patted one. There was just the one lone box overlooking the stage, a fine gold shield engraved in its paneling. Brigid recognized the shield—it was the House of Hanover, the same shield that she had seen on the map that had led them here.

Briskly, she located the only exit, an arched and curtained doorway that led to a narrow flight of tightly spiraled stairs, doubtless to best use the underground space efficiently. With a word to Grant, Brigid made her way into the stairwell, investigating where it led.

On stage, Kane continued to encourage the naked man to converse, but the stranger was having none of it. As a magistrate, Kane had handled difficult people, reticent prisoners and people in altered states of consciousness, and he knew the procedures for dealing with them. He recalled his training, continued to speak gently to the man, encouraging but not forcing him to speak.

This close, Kane could see the thing on the man's hand contained a name tag, like something one might place around the collar of a pet. Beautifully decorated at its edges, the tag's center contained a string of numbers along with the name Harold.

"Harold?" Kane asked. "Is that your name? What do they call you? Hal, maybe? You look like a Hal to me."

The naked man said nothing. He just continued to stare at Kane with those strangely wounded, empty eyes.

BRIGID FOUND THE FIRST of the bodies a quarter turn around the spiral stairwell, though she could smell it before that. Even so, she jumped when she saw the figure lying there, sprawled on the stairs, feet above his head, limbs protruding at awkward angles. It was a man, his skull crushed at the sides, forcing his terrified features into a compact narrow block as if he was staring through the gap between close-set buildings.

She held her blaster on him for a moment—nonsensically; aware that the man had to be dead. His skin was tinted blue from blood loss and there was a film over his staring eyes. She took a step over the body, trying not to look at the gaping wound that had colored his chest the hideous brown of dry blood, and peered farther up the staircase, her blaster thrust before her. She used a TP-9 semiautomatic, a bulky hand pistol with a covered targeting scope across the top finished in molded matte black. The grip was set just off center beneath the barrel, creating a lopsided square in the user's hand, hand and wrist making the final side and corner.

Slowly, gun unwavering before her, she continued to ascend the stairs.

BELOW, GRANT WAS EXAMINING the auditorium where the stage was constructed. It was a small space, but the high ceiling gave a sense of grandeur and would help carry sound around the room. Besides the twin rows of velvet-backed seats, there were wall lamps that could be manually dimmed, and a curtained area at the side of the stage itself. Grant pushed back the curtain using the end of his blaster, nudging it aside. The metal curtain rings squeaked discordantly as they inched across the brass rail.

Behind the curtain, Grant saw a small, unlit room where costumes hung on racks, both male and female though all of them appeared to be of a similar size. The similarity of costumes indicated to Grant that the stage players were a tight cast, taking multiple roles and being recast with each new production.

A shelving unit near the back of the room contained clothbound manuscripts. Grant grabbed one at random and flicked through it, tilting its pages slightly to catch the light from the stage. The pages contained details of a play, stage direction and dialogue written out in hand. The penmanship was exquisite, great looping letters within which beautiful cameos and artworks had been drawn. It was something that could not be artificially reproduced.

ON STAGE, KANE CONTINUED trying to reassure naked Harold. The man watched him with his duo-toned eyes, no sign of understanding behind them.

BRIGID FOUND THE SECOND CORPSE at the top of the winding staircase, sprawled against a wall with a hunk of his chest in ruins on the floor between his open legs. He was a stocky man and his eyes had been gouged out and his skin had been flayed, great rents of it torn from his face and hands. Brigid gagged when she saw this. The man had suffered at the hands of his torturer; of that there could be no question.

The walls here were a pale gray color, lit once more by the inconstant glow of gas lamps on elaborate wall brackets. There was an open doorway to the left and a line of closed doors on the right. Each door had been painted with representations of flowers, creeping plants winding down the height of the wood. Taking a closer look, Brigid saw pixies or fairies playing among the flowers, playing pipes and drums as they danced on the leaves.

Brigid glanced in the open doorway, acknowledging a large room that looked something like a gymnasium. The room was unlit and Brigid was determined to come back to it once she had confirmed what was behind the painted doors.

She peered behind each door in turn, confirming that no one was lurking there and that there were no more dead bodies. Behind the doors were rooms, each containing a large double bed and a desk with a lamp with a decorative shade. The beds and the lamps looked ancient, recalling Victorian England. There were trinkets in each room, mechanical jewelry boxes with clockwork dancers that would pop up when the lid was opened, books containing aged photographs and drawings, a great atlas showing the world as it was in 1895. Each room contained a partitioned area with a wardrobe-cum-dressing-room. Brigid took a moment to riffle through the clothes hanging on the rail of the first, discovering long dresses in the ornate Victorian style. Her heart sank, recalling the way that Grant had described his attackers in the Panamint factory.

The final room contained bathing facilities along with a toilet, scale marring the porcelain sheen, newly deposited feces and urine spattered against the floor.

After a quick sweep, Brigid left the side rooms and checked the end of the corridor, where the tunnel bent sharply to meet the one that she, Kane and Grant had used to reach the theater box. There was no one else here, just one last room to check.

She strode back down the corridor, boot heels echoing on the floor tiles, and made her way to the open doorway that waited to her right. TP-9 still in hand, Brigid used her free hand to activate her flashlight before stepping through the doorway. The beam of light played across a large, almost square room that contained various items of training equipment. The gear was old-fashioned—no, not old-fashioned, Brigid mentally corrected, simply old. There were leather punching bags, wooden vaulting horses, ropes and a marked-out sparring ring.

And there was something else, too. Brigid's beam passed over a metal plate on the wall, and she moved the flashlight back to check it more carefully. Wide as a door, the brass plate stood taller than Brigid and it seemed at first glance to contain a face. On closer inspection she saw that the "face" was actually an effect created by two round control knobs and an oscillator scope that ran beneath them like a mouth. There were other dials and knobs on the wall plate, several level indicators held behind glass.

Brigid reached forward, turning the most prominent dial, a black knob that rotated with a clicking noise. As she did so, soft lights illuminated the doorlike metal slab from above and within the casing itself, and she heard the crackling recording of a man's voice emanate from a single speaker at the midpoint of the plate.

"Welcome to the WarCreche, Dorian. Opponent selected. Sequence begins."

TWENTY FEET BELOW BRIGID, Kane was still kneeling on the stage before the eerily silent figure he had found there.

"Can you talk?" Kane asked. "English? Um…*parlez-vous Français?*"

Nothing.

Dammit, he was running out of ideas. The guy continued to stare at Kane, his eyes flicking down to the automatic pistol that he held in his right hand. Maybe the gun was frightening him, Kane figured. He held his hand up before the man's face, making a show of it, the barrel pointed away at the ceiling. Then, with a long-practiced flinch of trained wrist tendons, Kane commanded the Sin Eater back into its hidden holster.

"There," he said. "I put it away. The blaster's not going to hurt you."

Without warning, the man reached forward and grabbed Kane by the neck with both hands, driving him down onto the stage with all his weight.

Chapter 14

Brigid stepped back as the gymnasium-style room came to life, bright lights illuminating every corner. The strange wall plate was alight, too, its indicators rotating in their dial casings, the oscillator showing a wave form, a thick black line drawn on off-white paper.

There was someone else in the room, too, Brigid realized, and she spun automatically to face them. The figure wore loose, colorful silk robes and had a yellow pallor to his flesh. A long sword was sheathed at his belt. He looked inhuman, a stylized representation of a man, tall with broad shoulders.

"Hi, there," Brigid began uncertainly. "Now, just where did you appear from?"

Brigid felt trepidation as the figure strode across the gym toward her, face fixed in a cruel expression of hate, not saying a word. The lights had altered around her; they flickered continuously at a level Brigid was aware of only subconsciously, and suddenly she had the impression she was standing in a wild jungle, great ferns arcing above her to create a canopy of lush green.

The silk-robed figure was still striding, drawing his glinting sword from its sheath as he hurled himself at Brigid. She sidestepped, ducking under the figure's first attack without hesitation.

Behind her, a second figure appeared through the thick foliage that now defined the space, lunging with his own sword as Brigid leaped aside. This one looked just like the first, a fixed, grim expression on his face, a coned hat propped over his dark, braided hair. The two-foot sword cut just to Brigid's side, and the flat of the sword slapped against her flank with a solid rebound. Brigid grunted with the strike, dropping down out of the path of the next swishing arc of the sword.

"They're samurai," Brigid realized, speaking to herself. Stylized representations of ancient samurai.

Another blade sliced through the air and Brigid felt the brush of falling leaves against her arm as she dodged aside.

"What the heck did I walk into?" Brigid muttered as she tossed aside her flashlight and swung her blaster round to bear on the first of the opponents.

ON THE TINY, gas-lit theater stage, Kane struggled with the naked man as he pressed his fingers into Kane's windpipe. The man was strong, superhumanly so, and it was all Kane could do to grasp the man's wrists and keep him from crushing his throat.

"Git…" Kane muttered through strained lips.

The bald man loomed over him, pushing harder against Kane's neck, bringing all of his weight to bear as he tried to strangle the ex-magistrate. The man's lips were pulled back from gritted teeth, the whites of his eyes wide, creating a complete white ring around his mismatched irises, blue and brown. There was something about his eyes, the look not of intelligence but that of a wild animal, one that had been caged too long, had turned on its master.

Beneath Kane, the bare boards of the stage felt hard and unrelenting. He had been strangled before, by men and by other, stranger creatures. The strength in this man's arms surprised him. The rational part of his brain tried to figure out how this seemingly normal man could be so strong. He remembered what Grant had said about the strangers he had faced in the factory, recalled how swiftly Grant said they had moved, how their stamina seemed far superior to a normal man's.

Kane shifted his grip, struggling to find the leverage to push the man away, hands grasping up and down the man's bare arms as he strove to gain purchase. His face was already turning beetroot-red with the pressure, yet he was unable to get any force into his response.

"Don't…" Kane requested, but the word came out like a whine, barely a word at all.

His throat was aching now; it felt for all the world as if he was trying to swallow liquid concrete before it dried. In another minute I'll be unconscious, Kane realized, then after that I'll be dead. Unless I can do something—now!

UP IN THE GYMLIKE ROOM, Brigid Baptiste found herself meeting attacks from every side. There were six of the stylized samurai warriors now, their faces fixed in horrific masks, their blades glinting in the thrumming lights as they cut through the air.

It was eerily silent despite the number of attackers. Brigid brought her blaster around and targeted the first of them, sending a clutch of 9 mm parabellum-sheathed steel at a samurai figure in fluttering bloodred silks. The samurai's blade whipped before him, slicing the air in a multiple flash of receding bullets.

"Did he…?" Brigid muttered incredulously. "Did he just cut my bullets out of the air?"

There was no time to find the answer. Already the faux samurai was upon her, his two-foot blade swish-

ing down to meet with the center of her skull. Brigid
dropped, letting her body sag as she kicked out with her
right foot. The foot connected, delivering a punishing
blow to her foe's left knee even as his blade cut through
the empty air where she had stood. The samurai tumbled
back, tripping over himself as his leg gave way.

So, they're immune to bullets, Brigid realized, but not
to physical assault. Interesting.

The beautiful redhead brought herself back to her feet
as more samurai approached, nudging past the thick foliage with their cruel blades. Brigid spun as seven ugly
masks burst through the greenery, arms sweeping as
one, seven razor-honed swords swishing toward her.
Surrounded, she did the only thing she could do—she
leaped, reaching out with her empty hand and grabbing
a handful of overhanging branch, dragging herself up
into the nearest tree.

The samurai watched her depart, their blades cutting
silently through empty air, one blade clipping the heel
of her boot with a clank as she pulled it out of reach.

There was something going on here, Brigid realized
as she pulled herself up higher into the tree. A minute
before, she had been in a gymnasium, working that metal
plate thing she had found on the wall. Then the plate had
spoken, describing this as the WarCreche and addressing her as…*Dorian?*

Below, the samurai were pacing around the tree,
watching like cats to see if Brigid might slip. They had
the right idea, she concluded—sooner or later she would
have to come down, and when she did there would be no
escaping the cruel justice of the samurai's blades.

KANE COULD FEEL the pressure on his throat like a vise,
constraining his breathing, cutting off his air supply.

Above him, the deranged figure he had come to think of as Harold wore an insane expression, haunted eyes wild with animal rage.

Kane had been trying to remove the man's hands from his throat, but it was no use. Harold's pounce had given him the leverage, and he was strong as all get-out. Kane could feel his own strength ebbing, could feel that burn in his lungs where the desire to take another breath became pressing. Caught by surprise, Kane had expelled his breath when Harold had leaped onto him with such suddenness, had had no chance to take another.

Kane let his hands slip, sweat moistening his palms as his knuckles rapped against the wooden stage. The whole battle was almost silent, so there was no chance that Grant—just feet away—would hear while he searched in the little dressing room. Well, screw that, Kane thought. He'll hear this and when he does he'll come running.

With that, Kane's arms whipped up and his open hands slapped against the sides of his attacker's head with as much force as he could muster, letting out a great clap as he cupped them over his foe's ears. As he did so, Kane also tensed the tendons in his right wrist in a specific, well-practiced way, calling forth the Sin Eater pistol he had sent away to its holster just minutes before.

As Kane's hands drew back from the vicious strike against his foe's skull, the Sin Eater materialized in his right hand, his index finger locking in the curve of the trigger, sending forth an angry flurry of bullets.

Ten feet away, Grant heard the noise where he stood examining another play manuscript, this one even more ornate than the first. He spun to face the open doorway, pushing the heavy drape back farther and eyeing the scuffle that was occurring on the stage.

"Kane? What the—?"

Grant didn't finish the sentence. Already the naked, bald-headed figure on stage had turned his attention to him, and Grant saw that he was smiling like a loon. Grant watched in horror as the man gnashed his teeth before opening his jaws wide and dipping his head down toward Kane's exposed throat.

CLINGING TO A BRANCH, Brigid tentatively leaned out, bringing her TP-9 semiautomatic in line with the pacing samurai's heads. "Here goes nothing," she muttered, squeezing the trigger and sending a burst of 9 mm slugs into the crowd of patrolling warriors.

As one, the samurai raised their swords to a high, horizontal position, and Brigid watched incredulously as her bullets were repelled. That was impossible—wasn't it?

She clung to the tree, trying to figure out what to do. Her Commtact was no use underground like this; she tried it quickly but there came no response, not even from Cerberus headquarters. She had to think.

It looked like a jungle for sure, but there was something missing. The smell. This jungle had no scent, despite all the lush greenery that was apparently growing all around her. Brigid had been in jungles before. She knew the smells, like mulch and dew and sweat—but she wasn't sweating. It should be hot here but she wasn't sweating, not unduly, certainly no more than the shadow suit could compensate for.

It was an illusion, then, somehow generated when she had turned the dial on the metal plate. Some kind of virtual-reality program perhaps, like the dream structures she had entered in the backstreet dream factory in Hope.

Nuzzled in the safety of the high branches, Brigid looked around. The door was still out there somewhere, doubtless hidden by the illusory trees. If she could reach that, maybe she could exit? But if this was some training program, would it allow her to exit? Wouldn't it block her, to prevent a participant's accidental egress during battle?

Think, then. Another answer. The wall plate, the one she had tinkered with, had switched on. Any machine that could be switched on could be switched off again, right?

"Program," Brigid called out in a loud voice, "shut down."

Nothing happened.

"Switch off."

Still nothing.

"WarCreche—this is Dorian. End training simulation."

Nothing.

Below, the samurai warriors continued to wait patiently for Brigid to drop from her perch.

ONE LEVEL DOWN, Kane turned as the bald head lunged toward him, jaws wide, ready to bite his throat. Still in the grip of the deranged figure crouching over him, Kane felt the man's teeth graze his neck.

As sharp teeth nuzzled against his exposed throat, Kane heard a distant explosion—the boom of Grant's Copperhead subgun. Seemingly at the same instant, the grip on his throat was relinquished as the naked man went tumbling backward, a stream of bullets drilling against him one after another.

Grant stood at the side of the raised stage, one booted foot on the stage itself as if to climb up, holding the trigger of the Copperhead down on continuous fire. A rapid stream of 4.85 mm slugs slapped against the bald figure who had attacked Kane, striking against his head and shoulders, knocking him back across the stage with the force of their impact. The naked man scrambled back with each strike as if he was being hit with a water cannon, his body trembling as the bullets struck.

Grant stepped up onto the stage, still holding the blaster on Kane's attacker. "Get back," he snarled, "you evil sack of crap."

Lying on the stage in a semidelirious state, Kane struggled to take a breath, feeling the rawness in his throat as if it was sandpaper. He rolled and spluttered, forcing himself up, striving to inhale. The air hurt his windpipe and made him cough more, great whooping splutters as he tried to hold some air in his lungs.

Grant's gun was cycling around rapidly, and he had maybe five more seconds before the ammo clip ran out. Before him, the naked figure was now at the back of the stage, jostling in place as the bullets lashed him, snatching at them like insects as he tried to fend them off. Grant took another step forward, expending the last of the Copperhead's clip as he brought himself right up to the struggling figure.

He may look like a man, Grant realized, but he was certainly something more than that. No man could survive the impact of that many bullets; it was simply impossible. Shell casings lay all about the stage, littering it like cherry blossoms fallen in the wind, a great carpet of steel flecks.

Grant felt the trigger pull just slightly, heard the abrupt silence as the Copperhead ceased firing. He stood over the crouching figure, eyes narrowed as he watched it. And the figure was an "it" in Grant's mind; he refused to think of something that could survive such an assault as human.

The thing looked up at Grant with its mismatched eyes, fear showing in its hairless features.

WHOEVER HAD DESIGNED this WarCreche, whatever it was, had clearly meant for the participants to complete the task before it shut down. The task being deadly battle with opponents who were only too happy to exploit a weakness and maim or perhaps even kill whomsoever they perceived as an enemy. And right now, they perceived Brigid as one.

Her blaster wasn't doing anything, Brigid realized, just making dents in the gymnasium floor where it lurked beneath the illusory jungle. Reluctantly, she flipped on the safety and shoved the TP-9 back in its holster.

Twelve feet beneath her, the samurai were milling about, pacing in silence as they waited for their prey to drop. However this illusion had been created, their swords seemed plenty real enough.

She needed to get to the control panel, dial herself out of this simulation, shut down whatever the hell it was she had powered up. Brigid's head flicked back and forth, her hair drawing over her face as she searched for the bronze plate in the wall. The jungle appeared dense, greenery in all directions and as far as the eye could see. It was an illusion, though—it simply had to be. There had been no rush of the teleport, no momentary physical uncertainty as her body was discorporated before rematerializing here in this jungle, and there was surely no jungle under the ground like this—not here. No, she was sure of it—she was still in the room that the recorded voice had referred to as the WarCreche.

"Find a wall," Brigid muttered to herself, "and follow it." A simple and elegant solution.

Grasping the thick branch that loomed ahead of her,

Brigid swung herself once, twice, three times over it like a gymnast on the bars, picking up speed before launching herself down toward the waiting samurai. She struck the foremost samurai high in the chest with both feet, slamming into him with the impact of a runaway freight train.

Without a word of complaint, the samurai-thing went down, crashing into three of his colleagues as he plummeted backward to the ground.

Brigid landed in a crouch beside the fallen samurai warriors and sped away, legs pumping, arms stretched out before her to feel her way. Low-hanging tree branches and tall ferns blocked her path, causing her to think quickly, weaving a new pattern even as the remaining samurai hurried after her. Up ahead there was a solid wall of foliage, more like a hedge than something that would naturally occur in a jungle. That had to be the wall, she realized, that or something just behind it.

The samurai were catching up, cutting through the plant life as though it were weightless. Perhaps it is, Brigid realized. Perhaps only I see it.

Then she was at the hedge and instead of turning away from it, she leaped, powering her body in a two-step spring that took her to the top of the towering green eight feet above the ground. Her hands slapped against the sky that waited behind it with the sound of flesh slapping brick. It was the wall, disguised as the sky, hidden within the projection.

From her position atop the hedge, Brigid scanned left and right, narrowing her eyes to try to filter out the flicker that seemed to be generating the unreal environment. It was there when she blinked, a momentary afterimage of the unlit gymnasium, shadow figures moving within it. The image was too momentary to fully process, but Brigid realized right away that she was in some kind of interactive virtual environment, as she had guessed, one that required props to function. Despite the conviction and speed with which the illusions were cast, the whole thing was little more than a funfair ride, shadow and light used to cast images in the viewer's mind.

Brigid's eidetic memory granted her an incredible spatial awareness, enough that she might locate the brass panel within those split seconds before her blinks resolved back into the illusion.

Blink. Look left.

Blink. Look right.

Blink. Left again.

Blink.

There. She spied the panel gleaming against the wall, just as she had left it, and she fixed it in her mind as the illusion took precedence, filling her eyes with the fluttering image of the jungle like a flip-book animation.

Knowing what she was looking for now, Brigid saw the way the hedge became a knot of branches, a wide tree trunk, a thick clump of bushes. She saw the way that the illusion projected over the walls, disguising the true proportions of the room. Knowing was half the battle.

It took a minute, ducking and weaving, slipping under drooping branches, vaulting over others, always keeping just three steps ahead of the relentless samurai warriors with their fixed expressions.

When she reached it, Brigid still could not see the door-size panel. It existed only in her eidetic memory, its position fixed in place, each dial and knob and lever crystal clear in her mind's eye. She reached forward, clawing for the black knob she had clicked around a quarter turn to set the simulation in motion. She couldn't see it—all that appeared before Brigid's eyes was a wall of leaves, their thin veins drawn sharp by the sun's rays. But she felt it, forced herself to feel it as she held the dial. Behind her, two samurai had broken through the curtain of vegetation and were bringing their swords to bear, held high in preparation to behead her.

"Please work," Brigid muttered as she twisted the dial back in the reverse direction, resetting it to how she had found it.

From the speaker in the wall panel before her, that same crackling recorded voice burst out.

"Simulation concluded," it said, structuring the words into syllables, each one shouted. It sounded like an old-fashioned sergeant major, the type Brigid had seen in ancient entertainment vids, the type Bill S. Preston Esquire had so desperately fought to avoid when his dad threatened to send him to military school.

Behind and all around her, the simulation flickered and died, the vines turning back into ropes, the thick tree branches becoming just a pommel horse and a punching bag once more. The samurai warriors waited immobile, only they were no longer samurai—just blank-faced automatons holding pipelike staves in their clumsy hands.

It had felt so real.

Brigid studied the control panel before her, the lights dimming to nothingness. She bent down, retrieving the discarded flashlight she had dropped earlier, playing its beam across the shiny metal plate. It looked ancient, the design all elaboration and hand-crafted workmanship. A tiny plaque at the bottom read Made in Colchester, England, 1895.

The words, embossed on a brass tag, had been buffed almost flat, and beneath them lay the royal crest indicating the builders of the machine served the British Royal Family.

"WarCreche," Brigid repeated, running the strange

word around in her mind. "Some kind of virtual training environment for elite soldiers, maybe?" What was it the machine voice had called her? "Dorian. As in Dorian Gray perhaps?" Well, that made as much sense as anything else she could come up with.

Brigid backed out of the silent gymnasium and headed for the staircase. It was time to share her findings with Kane and Grant.

KANE AND GRANT had troubles of their own.

The mysterious Harold was still crouched at the rear of the stage, warily eyeing Grant as the hulking ex-magistrate reloaded his Copperhead. Kane was only now pulling himself up from the floor, and it took him several goes to get the words out to speak to Grant as he aimed his Sin Eater—albeit somewhat haphazardly—in the direction of his attacker.

"Wh-what…kept y-eugh?" Kane croaked.

"Didn't realize you had trouble out here," Grant said as he slid the new ammo clip home. "You should have said something."

"Little…difficult," Kane admitted in his strained voice. "Bastard had my…windpipe shut."

"You okay now?" Grant asked without taking his attention from Kane's attacker.

"Getting there," Kane said after a moment's hesitation. "Sore as hell, though."

"There's water back in the Mantas," Grant reminded him. "You want to go back?"

"In a bit."

The unclothed figure remained in place, watching Grant's blaster with obvious concern.

"Yeah, that's right," Grant said, motioning slightly

with the Copperhead, "I got no bones about shooting you. None at all."

On his feet now, Kane looked swiftly about the little stage area for something to bind his attacker. His eyes fixed on the curtain pull, a thick rope colored a dull gold, and he drew his knife from his boot and hacked through it in three quick strokes. A moment later, Kane was standing next to the man who had attacked him, making it very clear what he was going to do and warning him not to try anything.

"You don't want my partner to shoot you again," Kane said, his voice still hoarse. "Not while you're naked anyway. He's liable to shoot you in the crotch, something I don't think even you're going to recover from quickly."

Without replying, the naked man held his hands ready to be bound, and Kane looped the rope over him to make sure his ankles were bound, too.

"So what are we going to do with him?" Grant asked. "Can't shoot him. Not easily anyhow—I got an empty ammo clip that proves that."

Kane cleared his throat to answer, but before he could, Brigid Baptiste reappeared in the doorway at the rear of the theatre.

"Hey, guys," she said.

Kane looked at her, irritated. "Where the hell did you get to, Baptiste?" he croaked. "This ass almost punched my ticket down here while you were—"

"Kane, I've found something," Brigid said, stopping him midflow. "I think it's important."

With their prisoner tied in one of the chairs, Kane and Grant followed Brigid up the staircase, past the dead bodies.

Chapter 15

"It's called a WarCreche," Brigid explained. The three Cerberus warriors were standing together in the gymlike room, huddled around the brass instrument panel that was sunk into one wall. The eerie, faceless mannequins had disappeared back behind the cabinet doors that lay flush against one wall. "It's some kind of ancient training facility designed to test soldiers."

"How old?" Grant asked.

"Over three centuries," Brigid said, pointing to the worn plaque. "Says it was built in 1895."

"How does it work?" Kane asked.

"It employs the principles of theater to generate a virtual environment, using an advanced form of hypnotic suggestion."

Grant shook his head. "Boy, you sure said a mouthful…."

"I experienced it firsthand when I accidentally switched it on," Brigid explained.

"'Accidentally'?" Kane repeated, his dubious tone clear even with his newly gravelly voice.

Brigid raised an eyebrow as she smiled. "It was pretty obvious how it operated," she said. "I wanted to see what it did."

"And what did it do?" Grant asked.

"It uses flickering light to fool the brain," Brigid explained, "similar to the kind of strobe effect that has been known to set off seizures in epileptics. That effect, coupled with some rather dazzling automatons—"

"Robots," Kane translated.

"—creates a kind of training field where combat prowess can be honed and tested."

Kane whistled incredulously. "And it's been down here all this time," he said.

Brigid nodded. "We've no reason to think otherwise."

"Then who's it for…?" Grant began. "Or do I already know?"

Brigid nodded again. "Yeah, I suspect it's your ambushers from the factory. There are clothes in the bedrooms that match the styles you described."

"But they're—what?—soldiers?" Kane asked.

"The brain of the WarCreche called me Dorian," Brigid explained. "I suspect that's a general name for the people that Grant met, like a designation or rank."

"Dorian…? Dorian…?" Kane rattled the word around thoughtfully.

"Dorian Gray was a character from a story by Oscar Wilde, an Irish playwright best known for his exceptional wit," Brigid filled in. "In the story—*The Picture of Dorian Gray*—the lead character has a supernatural portrait of himself which ages in his place, allowing him to remain a young man. He uses this incredible gift to enjoy a rather excessive lifestyle until the picture is discovered and the spell lifted."

"How does this relate to this WarCreche and the people who attacked me?" Grant asked.

"For all intents and purposes, Dorian Gray was an immortal," Brigid said. "I suspect that someone—maybe the British government—was experimenting with immortality around the same time as the story appeared, and that this facility contained the results of those experiments."

Kane looked unsure. "That's a lot of speculation based on not very much," he said warningly.

"The connection to Dorian Gray is obvious," Brigid said. "How many famous Dorians can you think of?"

Kane nodded reluctantly while Grant grumbled an agreement beside him.

"To achieve genuine immortality would require incredible medical advances," Brigid said. "The only other way to do it—and perhaps a more realistic one—would be to engineer something at the fetal stage, while it was still developing in the womb. Either option requires huge amounts of money, money that, historically, is only available for military purposes."

"But if you combine the two…" Kane said, seeing where the distaff member of the group was going.

"Exactly." Brigid beamed. "Supersoldiers. Immortal, impervious to attack, stronger and faster than an ordinary man." She turned to Grant. "Is all of this starting to sound familiar?"

"Yeah," Grant growled. "A lot like what me and Shizuka… What put her in the infirmary."

Kane looked around the dark WarCreche, light trickling through the open doorway. "So what now, Baptiste?"

"We have some names," Brigid said. "We may be able to track down more information through the Cerberus database."

"One thing confuses me," Kane admitted. "You said this looked like a British project—what's it doing here, buried under a mound in Luilekkerville?"

"That's a good question," Brigid agreed, "and one I don't have an answer to."

"Here's another," Grant groused as the trio left the

room. "How come they didn't show up before now? If they've been here since eighteen-ninety-whatever, what made them come up for air?"

"Our late grave robbers disturbed them," Brigid suggested, "but that doesn't explain why they didn't emerge before then. From what you've told us, these Dorians are naturally inquisitive."

"Yeah," Grant said.

"So how do you keep inquisitive supersoldiers from turning on their own troops?" Kane asked. "You have to have a way to contain them. Bunkie on stage back there is one of them. I'd lay money on it. The way he came at me and shrugged off Grant's bullets, there's no question that he's something more than human."

"And nuts as a jackalope on jolt," Grant muttered.

"Why didn't he leave, too?" Kane wondered. "The door's open, so what kept him down here?"

The group were back at the staircase now, and Grant led the way down with his subgun poised ready, stepping carefully over the pale corpse that littered the winding steps.

"If the evidence is to be believed," Brigid said, "then they've been down here a long time. While it began as a training facility, this place may have become a prison, either accidentally or on purpose."

Kane was shaking his head. "People don't get imprisoned accidentally. Not like this anyway. Someone's thrown a lot of money at setting this hole up for them. A *lot* of money."

"They may have been forgotten," Brigid mused. "It's been a long time."

Grant turned back to the others as they reached the foot of the stairs. "Trapped down here all that time— what do you figure that would do to someone?"

"Make them mad." Brigid said it almost flippantly, but the resonance of her words struck her.

"Yeah," Grant said, emerging from the stairwell with his blaster pointed at the stage. "That's what I thought."

The naked figure whose wrist tag called him Harold remained where they had left him, tied to one of the seats in the little auditorium. He seemed to be crying again, head ducked down in shame.

"Mad immortal soldiers," Kane muttered, looking over to the broken figure sitting where the audience should be. "Inbred and insane, with three hundred years of crazy rattling around in their immortal fucking heads. Yeah, this is going to end well."

Together, the group approached the remaining immortal where he sat rocking in his seat. He had calmed significantly since he had attacked Kane. He seemed almost to have become entirely reclusive once more.

THEY DID ONE MORE SWEEP of the underground facility before leaving, finding clothes for the naked man before escorting him up the tunnels that led to the surface. The corpses could stay down there, since there was no way for either Manta to carry the extra weight and frankly they were too long dead to go through the hassle of burying them. Once they were out, Kane reasoned, they could seal this place up and that would be the end of it, at least until they found the so-called Dorians and figured out what to do with them.

But as it happened, getting out with their mentally altered prisoner proved a lot more difficult than they expected. Harold made it along the final tunnel with ease, clearly intrigued by where he was going, almost as though he had never seen it before.

It was still light up there, the last of the afternoon sun

painting the sky a peach-skin pink through the manhole opening. The effect created an almost luminous circle in the roof of the tunnel.

"I'll go first," Grant said, while Kane held his Sin Eater locked on Harold's hairless head. "More chance he'll rabbit once we're out in the open, so I'd rather have the Copperhead trained on him once we're outside."

Grant climbed swiftly up the ladder rungs, swinging himself over the lip of the manhole and out into the grassy area beyond.

But despite their urging, Harold refused to move. He just stared at the ladder rungs in bewilderment.

"What is it, Baptiste?" Kane asked. "What is he having trouble with?"

"I don't know," Brigid said, looking all around. "It's almost like the way a rodent reacts to a sonic repellent. It doesn't know why it feels compelled to turn away, yet it does so anyway."

"But what's he turning away from?" Kane asked.

"Something…" Brigid said, looking all around for a speaker, some device that might emit a sonic prompt.

As Brigid searched, Grant peered down through the entryway, swinging the muzzle of the Copperhead down below the circular opening. "Hey, what's keeping you guys? Rough-'n'-tumble there giving you some trouble?"

As if triggered, Harold suddenly reached for the ladder and began clambering up its rungs, a broad smile stretched on his docile face. It was as though he was seeing the hole for the first time.

"Something I said?" Grant asked, pulling himself back out of the way.

Harold stopped, and the confusion reappeared on his face. Grant was looking down at him, and he had the distinct impression that Harold quite literally could not see him. He seemed to be focused on something right in front of him, as if the door was still sealed an inch from his nose.

"Grant?" Brigid called up. "What did you touch?"

"I didn't touch nothing," Grant objected.

"You did something, buddy," Kane rasped, his voice still a little raw. "Big man there isn't moving, and he was a moment ago."

"It's something you did, Grant," Brigid reasoned. "Repeat your actions… No, forget that." She closed her eyes, replaying in her mind's eye the exact movements that Grant had performed just moments ago. He had leaned in, dangling the barrel of the Copperhead over the lip of the entryway. Dangling it over…*there.*

Brigid saw it, an innocuous symbol drawn on the base of the opened door cover. No, it wasn't drawn—it was engraved in the metal. Once she had spotted it, she saw another one, this time engraved on the complex workings that hinged the door open, the weight and counterweight system of cogs and pulleys that must have made opening the door possible despite its weight and bulk.

"Use your coat to cover the door," Brigid said.

Grant was bemused but he didn't argue; he simply removed his long duster and hung it over the open manhole round where it stood upright within the depression. His coat acted as a curtain over the strange engraving, and almost as soon as he had masked it, prisoner Harold seemed to be happy to climb out of the subterranean lair and out into the open.

Keeping his distance, Grant framed the strange figure in the sights of his Copperhead while Brigid and Kane climbed to the surface before closing the cantilevered trapdoor in the earth. It was not hidden as such, but surrounded by trees and sunk in the ground so it would pass a casual inspection. No one would come here unless they knew what they were looking for.

"You think you can cope with fun boy here in the back of your rig?" Kane asked as Grant slipped his arms back into his coat sleeves.

Grant eyed the strange figure of Harold shambling around in a circle, staring at his own feet. "Maybe we should sedate him," Grant concluded, "just to be safe."

Agreed, the three Cerberus warriors escorted Harold to the Mantas, reporting their initial findings before taking off and heading back to home base. Behind them, the eternal sun continued its lazy descent toward the horizon, eking out the last of its rays.

Chapter 16

"The symbol is a kind of *fnord*," Brigid explained to the assembled throng in the Cerberus cafeteria.

Kane, Grant and she had returned to Cerberus fourteen hours earlier, over which time they had placed Harold in the facility's holding pens and caught up on sleep before tackling the problem fresh.

Right now, the three allies, along with Lakesh, Donald Bry and Reba DeFore, had commandeered a table in the large cafeteria area of the Cerberus redoubt where they were discussing their findings over a late brunch of pastries, toast and fruit preserves. The cafeteria was a large room incorporating several long tables with wipe-down surfaces and fixed seats, along with a few smaller tables that might be considered a little more cozy. The redoubt had started life as a military base, and rooms like this were designed with the army in mind. As such they were more functional than homey.

The serving area dominated one wall of the room, behind which the huge kitchens were located, a line of hot drinks dispensers arranged in one corner. The walls had been painted in bright colors but that paintwork was chipped and scarred just now, evidence of the assault that the redoubt had suffered at the hands of Ullikummis and his troops. During that attack, the whole cafeteria had been smothered with a web of living rock that had adhered to the walls like creeping ivy. The rock had been removed, but the repaint had yet to be completed.

"A fnord is a piece of neural programming that can be hidden in the processing centers of the human brain," Brigid continued, "to effectively hide something that the programmer doesn't want to be seen."

"And that's the engraving we saw on the underside of the trapdoor?" Grant asked.

Brigid nodded. "I think so."

"But we could see it," Kane pointed out.

"We weren't the subject," Brigid said. "Presumably, it was meant for Harold and his friends."

"Who got out," Kane reminded her, and Grant nodded in agreement.

"I've been thinking about that," Brigid said. "A fnord is a theoretical word or sign that cannot be seen by the viewer but causes a subliminal reaction, usually revulsion. We saw that in our subject—Harold—and we may speculate that the other subjects from that underground facility would have a similar reaction, in essence unable to see that there was a trapdoor right above their noses.

"However, once it was opened by Ms. Blue's associates—" Brigid shrugged.

"They broke the spell," Lakesh finished with poetic license.

Kane took a swig from a glass of fruit juice before speaking. "The door was open when we got there," he said, "but Harold was still inside. And he wouldn't come out until we covered this...fnord thing."

"My observation suggests that Harold's one very disturbed man," Brigid said. Beside her, Reba DeFore agreed, flicking through the sheaf of papers that she had already compiled in her medical assessment of the prisoner. "Once the door was shown to them, the others could see past their programming and exit their lair. But Harold—?"

"His mind's not in a good place," DeFore seconded. "From my initial assessment, I'd say he's closer to a wild canine than a man at all."

Kane looked pensive. "You think he was always like that?"

"If he was, then someone was taking good care of him until very recently," Brigid surmised. "The clothes, the bathroom, the way in which everything had been kept— it speaks of a level of organization and cleanliness that Harold isn't capable of."

"It may be that someone did this to him," DeFore said, "either by accident or on purpose. Tapped into his mind and left him…spaced-out."

"Why do you say that?" Lakesh wanted to know.

The medic looked across to Grant guiltily before turning to her papers and finding the relevant page. "I've been examining Shizuka while she's in my care," she explained. "While she took some physical damage in the scuffle in the Panamint factory, there's no specific evidence of trauma enough to put her into a coma. I think either something touched her mind in such a way as to make it shut down, or she received a specific order to do so."

"Which amounts to the same thing," Kane said, shaking his head regretfully.

Grant looked across the table, aware that all eyes were on him. "It's okay, people," he announced, "I'm an adult. You can discuss Shizuka's condition around me."

DeFore nodded gratefully. "It could be that the subject in our holding pen—Harold—has suffered the same basic psychic attack."

Despite his outer calm, Grant felt his stomach sink.

Harold was an imbecile, little more than a savage, a rabid animal. If the same should happen to Shizuka, if she should wake up in that state—well, Grant didn't know what he would do, but he would have to do something.

Officiating the meeting, Lakesh turned to his second-in-command, the copper-curled, tousle-headed Donald Bry. "Donald?" he prompted. "Would you please share with everyone what you've found out?"

Bry nodded, referring to his own notes before he began. "Once you guys had confirmed the site as the correct location," he said, flicking his gaze from Kane to Grant to Brigid, "we set up a database search on the area in question, deeds of ownership, planning applications, et cetera.

"We had to do some digging—" Bry laughed nervously at his unintended pun "—but it eventually became clear that the land was owned, through a series of dummy companies, by the British Crown."

Kane looked surprised. "How is that possible?"

"The land was purchased in 1895 while Queen Victoria was on the throne," Bry explained, "where it was immediately designated a site for scientific research. An American professor—one Edgar Howard—was involved with the setup, which he dubbed the 'Gray Area' as a kind of joke."

Brigid nodded in understanding. "*Dorian Gray* rears his head once again," she said.

"Professor Howard," Bry continued, "was a pioneer in the field of early genetic research. Initially self-financed, he first turned to the U.S. government for funding in 1887. However, his experiments were ruled as too barbaric and that funding dried up, so he traveled to the British Isles, where he petitioned Her Majesty's government, specifically the ministry of defense, for financing to continue his research. This was in the winter of 1893, at the peak of the British Empire, one of the most successful military machines the world has ever borne witness to.

"It seems that the M.O.D. saw potential in Howard's research and commissioned him to explore the concept of a superior soldier, funding his research first in Britain before transferring to his native U.S.A.," said Bry. "Harold and his colleagues appear to be the result of that research."

"Supersoldiers," Kane muttered, shaking his head.

"It tallies with what we found underground," Brigid reminded him. "The WarCreche simulation was obviously designed to hone combat instincts as a practice room for warriors."

"Howard breeds artificial humans," Bry continued, consulting his notes, "who are designed to have superior intellect, stamina and endurance to the average man. In simple terms, his artificial people are immortals, the first of a line of unstoppable soldiers for the British Empire.

"But there's a snag. Just before Howard is about to go into full production, he starts to see a disturbing rise in the aggression levels in his five subjects. They're quick to anger and they often fly into what he describes in his notes as 'insane rages.' In March of 1897, one of his new men turns on him. He attacks Howard and has to be pulled off and shot by the on-site security. Of course, the Dorian, as Howard's now dubbed his genetically engineered men, is too strong to be shot, and it takes a total of 418 rounds to put the man down."

Kane cursed, while the others at the table looked horrified, all except Grant, who seemed placid.

"They tried to burn the corpse but it simply would not die," Bry continued. "Net result—Professor Howard now has five unkillable, superintelligent would-be soldiers on his hands who could potentially turn on him at any moment."

"And they couldn't kill them," Brigid checked.

"Exactly," Bry confirmed. "They had been engineered to be immortal. But Howard's smart—smart enough to have built a fail-safe into his creations, a command which they cannot counteract. According to Howard's logs, he genetically placed a hidden piece of neuro-linguistic programming in their makeup, what he refers to as an 'evolutionarily engineered blind spot'…"

"Catchy," Kane muttered.

"The thing that Brigid calls a fnord," Bry concluded. "Howard's team lock the immortal soldiers in their research bunker, bury it, landscape the area and hide them away."

"For three hundred years?" Kane asked. "How did they eat? *What* did they eat?"

"The Gray Area facility was designed to be self-sufficient, much as our redoubt is," Bry explained. "It recycles air and water, while food is best not thought about. Keep in mind these soldiers, these Dorians as they're called, are able to survive in extreme conditions with no physical decay. They can go for months without nutrition."

"So they couldn't even be starved away," Grant growled.

"What's more, they're very intelligent," Bry said. "I read through the reports Professor Howard left. He was very set on creating an intelligent army, one that would appreciate the arts and the sciences along with their designated role as upholders and enforcers of the law." He sent a significant look to Kane and Grant.

"Supersmart magistrates," Kane realized. "That's what we're looking at here. Isn't it?"

Lakesh nodded once, sorrowfully. "From what Grant related of his encounter with them, I suspect that three hundred years locked up in that bunker has made them a little…eccentric."

"YOUR PLEASURE GARDEN is wilting, Cecily," Algernon said as he peered up from his work with the bomb.

The four Dorian soldiers had discovered a little oasis of greenery at the edge of the Mojave Desert and acquired it for their own. The neat little garden ran in a long strip down one side of a tiny settlement of a dozen properties, which was secluded and unlikely to be noticed. The locals had tended small plants for cooking there and others simply for the joy of it. That was, until three days ago when the four strangers had arrived in their great flying vehicle and brought havoc to the village—havoc in the form of art.

It had been Cecily's turn first and she had taken to the task with great aplomb, sending tendrils of thought into the curious locals before switching their minds off with a jerk, like an assassin breaking a man's neck. The people had been left standing, seemingly untouched, and Cecily had carefully placed them around the pretty, well-kept oasis, stripped naked, taking hours over the angle of their arms, the inclination of their heads. One group—a youngish man with a woman of similar years, had been fixed into a lover's embrace, with static children dotted around them as if playing a game of ring-a-rosy.

But now the "lovers" were starting to smell, their once bright flesh turning pallid, no longer able to capture the sun's tanning smile.

Algernon was crouched on his haunches, working at his special project, building up its exterior shell into something fearsome and awe-inspiring as befit its content. He had discovered a graveyard nearby, its name plaques repeating the same last names over and over again, local families who never left the area. He had cracked open the coffins and assumed the rib cages of a half dozen of the more-rotted corpses, which he now placed like armor around the length of the gleaming metal shaft. But while Algernon could never be accused of being squeamish, even he drew the line at smelling three-day-old children moldering in the sun.

"It's a part of the great experiment that is my art," Cecily informed him as she flounced over from the bench where she had been sitting, feeding gulls. "A living thing, whose decay reflects the seasons."

Algernon shot Cecily a look. "You're bluffing."

Cecily turned away as she began to blush, fanning at her rapidly reddening face with one hand. "Is it so obvious?" she asked.

Algernon nodded. "Hugh and Antonia suspected as much yesterday but they didn't have the heart to tell you," he said. "I wouldn't have, either, but the pungency of dead people is rather interfering with my concentration."

Cecily had the good grace to feign additional embarrassment. Thankfully, Hugh and Antonia had found somewhere else to be, doubtless frolicking behind the closed doors of one of the abandoned properties that made up the village.

Weaving through a group of statuelike people as if dancing, Cecily peered back over her shoulder and laughed. "My pleasure garden was good while it lasted, wasn't it?" she asked.

Algernon had his head down, back at work on the missile. "I appreciated it," he said, "and I believe that the others did, also."

With a flutter of her skirts, Cecily danced over to

where Algernon was sitting. "And this is your contribution to our grand exhibit?" she asked.

Algernon glanced up at her as he tightened the screws that would hold one of the rib cages in place, like the segments of a caterpillar. "I cannot honestly take the credit," he said. "It really came from Hugh's suggestion. I'm no artist, but I like making things. Silly, as you know."

Cecily shook her head. "Our own Hephaestus. But you've already done so much," she said, peering over to the flying machine where it had been docked.

"Nonsense," Algernon scoffed. "The devil finds work for idle hands. And you know how much I loathe that."

"The devil?" Cecily chirped.

"Work, dear," Algie corrected.

IT WAS LATE AFTERNOON and Kane found himself wandering the redoubt's subbasement level. Grant was holding a vigil over Shizuka's comatose form while Brigid had buried herself in cataloging the tech they had recovered from Hope, which left Kane at loose ends. He had spent an hour in the facility gymnasium pumping weights, another forty-five minutes or so on the target range honing his skills with his favored handblaster, the Sin Eater. But Kane had been restless, unable to concentrate. He got like this when there was action looming, when he knew a threat was out there that needed to be dealt with. He was a man of action, schooled in it from a young age, poised like a coiled spring to face any danger. Waiting had never sat well with him; his body strove to be *doing,* a dog waiting for the stick to be thrown.

Wide enough to fit a motor car, the basement corridor was painted a dusty shade of white that looked dull and soulless under the artificial lights. All hard surfaces, the corridor echoed as Kane stepped out of the elevator and paced along it, searching for the holding cell where Harold was being kept. Behind him, the elevator doors closed with a huff, the echo of the motor almost subliminal.

A group of porters were hefting the last of the dismantled dream engines into a storeroom near the elevator, and Brigid stood with them, helping them identify parts before filing them away. The dream engines had been taken from the illegal den in Hope, and it had taken three days to bring all the parts over and catalog them for storage. After releasing the muties, the Cerberus cleanup squad had also found a great stash of glist, distilled for maximum effect, which they had seized and brought back to Cerberus for safe disposal, removing it from Hope so that it could do no further damage to potential addicts.

Kane stopped before the open door, a great shutter that could be rolled aside to open almost the entire wall of the storeroom area. "Hey, how's it going?" he said in acknowledgment.

"Lot of gear here," Brigid told him, glancing up from her scratch pad over the rims of the round-framed spectacles she wore for reading work.

"Is there much we can use?" Kane asked.

"Sure," Brigid told him with a smile. "Donald's already given the VR engine a once-over. There's some powerful computer processing here for when we need it."

Kane turned toward the corridor, indicating the bank of interrogation rooms. "Any word from our newfound friend?"

"Who? Harold?" Brigid asked. "Last I saw, Reba was trying to get him to speak. I watched for a while, but it was all pretty tedious."

Dropping her pad down on one of the crates, Brigid accompanied Kane for the short walk to the interrogation room where Harold was being held. The room had a single door beside which was a large observation window fitted with one-way glass. Brigid and Kane peered through it, pitching their voices low.

Harold was sitting in a low, comfortable chair, both wrists affixed to its arms by separate handcuffs. His clothes had been replaced with a simple jumpsuit, similar to the ones worn by the Cerberus personnel, only in a burnt-red-orange hue to distinguish him as a prisoner.

Reba DeFore was sitting in an identical chair opposite, asking him questions and ticking off the answers with her pen.

"Do you know what year this is?" DeFore asked. There was resignation in her voice, the kind that comes of asking the same question repeatedly and getting no response. Sure enough, Harold continued to stare at her, his jaw open wide, a string of drool gathering slowly at the corner of his mouth. "What year is it, Harold?" DeFore repeated after a pause, but there was no reply.

"Is this what he's been like?" Kane asked Brigid, poking a thumb at the one-way glass.

"Thrilling, isn't it?" Brigid said with a note of sarcasm. "Why do you think I was cataloging parts?"

In the interrogation room, DeFore had moved on to another question. "What's your name? Is it Harold? Is that your name?" She repeated variations of the same question for almost two minutes, giving the prisoner ample time to respond. Harold continued to sit there, staring and drooling.

"Whatever they did to Harold, it seems to be permanent," Kane observed.

"His mind's gone," Brigid agreed. "Broken. Reba could still be asking the same questions a year from now and she won't get a better response."

Chapter 17

The edge of Hope

The Pacific Ocean stretched out like a blue glass carpet, lapping against the western edge of the fishing village. Piers jutted into the ocean from the shore, reaching out like splints, as if holding the water at bay. Fishermen sat there with rods twitching in the water, their boxes of bait carefully hidden from thieves. Many of these fishermen had been working these waters for years, either for pleasure or to supplement their larders, or more oftentimes both. Lately, with the influx of refugees, more people had taken to fishing these waters, filling the piers and skimming the ocean in barely floating boats, jerry-built things constructed of old packaging, strips of abandoned buildings and the salvage of other, older boats. To eat was to live, and Hope had so many who yearned to live, even as crime blighted their every waking hour.

One fisherman was in fact a woman, her name Harper Wright. Harper was forty-five with three teenage kids and she had been fishing these waters since she was their age. She had a spot on the creaking wooden jetty that she thought of as home. She had spent so much of her life here, come rain or shine, that she knew every splintered crack, every stain in the wood, and she could tell you how much each split had grown in the years since she had first come here with her brother. Harper had seen fish as long as a man's arm span, seen seals bask in the sun on the cold winter days and witnessed people cutting open sharks on this very pier on three separate occasions— one of them disgorging a dead toddler whose body had been swallowed whole and remained in one piece despite his ordeal, the skin turned a puffy white where the salt-water had bleached it. Her hair had once been russet-red but now it was streaked with lines of iron-gray, and the lines seemed to get wider and more populous every time she looked in the mirror. She had seen a lot and she had fed her family through it all, even when the refugees had come and tried to take a whole lot more than was right. But in all that time, Harper Wright, forty-five-year-old fisherwoman, had never seen anything like the sight that caught her eyes now.

It seemed to glide on the horizon with the setting sun at its back, a great oval colored the silver-white of a heron's feather, dawdling thirty feet above the undulating waves. With the way the waves played beneath it, it looked as if it was swaying, creating the illusion of a ripple to the great white bulb as it hovered above. The sun painted that white surface with indifferent streaks of orange and peach, like a child's finger painting on a plain canvas, exaggerating the sleek curve of the gigantic surface. There was something depending below that oval, too, a long, dark box like a coffin, held in place by dangling wires that looked delicate from this distance but were each the thickness of a grown man's torso.

And with the great pale blot on the sky came noise; rhythm, music, emanating from somewhere within its silver hide. As it drifted closer, making its languorous way toward the shore, the music became more distinct, the sounds of strings and wind instruments, a deep bass drum keeping time.

It was an airship, Harper realized, but one unlike any she had seen before. She had seen pictures of airships, but they had not been like this. The basic structure was the same, the gigantic hydrogen balloon with the passenger rig hoisted beneath it. But there the similarity ended. The balloon featured a great web of steel struts, huge vents and spines poking from its sides at odd angles, a network of catwalks running from top to tail. There were huge pipes hanging from the undercarriage, too, jutting out fore and aft like the horns of some wild beast.

And the ship sang, pumping out that music with the flourish of a great event. The music wafted across the shoreline, washing against the beach like the ocean's waves in an uplifting medley of sound.

ABOARD THE AIRSHIP, four immaculately dressed figures were watching through open windows, admiring the sensation their arrival was causing on the ground below.

"Look at them," Antonia trilled, pointing a white-gloved finger at the people on the beach. "They don't know what to make of us."

"They're so tiny," Cecily added with a chuckle, "like ants." She had changed the style of her blond hair. It was now piled in a twist around her head, a hat with a lacy veil propped somewhere in its golden architecture with the sly use of hat pins.

Hugh looked at her admiringly from the other side of the gondola, the mannequin resting beside him with its strings trussed over the chair Antonia had promised to renovate. "They are ants, dear Cecily," he reminded her, his eyes on the puppet's carved wooden face. "Insects whose tiny lives are of no matter to we here on this ship. We may burn them with magnifying glasses, should we so desire it. They have no say in our affairs, they live only to entertain us and to be educated by us."

Algernon was standing in the lower section of the craft where the pilot's controls were, waving his hands in the air as if conducting the musical recording that pumped from the dirigible's speakers, a rapier-thin sword in one hand doubling for a conductor's baton. "Perhaps we should make them dance," he said, caught up in the music.

"Yes, let's," Antonia agreed, leaning with her arms crossed on the sill of the open window, the wind catching her chocolate-colored hair.

Cecily joined her a moment later, and together the two women studied the people below as the airship sailed unhurriedly toward the strip of beach. "There, that one. Do you see?" the blonde woman said, pointing out a figure seated on one of the jutting piers. "Make her dance for us. Make her dance with all the rhythm of a goose."

Antonia eyed the figure that Cecily had identified, focusing her mind on the unsuspecting woman. It took a few moments to find her way, reaching out tentatively in the way that one might judge the weight of a football before throwing it. There were so many minds down there, each one babbling with thoughts, primarily concerned with what the airship was doing and where it had come from.

The woman took a moment to home in on, and once she had, it took Antonia another few seconds just to rummage in her wide-open mind to be sure she had the right person. She saw through the woman's eyes, a double sight, layered over her own like a painting on glass. The woman was watching the airship approach, trepidation prodding at her thoughts. Her name was Harper Wright and she had come here to fish.

HARPER WRIGHT WAS WATCHING the airship approach when she felt something pluck at her hair. She reached behind her, brushing at the back of her head to dislodge whatever it was, but there was nothing there. Shaking her head, she turned her thoughts back to the airship, its great shadow casting an inky blackness over the shimmering ocean surface.

Pick.

There it was again, that same feeling of something behind her, like a creature in her hair. She swept at it again, running her fingers through her hair and scratching at the back of her neck.

"You okay, Harper?" Old Taylor asked from his usual post beside her. Taylor was ruddy-faced with the prematurely aged features of a man who had spent too many hours sitting in the sea breeze waiting for something to bite. He may have been sixty-five, but could just as easily have been thirty. His grease-stained hat was pulled snug to his head, hiding any hint of the baldness that had taken over his once-full head of hair.

Harper looked at him, her face screwed up in irritation. "I'm... Something keeps scratching me," she said. "Can you— Would you take a look? Do I have something in my hair back here?" She showed him.

Taylor leaned forward in his chair, keeping one finger resting on the fishing line so he wouldn't miss a bite. "Can't see anything," he admitted after glancing over Harper's red-and-gray hair.

"You sure?" She checked, feeling the stab of claws or thorns again. Whatever it was, it itched like the devil.

The airship loomed over them both, its shadow drowning them in darkness.

"What in hell's name is that thing anyhow?" Old Taylor asked.

Harper looked up at it, stunned by its enormity. It was at least one hundred feet long, wide as the church that dominated the old village area of Hope. It was like the church in other ways, too, the spires like the church steeple remade through a fractured lens, a dozen spires writ across the sky by a madman's brush. The music was louder now, pressing down on them like a physical thing, changing the feel of the air. Old Taylor said something about the music putting the fish off their biting, but Harper couldn't hear him, not over the sound of the brass section, nor the scratching inside her skull.

Dammit, what the hell was that anyway? she wondered irritably as she clawed fingers through her hair again. There was definitely something there, but it felt almost like it was on the inside.

And then…

The pressure of fingers inside of your head. Like the realization that you have something caught in your tooth, the way you'll keep working it with your tongue, keep going back to it.

The ghost fingers pushed inside Harper's skull, pressing against her mind. Half standing over her seat, she stumbled, knocking the fold-up chair with her leg, causing it to go skittering across the pier. Old Taylor looked at her, wondering what she was doing. She stumbled about as if she was drunk, kicking into her box of bait, knocking the end of her rod so that it tipped up on its mount, drooping over the edge of the pier.

"Harper, what's got into you, girl?" Taylor asked, finally getting up from his seat.

Harper couldn't answer. The thing was in her head now, jabbing her like a pianist's busy fingers, tapping out a rhythm. She smelled something in her nostrils, a sweet, musky scent like a woman's perfume. The smell wasn't there, not really. It was Antonia's scent, the one she had dabbed behind her ears and on her wrists in delicate little touches like the brush of summer flowers. The woman was in her mind now, parting great slabs of her thoughts to make way for the jig. In that moment, she forgot the names of her children forever. Harper felt it like a blow to the head, a blow so hard it made her nose twinge, her eyes feel as if they would pop free from their sockets.

"Now dance," Antonia murmured as she peered over the side of the airship.

Below, Harper began to dance, arms and legs splaying in clunky rhythm, feet rising and falling in graceless stomps.

"What's the joke?" Old Taylor asked, reaching a grizzled hand for Harper's arm. She pulled from his grip, turning on the spot and raising her arms like a ballerina. "Harper?"

Peering from the airship cabin down at the cavorting fisherwoman, Cecily made a face. "She looks like a pachyderm pushed into a party," she observed.

Antonia looked at her colleague, squinting a moment to see past the angler's senses and into the cabin again. "Oh, please do allow me a moment to fine-tune things," she said. "I hadn't expected her mind to be quite so primitive. There."

Down on the pier, Harper began to move with improved style, her rhythm matching the rhythm of the music emanating from the leviathan above. Old Taylor's eyes bugged out as he saw the always-practical woman begin to leap and twirl, dancing across the rugged pier like a ballerina on stage.

"I never knew…" Taylor began, but he couldn't quite explain what it was he had never known about his long-time fishing neighbour.

Harper spun faster and faster, first on her left leg and then on her right, whirling around and around with the grace of a sycamore seed fluttering to the ground.

CECILY WAS ECSTATIC. "You have it, you really have it," she cried as Antonia made the simple woman dance.

Algernon shunted a lever on the side of the control column, locking the dirigible on automatic pilot before he strode across to watch. "I concur," he said with a brief, two-fingered clap. "You've made her really quite graceful."

Antonia smiled a knowing smile. "Merely phase one, my doubting friends," she said.

Suddenly, down below them, the whole pier seemed to take up the dance, young and old spinning in time, twirling around together, their steps perfectly attuned. Across the beach, more figures began to dance, pulled to their feet by the potent force wrenching at their minds.

Cecily was applauding now, too, her cheeks flushed with excitement. "It's wonderful," she said. "Like a Christmas card. All you need is ice skaters to complete the scene. A living, breathing Christmas card."

With a swish of her skirts, Cecily darted across the cabin to where Algernon sat, mock-conducting the music, and reached for his hand. "On your feet, Algie dear. A young lady should never dance alone."

Accepting the request in the spirit in which it had been made, Algernon tossed his blade aside and stood, joining Cecily in a lap of the cabin as the music played on.

But down on the pier all was not so wonderful. Harper Wright spun and spun, utterly out of control with the sharp nails pressed into her brain, yanking at her mind. She had all but lost consciousness, could no longer process what was happening to her. She whirled again, another two-step before butting against the wooden barrier of the pier. Red flew from her ears, crimson drops of her blood as her brain began to hemorrhage.

Around her, others were doing likewise, their dance steps becoming more desperate, blood budding from ears and nostrils as their brains went into meltdown.

"Tracking something," Brewster Philboyd said. He was sitting at his monitoring station in the main operations room of the Cerberus redoubt, watching the live satellite surveillance feed as it identified and zeroed in on an unexpected shadow over by the West Coast. Philboyd was a tall and gangly man with blond hair swept back from a gradually expanding forehead. He wore black-framed glasses above cheeks that showed evidence of acne scarring from his youth. Philboyd was an authority on astrophysics and had been deeply involved in securing access to the satellites that Cerberus had come to rely on for data. Cerberus used two satellites, repurposed from their original launch years before. One, the Keyhole Comsat, provided a communications relay for the Commtacts, while the Vela class brought a live visual of the globe from its steady orbit. Both satellites could be adjusted from the Cerberus ops room to be employed for a variety of surveillance tasks, but remained restricted by their positioning and by their simple lack of numbers.

The Cerberus team relied on plenty of other systems to complete their monitoring, from remote, unmanned stations that measured seismic disturbances to people on the ground who fed the ops room reports on a regular basis. However, the object that Philboyd's feed had spotted had been part of a specific computer-aided sweep as he scanned the areas where the Dorians had previously been seen, gradually expanding the surveillance window to try to identify anything that seemed out of place.

It was needle-in-a-haystack work, and everyone on the team knew that. But even a needle can be found, given enough time and personnel. This particular needle had taken three days to locate—and that was assuming it was the right needle.

Lakesh looked up from his desk at the rear of the ops room. "Mr. Philboyd?"

Brewster Philboyd ran his hand idly over his nose and chin as he analyzed the live information coming through from the satellite feed. "We have a shadow showing on the scan in the Luilekkerville region," he said as Lakesh strode across the room to join him. "Large. Could be an aircraft of some type."

Lakesh pulled over a spare seat from the empty desk beside Philboyd and sat, his eyes fixed on the monitor screen. The screen showed an overhead shot of the West Coast area, split roughly 70/30 between land mass and ocean. Although the clarity of the shot was remarkable, with the deep blue of the ocean and the tan-and-yellow mainland clearly defined, it took Lakesh a moment to spot the shadow that Philboyd had identified. At this scale, it was tiny, just a little stripe no bigger than his little fingernail, and shaped rather like a cigar.

"That's Hope, isn't it," Lakesh stated, recognizing the coastline of the fishing village.

Philboyd nodded. "Increasing magnification," he said

matter-of-factly as he entered a command on the computer keyboard, manipulating the image before them.

"What is it?" Lakesh asked as the image drew focus on the dark line hanging over Hope's shore.

"Comparative analysis suggests it's about a hundred feet long," Philboyd said, "and it's moving."

Without realizing, Lakesh squinted as if to get a better view of the object on screen. "Are you certain of that?" he asked.

Philboyd tapped at his terminal again and the image on screen split off into a smaller window as he brought up several moving shots of the same area from the past thirty minutes. Each shot showed the same coastline with a time code reference in the bottom corner. Two of them showed the mass located farther out to sea, while the third did not show the object at all. "It's taken a curved path from the north to bring it out over the ocean and approach from the west," Philboyd said, "keeping the sun behind it."

"A classic military maneuver," Lakesh stated absently. "Who do we have down there? Anyone?"

"Nobody at this time," Philboyd stated dourly. "The last of the cleanup crew left Hope over twenty-four hours ago. We have no one on the ground."

"Get Kane, get Grant, get Brigid," Lakesh instructed. "This is what they've been looking for. I feel certain of it."

Philboyd eyed Lakesh with concern. "It would take thirty minutes to scramble a team out there," he said. "By that time the...whatever it is, will have passed."

"No," Lakesh said with certainty, "it's traveling too slowly for that. Even if it leaves Hope it won't get far, and now that we have it we can track it."

"What if it's nothing?" Philboyd asked. "It could pose no threat and be completely unrelated to—"

"Alert Kane," Lakesh said, cutting the man off. "Scramble CAT Alpha and get them out there. We'll let them answer the ifs and maybes, Mr. Philboyd."

Chapter 18

Devastation. That was what Kane saw when he clambered out of the Manta and stepped onto the beach that ran along the once-beautiful shore of Hope. It was beautiful no longer. Now the sand was turned a dark shade of pink where blood had been muddied into it, pouring from the victims of the bizarre attack.

The victims lay groaning, their pleas wafting across the beach against the relentless swish of the waves. Their faces were covered in blood. It seeped from every orifice—ears, eyes, nostrils, mouth—rilling down their necks and across their shoulders, their chests. It looked as though someone had thrown dye over them, a rich scarlet so dark it was almost black. Kane drew another breath as he looked at the damage, estimating there were close to seventy victims lying here on the beach or bobbing on the waves.

"We need to check these people first," Brigid said as she hurried across the beach. "Find out what it is that we're facing here."

Kane wanted to argue but he held himself in check. She was right, much as it frustrated him to have to do still more waiting. His eyes scanned the body-littered beach, people's faces racked in agony staring back at him at every turn.

Brigid Baptiste was crouching by a nearby body—a

man of perhaps twenty with a shaved head—and she ran a penlight over the wounds to better see them in the dusk.

"It's okay," Brigid soothed as she ran the beam over the man's bloody features. "It's over now."

The man tried to respond but he just began spluttering, blood catching in his throat. He hacked the blood up, retching until a crimson line was spat across the sand beside him.

How Brigid had settled on him and not one of the numerous others, Kane didn't know. Bodies were strewed all across the beach and more limp forms floated in and out with the tide where they had fallen into the ocean. Twenty yards away, one of the piers was piled with bodies, one woman hanging over the side, dangling from fishing lines like a string puppet, her red-gray hair fluttering in the breeze.

"What happened here?" Grant asked as he made his way across the beach to join his allies. "Are they dead?"

"No," Brigid confirmed without looking up. "Not yet."

"So much blood," Kane muttered, his gaze sweeping across the darkened sand. He had seen terrible things in his life, both as a magistrate and in his field role with Cerberus. Man's inhumanity to man seemed boundless, and that was before factoring in the insane peccadilloes of alien infiltrators and the numerous other monsters Kane had faced and beaten. But this—this was on a scale he had rarely seen, and it wasn't like the bombing raid that had taken Beausoleil a year ago, leveling the ville in the space of a few minutes. No, there had been something understandable in that action and in the other travesties he had witnessed, something almost clinical and artificial in the way in which the attacks had been performed, the lives had been taken. But this was an attack on individuals, dozens of them, each left bleeding from the face.

While Brigid examined another victim, Kane trotted over to the pier and clambered up one of its struts until he reached the dangling figure of the woman. Close up, he could see the streaks of dried blood traced like webbing across her face, her mouth open, eyes closed.

"Ma'am, you okay?" Kane asked, ignoring the other groaning figures sprawled on the pier. "Ma'am?"

She didn't answer, not even when he prodded her. She was dead from massive brain trauma, the blood leaking from wherever it could as her brain collapsed in on itself.

Pulling a knife from its boot-mounted sheath, Kane cut the woman free from her fishing lines, watched as she tumbled into the ocean. It wasn't respectful, but it was better than where she had been left, hanging like that from her own fishing line.

Grant had made his way to the edge of the beach where it met a paved road, and he stood with one foot up on the foot-high stone barricade that marked the delineation between beach and road, gazing down the streets that led into Hope. The airship was waiting there, looming over the roofs of the houses like a storm cloud, its sleek lines turned a burnt-orange by the ebbing sun. He and Kane had not been able to land the Mantas any closer than the beach, the settlement had become so built up with the influx of refugees over the past twelve months.

Not everyone had been caught up in the human destruction. A number of people wandered about the streets in dazed confusion, while some had stopped to administer medical assistance or to simply give comfort to the wounded. Grant recognized one of the helpers as Mallory Price, a tall, gangly woman in her early fifties with disheveled blond hair cut close to her head. Price was a local physician who had worked with Cerberus before. When she spotted Grant standing at the edge of the beach, she nodded to him and beckoned him over, unwilling to leave the patient whose face she was suturing.

The woman's hair was shorter than Grant remembered and he commented on it as he walked over to join her. "What happened here, Mallory?" he asked.

"I honestly have no idea," Price admitted. "One minute it was a normal afternoon, the next there was this noise—music—and when I looked out my window, I saw this thing hovering there in the sky."

Grant scratched his shaved head. "Music? What kind of music?"

"Elgar," Price said. "Seemed to be coming from speakers set up beneath the airship."

Noting Grant's lead, Kane and Brigid had joined him and they acknowledged Mallory briefly before she continued.

"Do you think the music did this?" Brigid asked.

Price shrugged. "Can't say for sure, but whatever it was, it didn't affect everyone. It wasn't random, neither. It seemed to target specific people, more and more of them as it went on."

"And what did they do?" Kane asked.

"They danced," the local woman said, as if it was obvious.

Grant made a show of looking about him at the blood-spattered bodies. "Looks to me like they danced themselves to death," he growled.

Thanking Price, the Cerberus trio began striding down the street toward where the airship loomed.

"Everyone put in earplugs," Kane instructed as they hurried. "We'll stay in contact by Commtact."

Without hesitation, Brigid and Grant followed Kane's

lead, popping little earplugs from their field kits and slipping them inside their ears. After that, the moaning voices of the wounded dulled to a distant whine.

It had been just six minutes since they had landed the Mantas, and already it felt too long. Kane ran, leading the way down the tight street that led to the hovering airship, and Brigid and Grant kept pace. The streets were littered with wounded, just a few here and there, lying in bloody splashes as if caught in an explosion. Many of them were bleeding, red glistening on their faces, running down the side of their heads. They bled from the ears, the nose, the mouth, just like the people on the beach.

As they neared the airship, the Cerberus team saw fewer wounded. Instead, there were people standing and moving, jigging on the spot as if caught up in a grand dance. They twirled in place or spun together, taking one another arm in arm, fixed, rictus grins on their faces. Grant halted by one pair and put his arm between them, but they ignored him, batting his arm aside as they hurried through the intricate steps of their routine.

From overhead, it looked like a massive circle of dancers, each one moving in time, like peering inside the workings of a pocket watch. Several laughing figures strode through the center of it all at a wide junction where four streets converged. Kane drew back the moment he spotted them, hugging the outside wall of a sun-faded house and ushering his team to do the same with a motion of his empty hand. The Sin Eater had reappeared in his right hand automatically, though he held it high to his shoulder, analyzing what he could see.

"What is it?" Brigid whispered, the words boosted by the Commtact pickup and relayed to both Kane and Grant on an open channel.

"Two...no, make that three people, walking among the dancers, dressed kind of strange," Kane said.

He watched the figures—two women and one man—stride through the group of frustrated, whirring dancers, laughing and pointing as first one, then another of the dancers dropped to their knees, clutching at their heads in agony.

"They're our perps, all right," Kane finished.

"Three of them, or four?" Grant checked, subvocalizing the question and trusting the Commtact to relay it to Kane.

"I see three," Kane said. "Two hers and a him. Split up, we'll try boxing them in."

With a single word of acknowledgment, Grant and Brigid peeled away from the wall and headed in different directions, sprinting through the nearby streets, seeking alternate routes to the convergence.

Brigid took a right turn, then another, making her way around to the far side of the junction. She found a maintenance ladder attached to the side of a taller building used for storage and eyed it appraisingly. The ladder operated on a sliding system and had been bolted to the side of the building so that its lowest rung hung about nine feet above the ground, too high for the average person to reach with ease. Ideally, a workman would attach another ladder at ground level and climb up to the unit that was secured to the wall, but Brigid had no time for that. Figuring it for the most direct route to the Dorians, she ran at the wall and leaped, her firm muscles launching her with such force that she could snag the ladder's bottom rung with one outstretched hand. She hung there for a moment, twisting in the air before pulling herself up.

Sheathed in black leather, Brigid scrambled up the ladder like an insect up a wall, and within seconds she was atop the building's sloping roof, arms outstretched for balance as she sprinted across it toward the convergence of streets ahead and below. Looming very near above her was the airship, poised like the mythical Sword of Damocles, and Brigid eyed it from up close for the first time. Its body was intricately tooled, with elaborate patterns sewn or printed into the silver material of the balloon, a true work of art. Gantries and scaffolds ran across the balloon's surface like the rigging of a ship, with great pipes and spines poking from it in the manner of a surrealist hedgehog.

Brigid dropped down to the roof, snatching her TP-9 from its holster as she turned her attention to the street below.

MEANWHILE GRANT had turned left after he had departed from Kane's position, and he rapidly lost himself in a network of alleyways that cut into one another like a maze. Grant took a steadying breath as he made his way down the alleys, keeping his mind focused on where he needed to be. Around and to the left would bring him to the crossroads that was his target; he just needed to find the path of least resistance.

Coming up on his left, Grant saw an open doorway in a white stucco wall, and he turned into it as he reached it, almost knocking down a man washing dishes at a grimy basin.

"Just passing through," Grant said before the startled man could react.

Grant dashed through a doorway and into the next room of the building, finding himself in a large dining area. It was some kind of restaurant, the decor cheap and run-down, the food not much better, most likely catering to the influx of refugees that Hope had endured over the past year. As he hurtled through, weaving around the wide tables like a guided missile, Grant noticed one woman slump against the table, crashing headfirst into her meal, much to the astonishment of her fellow diners. Grant recognized the telltale traces of blood trickling from her ear holes, realized that the fatal music or whatever it was was beginning to affect the people in this place.

Keep moving, he told himself. Just get there.

KANE WAITED, back pressed against the wall, watching the eerie dancers as they whirled mindlessly to the soundtrack pumping from overhead. Despite his earplugs, Kane could hear the music, albeit muffled. The unwilling participants danced as if they had no strength in their limbs, moving like puppets. It was unsettling to watch.

The strangely garbed people in the midst of it all were laughing and talking among themselves.

"Look at the way they spin," said blond-haired Cecily, "like something you'd see at a fairground."

"Marvelous, is what it is," Hugh agreed. "You've outdone yourself here, Antonia. Truly."

The brunette's eyelids fluttered as she held the many dancers in her thrall. "Do you really think so?" she asked, fishing for more compliments. "It's challenging to keep so many whirling at once, like juggling batons."

"Some have fallen," Cecily admitted, a little embarrassed for her colleague.

"All part of the artistry," Hugh corrected with a joyful click of his heels. "Behold the dance of death, its participants mere fruit flies, whose lives are cut—" he slapped the edge of one hand into his palm with a slap "—abruptly!"

Kane's Commtact chimed to life as first Brigid and then Grant checked in. They were both in place, with a good view of the action.

Kane stepped forward, his Sin Eater held casually at his side. "Neat trick," he said. "Care to tell me how it's done?"

Cecily jumped with surprise, blushing delightfully as Kane stepped into view. "Mercy, have you missed one, Antonia?" she decried. "This one is not dancing, he's threatening."

"Yes, and the cad's holding a pistol," Hugh added, his keen eyes fixing on Kane's handblaster.

"There's another," Antonia told them, her eyelids fluttering more intently, "watching from…just above us."

Hugh turned his head, scanning the rooftops until he spotted Brigid crouched snugly on the roof of a white-painted building. "So there is," he said. "Well, Antonia, I have to say that this rather ruins the effect."

"And it was all going so elegantly, too," Cecily scoffed.

Kane could just barely discern the words, his earplugs keeping out all but the loudest of noises. But he heard the airship's speakers droning on, felt the thrum of the rotor blades as they kept it afloat in the sky. And he watched as the music played on, but everyone in the square—all thirty people there—suddenly dropped to the ground, clutching their heads in agony.

BRIGID DREW HERSELF CLOSER to the roof's edge as the dancers sank to the ground, watching in horror as their expressions told a story of pain. Most of the people in the street had dropped, all except for the three strangely garbed individuals and Kane pacing across the junction toward them. And then she saw the dark-haired woman, dressed in a lavish ball gown of sky-blue silk, turn her gaze directly toward her, brows furrowed in irritation.

The next thing that Brigid knew, something was ripping into her skull like a chain saw, and she felt her reasoning disappear as the burning agony took hold.

And then Brigid was falling, tumbling from the rooftop as all conscious thought disappeared. The bitch was inside her head.

Chapter 19

One second:

Kane saw Brigid trip over the rooftop three stories above, saw the way she was flopping like so much deadweight, her wild hair trailing behind her like a streak of fire. The shadow suit might provide some protection, he guessed, but never enough—not with the way she was dropping like a stone.

Kane was moving before he had even made the conscious decision, sending the Sin Eater back to its concealed holster to leave him with both hands free, legs kicking out to eat up the space between himself and Baptiste, his breath coming faster as the adrenaline pumped through his veins.

Two seconds:

Leaping over the fallen bodies of two dancers, legs thrusting out like pistons, eyes locked on the prize of Baptiste's plummeting form, arms reaching out to take her weight.

Three seconds:

Kane was beneath her, boots scraping on tiny flecks of gravel that had come loose from the roadway, his arms in position as Brigid's black-clad form dropped before the white wall, his legs braced for the impact.

Four seconds:

Kane felt his knees take the weight as Baptiste's flopping form landed in his arms, grunted aloud as he stumbled a half pace backward. She sagged toward the wall, but Kane yanked her back, rolling her in his arms. He let out the breath he hadn't realized he had been holding, wanting to say something to her.

When he looked at her, he saw that her eyes were unfocused, her face expressionless. She looked as though she was awake but dreaming, like those sad glist addicts in the dream factory they had shut down less than a week before.

Time sped up again, the rush of the everyday striking Kane with the suddenness of a gust of wind.

Kane turned then, suddenly conscious of a noise behind him and inwardly cursing the earplugs. It was laughter mixed with applause. The three immaculately attired Dorians were watching him with admiration, applauding his feat of agility.

"This one bears watching," Hugh said, though the words came muffled through Kane's earplugs. "Bravo, Antonia—bravo!"

"I wish I could take credit," the dark-tressed Antonia replied, her eyelids still flickering, "but my attention was caught in the ginger girl's mind."

Angry, Kane brought Brigid down gently to the ground, his eyes still fixed on the trio of strangers.

"Oh, look, young lovers dancing!" Cecily trilled as Kane turned with Brigid's body.

"Shove it," Kane snarled, and his right arm whipped up, the Sin Eater already back in his palm.

Cecily looked at the weapon for a moment, one perfectly plucked eyebrow raised in either astonishment or amusement, it was hard to tell which.

This close, Kane saw that the three supersoldiers were beautiful. Each of them had flawless skin and the ideal features of a statue from ancient Greece. Both the women were delicate yet strong, while the man's face had an androgynous quality that made him strangely alluring. The brunette in the sky-blue dress had her eyes closed—no, not closed, but almost so, her long lashes fluttering like the wings of a honeybee. Kane wondered if she was having an episode, perhaps an epileptic fit. He could worry about that later, once he was sure he had them covered.

Bringing his left hand up to join his right, Kane thrust the Sin Eater ahead of him in a two-handed grip, his lips set in a grim line. "Now," Kane began, "I want all of you to back against that wall, with your arms spread where I can see them."

Cecily laughed nervously, her eyes still fixed on the barrel of Kane's blaster. Beside her, Antonia's eyelids fluttered as she shoved the knife blade of her mind deeper into Brigid's, drawing the red-haired woman to her feet. With the heightened awareness of combat, Kane spied Brigid's movements behind him.

"You okay, Baptiste?" Kane asked without turning.

Brigid lunged at Kane, swiping at his back with the TP-9 still clutched in her grip. Caught by surprise, Kane sidestepped just quick enough to avoid the full impact of the blow, instead taking a sideswipe to his right shoulder.

"Baptiste?" Kane growled as he spun to face her. "What the hell are you doing?"

When he looked at Brigid, Kane saw the way her eyelids fluttered in time with the dark-haired woman's. There was a connection between the two of them, he realized; something the brunette was doing had changed Brigid, caused her to step from that rooftop moments ago—*and to take a swing at him now.*

Before Kane could vocalize his conclusions, Brigid lunged at him again, bringing her right leg up and forward to place it between Kane's legs. In an instant,

Brigid's leg had hooked Kane behind the knee, forcing him to stumble forward before the bone snapped. He found himself tripping into Brigid's arms, which she raised to grab him, bringing her free hand around his back and drawing him close.

And then they were dancing, blasters still clutched in their hands, Brigid leading the unwilling Kane in an aggressive tango across the bleeding bodies that decorated the junction.

BRIGID'S THOUGHTS had misted over while she was on the rooftop, a thin red veil oozing across them like a whisper of gauze. She could still see what was happening, but it was distant, as if she were viewing it remotely, her actions seen down the end of a long, long tunnel.

They're in my head, Brigid told herself. Her thoughts are in *my* brain.

Kane moved before her in a blur, the street swimming about her in a blotchy stream of intermingled colors like smeared paint.

Her head ached. She could not seem to affect her own movements, was only partially aware of what they were. Her body was being played like a puppet, each arch of her back, each stretch of her limbs dictated not by her but by the woman who had stepped inside her mind.

Donald Bry's research had revealed that the Dorians had superior intellect, but there had been no mention of extrasensory powers. Perhaps they had not been designed to have them, Brigid wondered, perhaps it was the unexpected result of leaving vastly intellectual immortals caged for three hundred years, left to develop their own idiosyncrasies, to find new applications for the abilities that Professor Howard had gifted them.

The pressure was like a vise on her brain. She could

feel her own thoughts being squeezed out as the woman crushed the last of her will. No, Brigid screamed, this cannot happen.

It had happened before, back when Ullikummis had overpowered the Cerberus installation and imprisoned Brigid. He had used a brainwashing technique to make her see the world through Annunaki eyes, to comprehend in a new and alien way. On that occasion, she had become someone else to cope with the psychic assault, transformed from Brigid Baptiste to Brigid Haight, her own dark aspect come to furious life. But it had been a trick, a carnival huckster's "swerve." She had used meditation to hide her mind, sealing it inside a protective bubble well away from the damage that Ullikummis was generating, keeping her true self safe.

When the time had come, Brigid Baptiste had reemerged from the shadow personality called Haight, resuming control of her actions. Kane, her *anam-chara,* her soul friend through eternity, had struggled to comprehend what had happened to her, and it had taken time for her to fully regain his trust.

Right now, as her mind struggled under the crushing weight of the other's psychic attack, Brigid remembered what had happened before, remembered her other self, the one called Haight.

"THEY DANCE LIKE FOOLS," Danner mocked as Brigid dragged Kane around the square.

"Like fools in love," Cecily corrected, her white teeth showing in a broad smile.

Hugh turned to her with an expression of disdain. "Must you always see romance in every gesture, Cecily, dear? This is poor art. Look around you—the participants in Antonia's little installation are being used up too quickly. It cannot possibly sustain itself."

"Aha, but isn't all art ephemeral, my dearest Hubert?" Cecily replied, the smile never faltering on her lips.

The Dorian called Hugh Danner thought about this for a moment, and a smile spread across his face. "You're right, of course," he realized. "Antonia has reminded us how our art must stand in this world. Like the momentary fluttering of a passing butterfly's wings." He swished the crimson tails of his frock coat behind him and gestured with outspread arms to the place he now thought of as the stage. "Talent borrows—but genius consumes!" he announced with a roar, his words echoing back from the walls of the buildings.

"Oh, that's simply inspired," Cecily said as Antonia continued to manipulate Brigid and her would-be swain in the dance of death.

KANE FELT THE PRESSURE build in his own skull as Antonia split her consciousness across the two players in her performance. It was as if his skull had been trapped between two great concrete blocks, a pile driver slamming against each one, crushing his skull in the middle. He *saw* and he *felt* but he could not *control*. Not any longer.

A hairbreadth from him, Brigid felt something change inside her own head as the Dorian's grip loosened just slightly. Antonia was concentrating on holding Kane in her thrall and in so doing she had slipped infinitesimally in her hold on Brigid Baptiste. Brigid locked on that tiny fracture in the near-absolute control, began to work at it with the last of her free will. To see as a human sees would do no good here, she knew. These people could conquer the human mind as easily as a man masters a docile pet.

Shift consciousness, shift outlook, break the hold. "Now," Brigid muttered, the word purring out between strained lips.

ANTONIA GASPED. "My…goodness," she stuttered, not quite believing what she had felt.

Cecily, who had lifted a dying man from the ground and was now dancing with him amid the human debris, turned to Antonia with concern. "What is it?"

"One of them," Antonia began, "the woman, I think, is not quite what she seems. There's something inside her. It's picking at me."

Hugh frowned. "How so?" he asked, watching the dancing puppets of Kane and Baptiste.

"She's actually fighting back," Antonia said, as surprised as he was. "I can feel her…in *my* mind. It's almost…inhuman, the way she sees things."

"Disengage," Hugh instructed, suddenly all business.

"Hugh, I can hold this simple mortal," Antonia scoffed, her eyelids still fluttering like papers caught in a hurricane.

"Disengage, I say," Hugh insisted. "Antonia, your art has come up wanting. Should you be hurt by one of your exhibits…"

Antonia screeched and fell to her knees, curtailing Hugh's instructions before he could finish.

"Antonia?" Cecily and Hugh called in unison.

HIDING IN THE RESTAURANT DOORWAY, Grant saw the woman in the blue dress sink to her knees. He had recognized the three strangers as soon as he had seen them—they were the same individuals who had ambushed him out in the Panamint mountains and put Shizuka into a coma. Holding his rage in check, Grant had bided his time, waited for the moment to strike. Raising the Sin Eater in his right hand, he targeted the other woman, the blonde called Cecily, and squeezed the trigger.

CECILY DIDN'T SEE the shot coming and despite her speed, she could not react fast enough to step out of its path.

Crouching on his haunches beside Antonia, Hugh turned as Cecily dropped, the shoulder strap of her dress shredding with the impact of the first bullet. "Silly?" he asked, his head whipping around to find the shooter.

Grant blasted again, sending a second 9 mm bullet at his next target, the crouching figure of Hugh Danner. The bullet sang as it cut the air, whipping across the open space as it drove toward its target. But Hugh moved faster, a superman bolting out of the path of the 9 mm missile.

From the shadows, Grant cursed as the bullet zipped past his target and drilled into the wall beyond. Danner had spotted him, and his muscular figure raced across the distance between them, a cruel sneer on his face. Grant inhaled deeply and squeezed the Sin Eater's trigger again, sending two more bullets at his foe. Danner weaved out of their path, brushing the second bullet aside with a fast-moving flick of his hand.

He was almost on Grant now, and the ex-mag ducked backward, turning back into the run-down eatery and making his retreat. The superior man followed, smashing the door back on its hinges with a loud bang, leaping over a table that cut across his path. Grant was at the far end of the dining hall already, legs pumping as he hurried into the cooking area. "Gonna need a bigger gun," he muttered to himself as he raced through the kitchen doorway.

Designed to be in the peak of human condition, the

immortal Hugh was catching up to Grant with every step, his movements a blur to the surprised customers. He was through the doorway and into the kitchen in a flash, blue eyes scanning the area for his target. There was a door ahead, wide-open and leading to the alleyways beyond. Hugh spied it and was hurtling through it, all in the space of a single thought. He found himself standing in a tight alleyway running crosswise behind the eatery, with no indication as to which way his quarry had gone. For a moment he stood there, a grim expression on his handsome face.

"Where did he disa—?" Hugh wondered.

Then something struck him across the back of the skull with a rich metallic clang, and the immortal man loped forward, striking the far wall headfirst.

"Behind you," Grant replied, holding the heavy cooking pot aloft like a batter at the mound. The pot steamed with heat where he had snatched it from the stovetop.

But Hugh wouldn't quit so easily. Even as he slammed into the wall, he was beginning to recover, the results of ancient bioengineering making him far stronger than he appeared.

Grant skipped back as the man sent a low kick at his shins, just barely stepping out of the path of that fearsome blow. He swung the heated pot around, its fourteen-inch circumference whooshing through the air as it came down against Hugh's flank.

Hugh grunted, shrugging off the powerful blow, but Grant could see he was having some effect. He channeled all of his strength into a swing, bringing the pot around in a wide arc before striking the rogue immortal in the jaw with a resounding clang.

Hugh fell back, slumping against the wall. Grant stood over him, bouncing on his feet with adrenaline, the heavy pot clutched in both hands. "Yeah," Grant snarled, "that's for Shizuka."

But as Grant stood there, someone dropped—almost literally—out of the sky, driving his heels into Grant's chest as he landed on the surprised ex-magistrate. It was Algernon, the tails of his coat trailing behind him, the rapier-like blade clutched loosely in one hand as he dropped from the airship to fell Grant where he stood.

Folding with the blow, Grant caromed to the ground, the pot-turned-weapon spiraling from his grasp. He had almost forgotten about the airship, and he had been so focused on defeating the dark-haired Dorian that the other's attack had caught him entirely by surprise. Grant felt his head sing as he slammed skull-first against the doorjamb, his sagging body sprawling on the ground.

"Hitting your opponent from behind, old man?" Algie scoffed. "That's just not cricket." He stood there a moment, watching as Grant struggled to cling on to consciousness, struggled—and failed.

BACK IN THE OPEN street section, Cecily was just pulling herself up from where she had struck the ground. Grant's bullet had snagged her shoulder, not piercing the skin but still rebounding from the shoulder blade with considerable force. She winced as she rolled the shoulder experimentally, feeling the bee-sting-like echo left by the bullet.

"Hugh?" she asked, peering around.

Hugh was gone, no doubt after her assailant like the gentleman he was. The two new dancers were still performing, though their movements had become erratic, bumbling against a wall. It was clear to Cecily that Antonia was no longer in complete control—what a wretched thing to happen to her up-to-now bravura performance in the little coastal town.

"Antonia?" Cecily called, peering about the crossed meeting of the streets.

Antonia was sunk to her knees, clutching at her head as her eyelids fluttered, her head reeling back and forth like a ship on a stormy sea. Cecily gasped when she saw her, scrambled across the paving stones to her friend's side.

"Antonia, what has happened to you?" she gasped.

Antonia spoke through painfully gritted teeth. "Inside…my head," she said. "Fighting…can't control."

Cecily peered over her shoulder at the stumbling dancers, turned back to Antonia and settled on a course of action. "Do as Hugh said," she instructed as she drew something from her little clutch bag, tiny beadlike pearls lining its edges. "Disengage from your performance. You have nothing further to demonstrate to us, not to your friends, not at the risk of your sanity."

Behind her fluttering eyelids, Antonia could see the strange world that Brigid saw. It had been a human's world when she had stepped into the woman's mind, but something had shifted quite without her realizing, and now the whole thing seemed nightmarish and obstinate; even its colors made no earthly sense. She had never seen anything like this before, not in all her years of experimenting inside the minds of the others, not even when she had blown out poor Harold's mind in a misjudged conjuring performance that had left him in a state beyond repair. Yet this woman had seemed normal enough. How could she slip into this new method of understanding?

TEN FEET AWAY, Brigid felt her shoulder nudge against the wall. But the feeling was distant, as if it was happening to someone else. The Dorian bitch was still inside her head, but her grip was looser now, which was why Brigid could feel her shoulder as it scuffed up against the rough brickwork. A part of her mind was engaged in recalling everything that Ullikummis had shown her, the way he had tried to reconstruct her thinking, reshape it into something alien to her. She couldn't remember it all, even her eidetic memory had limits—or more likely a part of her had chosen to forget the horror—but she could recall enough, sending it like a missile into her attacker's probing thoughts. Brigid felt her dominance ascend, felt the Dorian pulling away, removing her psychic tendrils from her mind. Brigid *pushed*.

ANTONIA SHRIEKED AGAIN, her fingers snatching through her hair, ripping a whole clump out without conscious thought.

"It's all right," Cecily cooed, using her delicate hand fan to cool her friend. "You're safe."

Antonia looked at her with eyes full of fear. "That woman…she's inhuman."

Cecily glared at the redhead where she had slumped against the wall of an unmarked gambling house, her beau crashed against her in a tangle of limbs. "Well, what did you expect? She dresses frightfully and her hairbrush evidently leaves much to be desired."

Swiftly, Cecily helped Antonia depart the scene of carnage.

Chapter 20

Brigid Baptiste awoke with a headache. No, she didn't awaken; she was already awake—but she hadn't been herself in a while. So in a way it was like waking up in the sense that her mind was reengaging with her body. She had been momentarily overwhelmed by the other woman's presence as it infiltrated her brain. She couldn't say how long "momentarily" had actually been—the experience of losing one's mind, even temporarily, plays havoc on one's sense of time. Only the brainwashing technique, slipping mental gears and putting another way of thinking into motion, had enabled her to fend off the other.

She was back now; mind, body and spirit all in the same place. And as for the headache—well, that was all hers, too.

When she opened her eyes—reengaging her optic nerves after the psychic assault—she saw that Kane was two inches away, both of them sprawled on the street like discarded toys. Brigid realized then that, in a sense, that was a pretty fair assessment. Considering themselves superior to mortals, the Dorians perceived every other man and woman as a toy, a plaything to be posed and manipulated for their own entertainment, to be discarded the moment boredom set in. Brigid saw that now, had realized it the very moment she had used her mind trick to push back against the psychic invader. It had given her an insight she hadn't had before, and now she realized just what it was the Dorians sought—and it surprised her to learn that it wasn't to be all-powerful conquerors, to wage war as they had been designed. Rather, the Dorians sought entertainment, a lull in the boredom of their protracted existence. They toyed with living humans the way a cruel child might toy with insects, crushing them, pulling their wings off, subjecting them to the sun's rays through the medium of a magnifying glass. The Dorians were seeking nothing less than freedom from the tyranny of their endless lives. And as she lay in the street amid the mass of assaulted and wounded people, Brigid wondered—is immortality always to be so cursed?

Beside her, Kane shuffled, eyes closed, a thin stream of blood worming from his nose down across his upper lip, trickling farther as gravity drew it inexorably toward the ground.

"Kane?" Brigid urged, her voice little more than a whisper. "Kane, are you awake?"

Inarticulately, Kane grumbled something, his head rolling a little. His eyes were still shut.

Brigid reached over to him—an action that seemed to demand all her effort, weak as she felt just now—and slapped her palm against his broad chest. "Kane—wake up," she called. "We need to…to keep moving."

It was hard to think still, even after she had forcibly ejected the Dorian woman from her mind. Everything, every movement, every thought, felt as if she was breaking the crust of a scar, bits of herself snapping away in painful rips.

Something crossed over the street at that moment, something huge and dark as it passed across the sun, a grand cigar shape above Brigid's face. She squinted against the sun, watched as the shadow glided off to the east with a sound like a cat purring, the faint strains of Elgar accompanying it. It was the airship, its bulging shape and odd fingerlike projections gliding through the sky like the ominous shadow of death.

Kane muttered something as the great airship slunk away on the wind, his voice sounding like a deflating tire. "What hit me?" he managed, the words slurring into one.

"Mind probe," Brigid told him, still lying flat on her back and watching the sky. "Telepath tried to puppet us. Kind of succeeded for a while."

Kane cursed, the expletive coming out of his dry throat like an explosive round, doubled via their linked Commtacts.

GRANT FELT AS IF he'd had an altercation with a steamroller. And a particularly ill-tempered steamroller, at that.

As he sucked in a lungful of air, Grant coughed and the coughing made him hurt right across his rib cage. His chest ached where Algernon had struck him from the air, making it painful to properly draw breath.

There was someone standing over him, Grant realized as he became aware of his surroundings once more. For a moment, Grant felt the fight-or-flight urge hammering at his brain until the figure leaned down and spoke to him.

"You okay?" the woman asked. She was maybe twenty-five, malnourished with a dirty apron and her long, straw-colored hair tied ineffectively back from her face in a ponytail that had maybe begun her waitress shift as a bun.

"I'm all right," Grant said, plucking the earplugs from his ears as he pulled himself up to a sort of crouch using the wall. His words sounded loud to his ears, and they came out with hard edges that made his vocal cords burn. "Did you…see where he went?"

"The men you were fighting?" the waitress asked, taking a step back from Grant as he stood, keeping her distance. "They left. The blond-haired one helped the other one. They went down there and then—"

"Yeah," he interrupted. Grant was ahead of her, putting the story together with his eyes. Both the Dorians were gone, and their airship no longer cast a shadow over the alleyway. When he looked up, he could see a peach sky where evening took hold. "You have water you can spare?"

The waitress nodded. "We're by the sea," she told Grant as he pulled his aching body erect. "Water's just about the only thing we do have to spare."

"WE'RE FACING PEOPLE who can think so hard that they can infiltrate a person's mind," Brigid stressed as she sat with her colleagues in the Cerberus ops center a few hours later. Her head was still reeling from the psychic attack, and she sipped at a cool glass of water and tried to work her way through everything that had happened in the past few hours.

It transpired that she, Kane and Grant had been left semiconscious by the battle in Hope, giving the Dorians ample time to make their exit. The immortals had been wounded—Grant was sure of it—but they hadn't realized quite how hurt the Cerberus personnel had been. "Otherwise they would have finished us," Kane surmised. As it was, they had made a run for it in their airship transport, leaving the Cerberus field team struggling to recover amid the groaning bodies strewed through the streets.

And that was another point of contention. While the Dorian-class soldiers had departed in their airship, theoretically in full view of Cerberus satellite monitoring, the airship had somehow slipped away from the fishing ville unseen, disappearing as if it were never there at all.

Now it was four hours later and Brigid, Kane and Grant had returned to Cerberus feeling disappointed, frustrated and just a tad sorry for themselves. They had joined Lakesh and the team as soon as their Manta craft had docked in the mountainside redoubt, and all three still showed the ravages of their brief skirmish.

"They were designed to be smart," Donald Bry reminded everyone, sounding uncertain.

"Smart, yes," Kane spouted, waving an angry finger in Bry's face, "but no one warned us they'd be able to get inside our heads. That was not something I signed up for."

Lakesh placed his hand on Kane's arm to restrain him, speaking in a calm voice. "No one signed up for any of this," he said. "These Dorians are loose, and it is apparent that our knowledge base for them remains a work in progress. Reba has produced some interesting information while you've been away and I've asked her to join us as soon as she can to present her findings to all three of you."

"Lot of good that will do," Grant growled as he rubbed at his aching shoulders. "We had them right in our sights and the desk jockeys here apparently lost track of their airship. I mean, it's an airship. How hard is that to track?"

"It wasn't just an airship," Brigid said before any of the operations team could defend themselves. "I got a close-up peek from the rooftop before that…woman went for a joyride inside my skull. The balloon was decorated with various spines and projections. I suspect they're used to somehow baffle tracking devices, creating a magnetic echo when they line up with any large metallic object in the vicinity."

Perched on the edge of his desk with a mug of now-lukewarm tea in his hand, Lakesh rubbed his chin thoughtfully. "What you're suggesting is that these spines lock on to the nearest object and create some kind of a feedback loop that feeds false data to our tracking system. Ingenious."

"Like I said," Bry pointed out, "they were designed to be smart."

"But smart people can get caught out," Kane reminded everyone. "They don't know how we're tracking them— didn't even know we were until we arrived. They got lucky, but we can work around that—right?"

Lakesh nodded. "Definitely."

Poised at the computer terminal that they had all gathered around, Brewster Philboyd tapped a few commands into the keyboard as he spoke. "We had the airship firmly in our crosshairs when you reached the location," he said, bringing up the satellite footage of the moment when the Mantas had landed. "It had been traveling languidly in a northeasterly direction. Estimates put it at around two miles per hour—that's slower than walking speed.

"But everything seemed to go south when it hit this point—" again Philboyd tapped his keyboard to bring up footage of the fishing port "—where we suddenly see a ghost report over here." Sure enough, a second airship seemed to have joined the first, lining up almost parallel and about a quarter mile away from the original.

"Couldn't you just keep tracking the first?" Kane asked.

Brewster tapped out more commands, bringing a time-lapse version of the footage from the next half hour of monitoring. "Easier said than done. A second ghost appeared three minutes after that," he said, "and all three seemed to converge here—roughly five minutes after your arrival."

"That's just before we reached them," Brigid said, eyeing the satellite image. "But that isn't where the craft was at that stage. It's about a half mile off target, give or take."

Kane shook his head. "It's the old shell game," he muttered. When he realized that the others were looking at him quizzically, he briefly explained. "Three cups and one ball. Ball goes under one cup, then they're mixed up. The punter has to guess which cup the ball's under, usually without realizing they're being had courtesy of a little sleight of hand. Known as *Find the Lady* when you play it with cards."

"Clever," Lakesh admitted, the frustration clear in his face.

"So," Grant growled, flicking his hand at the screen, "assuming we can find our rogue supersoldiers again, how do you propose we take them down?"

"Airship should be easy enough," Kane mused. "If we can hit them hard while they're still in the sky, the ship'll come down and the rest is mop-up duty. Right?"

Lakesh looked uncertain. "If you do that over a populated area, we could be looking at massive collateral damage," he advised.

"Keep out of the villes," Grant said. "Gotcha."

But Lakesh was shaking his head. "It's not that easy," he remarked. "If whatever's keeping it afloat is flammable, then there could be much more significant effects. You could start a forest fire, for instance, and Cerberus is simply not equipped to deal with repercussions on that scale."

"Could we tow it?" Brigid asked thoughtfully.

Lakesh considered this for a moment before he spoke.

"Getting close enough to snag it with a hook of some kind would likely prove difficult," he said. "Assuming that that could be achieved, then we'd need to factor in the airship's power in relation to a Manta's pulling power. Without proper data, that's impossible to calculate…."

"From what I saw, it moved slow," Kane said.

"Doesn't matter," Lakesh warned. "What we've seen so far is simply what these Dorians have allowed us to see. Remember the shell game. They're wily and they don't answer to anyone. It would be folly to assume anything about that airship at this stage."

"Then what?" Grant asked angrily. "Sit and wait? While Shizuka's keeping a bed warm in the sick bay?"

"No, my friend," Lakesh said gently, "that wouldn't do. These people are dangerous—there's certainly no question of that now, not after what you all witnessed in Hope. We need to provide a way to halt the airship that creates the least possible damage to anything nearby. Holing it might be one option."

Kane looked thoughtful for a few seconds, his eyes fixed on the false image of the airship that remained on Philboyd's screen. "So, how do we do that with the Mantas?" he asked, turning to Lakesh. "Seriously? Poke it in the backside till it pops?"

"I'd propose a somewhat more graceful solution," Lakesh said, "but in essence, yes."

Kane nodded. "Okay, we're going to need one big zit popper, then."

"And some fancy flying," Grant chimed in.

SITTING ON A STONE BENCH amid Cecily's garden of human statuary, Antonia was rubbing at her head. It still hurt there, where the redhead had sent a mental shunt at her.

The feeling of alienness disturbed her, its echo like an aftertaste she could not seem to get rid of.

"Does it still hurt?" Cecily asked as she came to join her friend at the bench. She was chewing on a long-stemmed rose she had plucked from one of the flower borders that lined the decorative and practical garden, tasting the petals with a look of vexation marring her brow. She could not decide if she liked the taste or not.

"Has the world moved on so," asked Antonia, "that all humanity has been lost? The woman's mind was wrong—it's plain to see that now."

Cecily chewed thoughtfully on a rose petal the deep red of blood. "Perhaps she lost her mind?" she suggested.

"How frightfully careless that would be," Antonia pointed out, still rubbing at her temple with the heel of her hand.

Just then, Hugh and Algernon came to join the ladies where they sat together on the bench. Algie had a smear of oil on his cheek from when he had been tinkering with the airship's motion camouflage projector, and he wielded an adjustable wrench, tossing it from hand to hand as though it weighed nothing. As he reached the bench, the blond Dorian turned and launched the wrench in an arc. It spun through the air before embedding itself fully three inches into the chest of a nude woman where she appeared to prance amid the fairy children. The nude tottered on static legs before caving to the grass with the wrench sticking up from her ribs like a lever.

"Oh, Algie," Cecily chastised, "you've ruined my composition."

"The woman was too thin anyway," Algernon justified as he took a seat next to Cecily and Antonia.

A look of disdain colored his face as Hugh Danner paced the pleasure garden with his arms behind his back.

His shoulder felt sore where Grant had struck him with the pot, and a dull pink bruise showed across the right side of his face, but already both were healing thanks to the miraculous genetic manipulation that his body had been subjected to before his birth in a glass tube.

Cecily, Antonia and Algernon knew his look, had seen Hugh pace like this before, like a tiger caged but still ready to pounce if given the narrowest of openings to do so. He was bridling at something, and little wonder— Antonia was still nursing the most ghastly headache after what the woman with the red hair had thrust at her during their mental contretemps.

"Our glorious festival is unraveling," Hugh announced, gesturing flamboyantly to the ripe forms posed all about them. "Your art looks positively ill, dear Cecily, while Antonia's magnificent effort was so short-lived as to be an irrelevance."

"Oh, Hugh, dear," Antonia chirped, "all art is an irrelevance. That's its appeal."

The handsome, dark-haired Dorian inclined his head in acceptance of her point. "Too true. And yet, our grand design seems destined to fall like a lame horse ready for pasture.

"I propose that we step things up," Hugh continued, "and bring to this gauche world the most glorious art it has ever borne witness to. Something that will 'pop.' Any suggestions?"

"Oh, Hugh," Cecily trilled, "you have always been the great innovator. You decide and we shall play along in whatever capacity you direct."

Hugh looked from one of his colleagues to the next, his fierce blue eyes searing into them as he decided what he might make his grand artistic gesture to the world.

"Something that pops, didn't you say, old man?" Algernon added with a grin. "I have been preparing just the thing."

Hugh nodded. "Then to work, my friends. We have art to create and the world is our canvas. Find me people. Lots and lots of people."

Chapter 21

Reba DeFore waited nervously in one of the laboratories of the Cerberus redoubt, tapping her pen against the side of the clipboard to which she had attached a ream of paperwork relating to the captured Dorian solider, Harold. Lab assistant Gus Wilson was poised on a high stool beside her, checking his own papers, and he peered up when he saw how DeFore was fidgeting.

"Nervous?" he asked in his unassuming way.

The Cerberus medic nodded, watching as almost two dozen experts came shuffling into the room to hear her speak, lining up along the back wall and taking seats at the workbenches among the test tubes and Bunsen burners. "I didn't expect to be giving my findings to so many people," she said.

Cerberus had become a haven for scientific experts since its reestablishment several years ago, many of them gravitating here from the Manitius Moon Base project, where they had been held in cryogenic stasis since the start of the twenty-first century. Kane had once joked that he couldn't swing a cat in the redoubt without hitting someone who would calculate said cat's velocity and angle of impact to ten decimal places.

DeFore felt relief followed by a tiny pang of guilt when she saw Kane and Brigid stride into the room. Brigid was knowledgeable but she was book smart, an archivist rather than an expert in a given field. And as for Kane, well, Kane was Kane. At least DeFore could be normal around those two. She was surprised that Grant, the third member of their usually inseparable trio, was not with them.

Kane held the door for Brigid before checking the corridor beyond for stragglers. Finding none, he pulled the door closed and stepped over to where Brigid stood by the fire extinguisher. "Woo-ee." He whistled quietly. "I didn't realize this show would be so popular."

Brigid flashed him a smile. "Standing room only," she whispered back.

"Next time we catch the matinee and leave the main show to the smart folks, Baptiste," Kane teased.

"Aw, but then we wouldn't get to dress up," Brigid shot back, keeping her voice low.

Up at the front of the room, DeFore was welcoming everyone and thanking them all for attending. "Our CAT Alpha field team brought the subject in after one of our people suffered in an encounter with four of his companions," Reba summarized.

Those familiar with the members of CAT Alpha turned to Kane and Brigid, and several asked if Grant was okay. "Grant's fine, but Shizuka took a nasty hit," Kane said quickly, glossing over her condition so that DeFore could hold the floor.

"A further encounter along with archival investigation informed us that Harold is part of a group of three-hundred-year-old supersoldiers known as Dorians," the medic explained. "The Dorians exhibit increased endurance along with powerful intellectual capacity, mind control and astonishing reactions. Harold theoretically shares these abilities, though some past trauma has left him unable to function at anything approaching standard human behavior, let alone superhuman. However, we may assume that he is physically similar to his broodmares, which means that the results of these tests should give an insight into what our field personnel are dealing with."

One of the scientists, a man called Perry, whose blond hair was prematurely streaked with white, raised his hand to ask a question. "Where did you say these Dorians came from?"

Briefly, DeFore outlined the background data with some assistance from Donald Bry before taking up where she had left off regarding the test results themselves. "It's been my job to catalog his physical attributes and test their limits," she explained. "I began by taking a number of genetic samples from the subject—skin, hair and blood—along with some minor invasive work regarding his bones and muscle makeup. I've also conducted an X-ray and CAT scan along with an internal probe to take samples of his digestive tract and lung capacity. We're still studying the results now, but we do have some initial feedback on the early tests."

DeFore turned the pages on her clipboard, searching for the data she had highlighted before the meeting began.

"Though the subject's skin appears human enough, testing shows that it's actually some chitinous material," she explained, "akin to the shell of a beetle. The skin is superhard and acts like armor, enabling the subject to deflect blows of significant force including—anecdotally, at least—bullets. I'd speculate that the skin is close to impenetrable, except to the sharpest of blades. I actually went through three scalpels trying to get a sample. As such, the subject may be considered invulnerable for all practical purposes, much as a bug can survive a drop from many stories above the ground and nonchalantly walk away."

"Great," Kane muttered, "we're fighting human beetles."

Brigid shot him a look to silence him.

"The subject is different from humans in other ways, too," DeFore continued. "Early tests show that his metabolism is far slower than a normal man's—and that's important because the documents relating to these Dorians refer to them as being immortal. The slowness of the metabolism means any possible wounds would take far longer to register. It also has the added advantage of placing less demands on Harold's digestive system—I'd estimate that any one of these Dorians could go two months without food or water.

"Having said this, the subject's ability to process and adapt to stimuli is remarkable. Once we finally did take our skin sample, I watched it heal completely in a matter of hours," DeFore said, thumbing through her clipboard to the correct page. "To be precise, 118 minutes and 12 seconds."

Several of the audience questioned this, and DeFore went through the figures carefully along with handing out a spectral analyses of the process.

"And there's another point about Harold that bears consideration," DeFore continued with a quaver in her voice. "Our field team have already encountered this facet of the Dorians' abilities—that they appear to have a form of mind control over other people which they can exert seemingly at will. This is not hypnosis, let me clarify—this is a full-blown psychic attack that leaves the victim traumatized and, in several cases, dead.

"Our subject's brain function is damaged, so I've had to make certain allowances with regards to that in my analysis," the Cerberus medic explained, "but it's clear that his neural pathways—that is, the things that facilitate thought transfer—are linked with infinitely more connective ports, in a far more elaborate web than we would see in a normal human being. In very simple terms, our subject thinks far more quickly than a man. Equating his thought process to ours would be like comparing our speed of thought to that of a pineapple."

The audience in the room laughed at this lighthearted comparison, despite its serious implications.

Once the laughter died down, DeFore continued. "The Dorians' ability to think faster may explain their facility for mind control. CAT Alpha's field report states that the mind control seemed to affect a number of people at once, up to twenty or so at any one moment…."

"At least," Brigid chimed in when she realized DeFore was looking to her for confirmation. "Plus, its echoes seemed to continue long after the Dorian we faced had passed. Kane and I were also subject to the same attack at the same time."

"Which means it isn't focused simply on one person," DeFore clarified. "The speed with which these people can think may be allowing them to switch minds and control more than one at once. In essence, I see this as controlling each individual in turn, perhaps twenty people one after another before rapidly turning their attention back to the first and reinforcing their influence there, a little like a man spinning plates."

With that, the meeting was adjourned and the room began to empty. Kane and Brigid remained behind, along with a few of the other scientists who had more questions to ask or who merely wished to help with the study.

Finally, Kane managed to corner Reba DeFore as she took a sip from a much-needed glass of water.

"You said something there about spinning plates,"

he said, "to explain how the Dorians control multiple minds at once."

DeFore nodded. "Yes, I can't see any capacity to divide their thoughts in such a way as to control more than one person otherwise, and you assured me that they managed to get whole families dancing on the waterfront."

"Yeah. So, if we could split their attention wide enough," Kane mused, "we might have an inroad to breaking that influence?"

"It's possible, Kane," DeFore agreed, "but I wouldn't choose to be the one to test the theory."

Kane gave a slow nod of his head in deadly earnest. Already he was considering new ways to stop these lunatics, trying to find a new angle with which to bring them to a standstill.

"While this may all sound outlandish," DeFore told Kane and Brigid, "we must remember that medical science has improved to such a degree that even the weakest human can thrive under reasonable conditions. In essence, our subject is a conglomeration of all that research up to the end of the nineteenth century employed on just one specimen, infinitely superior to any one of us in this room. They may be three hundred years old, but whoever designed these supersoldiers knew what they were doing."

"They built things to last in those days," Kane said bitterly. "Bully for them. Sucks for us."

Chapter 22

While his colleagues endlessly debated strategy, Grant took time to visit Shizuka in the Cerberus infirmary. He found the infirmary empty apart from the four Tigers of Heaven guards on silent watch. DeFore was presumably busy with performing further tests on the skin samples she had obtained from the prisoner, Harold. The lights in the observation room had been dimmed, creating a kind of nighttime feel.

Grant paced through the consultation room, his dark eyes fixed on the observation window where he could see Shizuka's silhouette, feeling his heart break with every step.

He passed through the consultation room and into the tiny ward itself, four beds arranged two for two against the walls in mirrored opposition to each other. Shizuka lay in one bed, a low light glowing beside her, bedclothes folded down to keep her legs and midsection covered, leaving the top of her chest, her head and arms free. The other beds were empty, leaving the room with that sterile smell of disinfectant masked with flowers from an aerosol. Two more Tigers of Heaven guards waited in silence, standing at the door in full armor, swords at their waists.

Shizuka lay statue-still beneath the bedclothes, her face bruised, her expression serene. She looked for all the world as though she were sleeping; a beautiful dreamer.

Grant pulled a chair over and took up a position at the

head of the bed, barely able to turn away from Shizuka for even a second. She had to be all right, just had to be. What was it Reba had said? *She's a survivor, Grant. She'll triumph over this the same way she's triumphed against every other foe she's ever faced.*

But those other foes had been living. They had been physical things, with faces and strategies and weak spots. But this thing she was locked in the grip of now, this coma—that was different. That was like a foe that had already dealt the killing blow; it was just a case of waiting for it to strike.

Grant shook his head, trying to dislodge the negativity from his thoughts. Brigid Baptiste had explained the mental attack she had suffered, describing it as a violent incursion into her mind. From the description, it was the same thing that had happened to Shizuka, he'd guess. Grant was no doctor. He couldn't perform brain surgery or track neurological pathways in a human body, but he knew what could happen when a person suffered a brain trauma. Sometimes they were vegetables when they woke up, unable to feed or clothe themselves, unable to speak. Sometimes they didn't wake up at all.

"She'll hear you," Grant muttered under his breath. It was a silly thing to say, but he felt somehow that by thinking the bad things that it would make them happen, encourage them to settle here, to change the course of Shizuka's life for the worse. He had thought he was above superstition until he was faced with Shizuka lying comatose, like a corpse waiting for embalming. It seemed that, when you came down to it, no one was really immune to superstition. Not even an ex-magistrate who prided himself on his practical approach and realism in the face of danger.

He reached out then and stroked her bangs back from

her forehead, looking at her closed eyelids. "You'll get through this," Grant told her in a gentle whisper. "You'll be all right and we'll do something, go somewhere. We'll find the time and we'll go to the places you always wanted to see, do the things you always wanted to do. We'll do that, Shizuka. I promise."

Reba DeFore found Grant sitting in the semidarkness of the observation room an hour later. She had returned from the labs where the meeting had been held, and had left her colleagues busily running a whole gamut of tests on the genetic material she had harvested from the Dorian prisoner, Harold. The Dorian remained heavily sedated on her instruction. Given all she had seen and been told of his brethren, DeFore was not about to take any risks.

She entered her office and switched on the computer terminal, preparing to compare the lab results with her previous findings. But as she took her seat, she became aware of another figure, sitting hunched over Shizuka's bed in the observation ward. DeFore started, recalling for a moment the way that the redoubt had once been infiltrated by the demented legions of Ullikummis, the stone god. She had suffered badly in that altercation, and while her physical scars had healed she still carried mental scars: the night terrors came to visit time and again, and sometimes her heart would race faster because of a shadow on the wall.

Clutching her chest, DeFore stared through the observation window and steadied herself. "Grant," she said quietly. "It's just Grant."

The buxom medic made her way into the ward and caught Grant's attention with a soft plea. "Do you need anything, Grant? I can turn the lights up if you like." Already she was reaching for the light switch.

Grant shook his head heavily as the overhead lights came stronger. "It's all right, Reba. Shizuka's not in much of a reading mood." He tried to make it sound light-hearted, but it still came out like a diagnosis, the kind where the doctor tells you you only have six weeks to live.

"How is she?" DeFore asked as she dimmed the lights back down.

Grant's attention was drawn to something as the lights faded, a shining streak propped up by the edge of Shizuka's bed: her *katana* sword in its sheath, the weapon of the samurai.

"Grant?"

"No change," Grant answered. "I spoke to her a little but…" He left the sentence hanging—what was there he could say? How many ways are there to say someone is dead while still alive?

DeFore checked the computer chart where it had updated in her absence. The monitoring system would alert her to any change here, and even in the labs she was no more than two minutes from her office and the ward. "She's fighting it, Grant," DeFore confirmed as she scanned the chart. "It will just take time."

Grant stood, bringing himself up to his full height, and strode across to where Shizuka's sword had been propped. "She'll be mad at me if she finds I've taken this," he told the medic as he reached for the ornate sheath. It was a deep shade of emerald so dark that it was almost black, tied with leather strips and patterned with beautiful gold filigree that ran down both sides and across its lip. Inside, the *katana* itself was twenty-five inches of sharpened steel, razor-keen and polished to mirror-perfect. The weapon had been the official weapon of the samurai class for hundreds of years, often referred to as a samurai's soul, and it was as much a part of Shizuka as her own right hand. Grant hefted it in its sheath, judging the weight.

DeFore looked from Grant to Shizuka and back again. "I won't tell," she said. "And I'm sure you'll keep it safe."

Grant nodded. "I will. It's time this blade took some revenge where its mistress can't."

With that, Grant snatched up the sheathed *katana* and made his way to the door. The clock was ticking. It was past time they found these immortal lunatics and dealt with them once and for all.

KANE AND BRIGID were in the subbasement armory searching for something that might have an effect on their superhuman nemeses.

The armory was a vast storeroom featuring row upon row of weaponry from antitank dragon launchers to simple hunting knives. The well-stocked armory had been a feature of the redoubt back when it had been built and subsequently closed down in the twentieth century, and much of the stock here was renovated from that original source. A further chunk of it had been acquired from other stashes, barony hauls and through plundering other redoubts that had been forgotten by history.

The cool, filtered air of the room and the shelves of goods made it feel a little like walking through a refrigerator. The walls still showed scorch marks where Kane had launched an antitank missile in the midst of the armory while fighting the invading forces of Ullikummis.

"What about a bazooka?" Kane suggested, hefting one of the dragon launchers in two hands.

Brigid shook her head. "Too much collateral-damage potential," she warned, "and we don't know if these Dorian soldiers could survive it anyway."

Kane's brow furrowed. "You reckon they can?"

"I know they're tough," she replied without hesitation. "And I know they can slip into our minds given half a chance. I don't much fancy the results if one of them gets ahold of our thoughts while we're wielding that thing."

"Point," Kane agreed, replacing the dragon launcher next to two identical units. "What we need then is something hard and fast, something that'll put these soldiers down without undue risk to the general populace."

"That's the sum of it," Brigid said, pawing through a few light submachine guns to see what they had in stock.

"Sounds like every other mag mission I ever went on," Kane grumbled as he looked around the brightly lit room for inspiration. It struck him a moment later, but it suggested an unlikely weapon. "I've got an idea," Kane called as he hurried away from Brigid through the neat shelving units.

"Care to share it?" Brigid asked as Kane disappeared between the shelves.

"No, it wouldn't work for you," Kane said. "It's too crazy."

Brigid rolled her eyes. "Oh, great—what did I expect?" she muttered as she watched Kane stride purposefully from the store.

Kane walked through the live-ammo room beyond without slowing, barely acknowledging the sentry on watch there as he left the rooms. The thing he had in mind was not to be found in the armory here, nor on this level of the redoubt. Instead, he made his way through the well-lit corridors and caught the elevator as one of the facility's cleaning staff stepped out of it, pushing a mop and bucket on wheels before him.

Inside the elevator, Kane punched the button for another level of the subbasement. He watched as the indicator showed his descent through the mountain. He could only hope that the tech boys would let him try his audacious idea, and that maybe they could help him work it the way he wanted to.

AN HOUR LATER, Kane, Brigid and Grant regrouped in the operations center, where Lakesh and his team continued to scour hours of satellite footage for any sign of the unique airship. It was a tiny object in terms of global footage, and the Cerberus staff concentrated their efforts on North America. If the Dorians had gone farther afield, then the net would have to be widened, but for now Lakesh was happy—well, relatively—to play the odds.

"Once we find them we'll transport them back here," Brigid explained, "using the interphaser to dump them in the mat-trans."

"That safe?" Grant asked. He held Shizuka's sheathed *katana* tightly in his left hand, nervously running his thumbnail along the gold patterning.

"The receiving chamber is a sealed box designed to withstand the pressures of matter transference," Brigid reasoned. "Until the door's been unlocked, there's no possible way to get out. Not even for a supersoldier."

"What if they break the glass?" Grant wondered.

"Impossible," Lakesh said confidently. "That's armaglass. It's thick enough to withstand a bullet."

Kane looked uncertain. "They could arrive armed with something more than a bullet," he pointed out.

Lakesh looked over to the tinted brown armaglass chamber that dominated the far corner of the room. "If they show any signs of breaking through, then we can activate the mat-trans and send them elsewhere, effectively dumping the problem."

"And setting them free again," Grant rumbled.

"There are redoubts that have been locked under water," Lakesh reminded the three of them, "and others that have been crushed under innumerable tons of soil, thanks to earth tremors. If it comes to it—which it won't—we'll find somewhere. Better still, if you can disarm them before you shunt them to us then this should not be an issue."

Kane scratched his chin thoughtfully, feeling the start of a new beard beginning to form there. "I have an idea about that," he told the group. "I think I can get them here without too much difficulty...."

"Kane, you—" Brigid began, but he silenced her with a wave of his hand.

"I'm not going to tell you, Baptiste," Kane said, "nor you, Grant. That Dorian bitch has already had her claws in your skull once and you managed to repel her. I figure odds are good she'll want some payback, and I don't want her seeing my idea sitting front and center in your mind when she decides to take a peek."

"I can fight her off," Brigid reasoned. "I've already proved that."

"All the more reason to suspect she'll come for you," Kane said, and that was as much as he would say, no matter what Brigid or Grant asked. "Just put your faith in the ole Kane magic and I'll make sure we get our man, as it were."

Brigid was clearly less than happy about that situation, but she let it go. She had known Kane long enough to trust his instincts, and they were *anam-charas*—soul friends. While she didn't always like the way he played things, she knew that he had good reasons for his decisions. Furthermore, she had to admit that Kane was likely on the money when it came to assuming that the Dorian called Antonia would be seeking revenge for what had happened out in Hope during their mental battle.

"What about long-term?" Grant wondered, his thumb working the groove at the top of the sword's sheath. "Where do we send them then?"

"The mat-trans can hold them," Lakesh reasoned, "and we can use another facility to teleport in food and so on. Longer term, however, we may be able to return them to their bunker and reseal it in such a way that they can never escape. I have a team looking into this option even as we speak."

"Any other ideas?" Kane asked. He could see that Grant was fidgety, uncomfortable with letting these people live after what they had done both in Hope and to his love, Shizuka.

Lakesh looked solemn, his eyes two haunted blue orbs in his dusky face. "We shall find a way," he confirmed. "We always do."

Before he could say anything further, an alarm tone went off at one of the computer desks and Brewster Philboyd leaped up with a cry of "Eureka!"

"Mr. Philboyd, what is it?" Lakesh asked, scrambling over to the taller man's desk. "Do we have success?"

Brewster Philboyd self-consciously adjusted his glasses to cover his embarrassment before he spoke. "We do. I've located the airship just to the east of the Mojave. It's well hidden—they're using some kind of motion camouflage with a phase interrupter, which, in layman's terms, means it appears to flicker in and out of existence. Cameras checked over this area three times without spotting a thing."

Lakesh leaned a little closer to Philboyd's computer screen, where the satellite image had been paused, identifying the cigar shape of the airship they were searching for. Kane, Grant and Brigid joined the two men at the terminal, examining the satellite image for themselves.

"How did you spot it this time?" Kane asked.

Philboyd shrugged. "Just lucky, I guess." As if to prove his point, he toggled the image back to the live feed. It appeared exactly the same but the airship was no longer visible. However, there were some telltale signs if one knew where to look—a hint of the great craft's shadow could be seen on a grassy area visible at the edge of a small cluster of buildings.

"What's the delay on this?" Brigid asked.

"Live feed," Philboyd confirmed. "So, no more than four seconds, max. It's as live as it's going to be with satellite bounce."

"And we think it's still there?" Kane queried.

"The ghost shadow indicates that something is still there and backtracking shows it's been static a few hours," Philboyd confirmed. "The only way to be one hundred percent certain is to put a man on the ground."

"Exactly what I had in mind," Kane assured him.

Seconds later, Kane, Grant and Brigid were running out the door and making their way to the docking bay where the Mantas were stored. Brigid had memorized the location coordinates where the airship had been spied, committing it to her incredible eidetic memory in a single glance. Lakesh sent a message ahead of them to get the Mantas prepped and ready for takeoff, as well as sending a full team to provide the weaponry and other materiel they would require for the mission. They were on their way.

Chapter 23

The passage of the Mantas was marked by the explosive gasp of the air-spike engines as they tore across the Mojave Desert toward the tiny settlement that Brewster Philboyd had located on the satellite image. Both Mantas had been fitted with one additional feature—a corded harpoon of the type used by ancient whaling vessels, located in a fixed unit on the undercarriage. The harpoon could be launched from the cockpit control panel, utilizing a canister of compressed air to give sufficient thrust to outrace the Mantas for a few seconds. They were limited by their targeting features, which was to say there were none—Kane or Grant could launch their harpoon only once each and, in essence, direct it using the nose of the Manta itself, firing the weapon in the exact same direction as they were flying at the time. The idea was that these harpoons could be used to pierce and tow the airship from any volatile area, but neither man held out much hope for the tactic, partly because there had simply been no time to test the harpoons.

The outlander settlement was made up of a dozen or so properties located close to the ghost town of Oatman.

Piloting the lead craft, Kane spit out a curse as he spotted the town. He may not have Brigid's photographic memory but he could recognize a place he had seen a photo of. This was the spot—the white-painted houses with their sandy pathways, the single-track road dusted with sand, the strip of green at the easternmost edge where the airship had been flickering on Brewster's screen. Oh, this was the place, all right. Just one problem—the airship was nowhere to be seen.

Occupying the seat behind Kane in the tight cockpit, Brigid Baptiste peered out the window. "Are we there yet?" she asked as she heard Kane cuss.

"Sure are," Kane told her as he slowed the Manta and began to descend. "But I can't see any sign of our supersoldiers."

The whole journey through the air had been completed in less than two hours, from takeoff at the Bitterroot Mountains to arrival here on the eastern edge of the Mojave.

"Careful, Kane," Brigid warned. "That camouflage technology they have rigged up could be playing havoc with your sensors."

"Sensors is one thing," Kane agreed, "but even trying to eyeball the airship, I'm coming up blank."

Brigid peered out the cockpit, scanning the horizon as she confirmed their position. Kane was right: there appeared to be no evidence that the airship had been here. Skipping any discussion with her partner, Brigid engaged her Commtact and requested an update from Brewster Philboyd at the satellite monitoring station. "Has our bogey moved in the last however-long-it's-been, Brewster?"

"Negative on that," Philboyd told her. "I can't see the airship but I can see its shadow. And your Mantas are just coming into view."

"We're just reaching the spot now," Kane confirmed, taking over the conversation from Brigid. "No shadows here. Can you give me a wider scan of the area, Brew?

See if you can pick up any anomalies that might be our target?"

"Roger that, Kane, I'll see what I can do."

Beneath his flight helmet, Kane ground his teeth as he waited, eyeing the ground with annoyance. The airship was not there; he was sure of it. Over their linked Comm-tacts, Grant was saying something similar, and Kane defused his obvious anger by confirming that Brewster Philboyd was checking into it back at Cerberus.

Below, the settlement looked normal enough. Well-kept houses painted in pale colors to reflect the pun-ishing brightness of the desert sun. Roads nudged with sand where the desert continued its encroachment, inch by inch, speck by speck. But there was something else, something that nagged at Kane in the back of his mind. Despite the unusual sight of the Mantas in the skies, the streets were utterly empty. No one had come rushing out of their property to see what all the noise was about. No one was working in their garden or out buying food and just happened to look up. It was deserted, empty, devoid of all life. And Kane didn't like it.

"Whole town's dead," Kane said.

"How's that?" Brigid asked.

"Check for yourself," Kane instructed as he did a low swoop of the main street. "Despite the noise we're kick-ing up, no one's come out to investigate. Like there's no-body left to come out to play."

"That is strange," Brigid mused. "Kane, what if some-thing happened to them? Do you think…?"

"Demented supersoldiers who get a kick out of kill-ing people in strange ways," Kane said, "coupled with a ghost town that doesn't even have a roof tile out of place. Yeah, you bet *'I think.'* I think a lot, Baptiste, and none of it good."

"Bring us down," Brigid instructed.

"You read my mind," Kane told her, though perhaps it was not the most tactful choice of phrase given their recent experience.

KANE LANDED CLOSE to the strip of garden, while Grant kept airborne, circling the little cluster of buildings and keeping a close vigil on the skies for any sign of their target. The cockpit of Kane's Manta was open almost as soon as he landed, and he and Brigid leaped out, blasters in hand, ready for anything.

The settlement was colored by the whining sounds of the desert winds in the distance, a sound like emptiness. Stepping from the sloped wing of the Manta, Kane eyed the nearest of the buildings, waiting for signs of movement. None came.

Brigid called to Kane as he began to trudge over the street. "Kane, the garden—look at it."

Kane turned, examining the strip of grass and trees more closely than he had when he had exited his craft. His point-man sense had not suggested anything out of order, just some trees, flowers, a handful of statues arranged amid the greenery. But as he looked again, Kane saw that the statues were far too lifelike; they looked almost like actual people, unclothed and posing as if waiting for a photo to be taken.

Brigid was already at the garden's edge, pushing open the gate. The green space was surrounded by a decorative fence made of metal arches that reached midway to Brigid's hips, the gate just slightly taller, causing her to dip down a little to work the catch.

The statue people waited as Brigid entered, none of them moving. Kane was behind her now, his Sin Eater in hand, scanning back and forth for any signs of an ambush. "Be careful," he warned.

Brigid had her own weapon, the trusty TP-9, held warily in her right hand, carefully using it in time with her own line of sight as she watched the static figures. They stood on the grass, barefoot and mostly naked, a few wearing slips of material draped artistically around their motionless forms. They were neither hiding nor moving, but just stood waiting in their little groups, young and old, adults and children, a monument to the varieties of the human body.

There were fountains here, too, simple monuments made of stone or sheet metal, simply tooled into shape by a deft hand. The fountains tripped musically on specially arranged surfaces, the water playing songs that rippled like moonlight on the ocean.

Another noise came from the edge of the garden and the two Cerberus warriors spun, prepped for an attack. A Jack Russell dog, two feet from muzzle to tail, dirt and leaves caught up in its tangled fur, came bounding out of the cover of bushes, something caught in its mouth. It stopped before Brigid as she eased her finger off the trigger, dropping the thing it held at her feet. It was a stick, and it was almost as long as the dog was.

Brigid leaned down, holding her open hand out to the dog and letting it sniff her. "Who do you belong to, boy? Where's your master?"

The dog yipped once before scampering back to the dropped stick and running in a circle on the spot, almost chasing its own tail.

"The mutt wants to play," Kane said as he strode up to join his partner.

Brigid looked at it. "Looks pretty well kept, but he needs a bath," she observed. "I'd guess he's been forgotten about for the last few days, like his master went away."

Kane nodded in agreement. "You reckon he belongs to the Dorians?"

"No," Brigid replied. "He belongs to one of these people, the folks who used to live in this little spit of a town." As she said it, she was gesturing to the nudes around her where they stood statue-still. Kane looked at them with new comprehension.

"You think they're...?" he began and stopped, realizing that she was right. They were people, living people, trapped in time. "What happened to them?" Kane asked.

"Something bad," Brigid replied as she padded over to the nearest group of "statues," the eager dog following along at her heels. "The Dorians have exhibited the power of remote mind control. I suspect they used that here, to take control of this settlement."

Doing a quick head count, Kane figured there to be about thirty people in total standing in the garden, including eight kids and a couple of teens. "Dozen houses, thirty people," he calculated. "Matches pretty well. This is probably everyone who lived here. Turned into living statues."

Brigid had placed her hand to the throat of one of the "statues," feeling for a pulse. After a moment she regretfully removed her fingers and tried the next one to the same result. "Not living," she told Kane. "Maybe when they were put here, but they're dead now."

Kane's eyes roved over the nude figures. For the most part, they still looked alive. There were no signs of decay, and their eyes remained open and glistening. A few of them smelled a little off, like milk on the turn. "They died with their eyes open," he said, sickened. "Locked in place like this, unable to do anything but die."

Brigid swallowed against a throat gone suddenly dry. "We should check them all," she said, "just in case. There may be some survivors."

But there weren't. Fifteen minutes to check each of the posed figures confirmed that. It was a travesty, as heart-wrenching as any the Cerberus warriors had seen.

KANE AND BRIGID were making their way back to the Manta when the call came over their Commtacts. Brewster Philboyd had found the airship again.

"I backtracked and reversed the search parameters," he explained, "to try to track the wind pattern left by the airship's passage."

"That's great work, Brewster," Kane said bitterly. "But where is it?"

"Sorry," Philboyd apologized, "got a little too excited about it all, I guess. The airship is about sixty miles to your west, moving on an almost straight westerly course."

Linked in on the Commtact exchange, Brigid was already calculating the craft's location. "It's heading for Luilekkerville," she said with a gasp.

"Correction," Philboyd told her, "it's already there."

Brigid slipped in behind Kane in the cockpit as he slunk into his seat and adjusted his flight helmet. A moment later the bronze-winged craft was taking to the air once more, joining Grant's matching vehicle as they sped toward the West Coast and the missing airship.

THE AIRSHIP CARVED its slow path above the towering walls of Luilekkerville, drifting ominously toward the sinking evening sun. No music blared from its speakers this time; it simply glided across the blue-pink sky like a scar, some mighty, silent predator looming above the stunned populace.

On board, Hugh Danner rose from his golden throne and paced to the side door. The interior of the craft was still rudimentary—Algernon had a beautiful design sketched in his notes, but he was easily distracted into other projects and, what with Hugh's request that he look into that atom splitter bomb and the subsequent trouble he had had sourcing fissionable material, the upshot was that the inside of the gondola still looked more like a submarine hull than the gentleman's club he had in mind. Thus, for now at least the golden throne that Antonia had repainted would have to suffice.

Antonia and Cecily made do, using a low bench secured to the hill to gaze through the windows—open and not yet featuring any glass—at the massing crowds in the streets below.

"They love us," Antonia said excitedly, "and they fear us. They can't wait to see what we are!"

Up front of the hanging metal gondola, in a lower section separated by a short ladder, Algernon was standing at the pilot's podium controlling the airship. The noise of the rotor hardly reached all the way here, leaving the pilot's cubbyhole ominously silent. "We're coming up on the center now, old man," Algernon called back, his refined voice carrying through the passenger cabin behind him.

Hugh nodded, an alligator's smile fixed on his lips as he opened the passenger door. The wind buffeted against him immediately, but Hugh merely stood there, looking down at the ville below, his dark mane of hair whipping about his head. "For your entertainment, fine ladies and gentlemen of my acquaintance," he began in an announcer's voice, "I present a play. A play about the ultimate war—the war between man and his nature. If you cast your eyes below, the play shall begin, and you shall see the opening act, where man fights his inner beast."

Cecily and Antonia applauded delicately, silk gloves whispering against one another in delight.

Then Hugh stepped out of the open passenger door and strode onto the scaffold that waited beyond. The whole of the airship was caged in this scaffoldlike structure, a series of gangplanks and bridges that had been designed to hold the porcupine-like defense spikes in place. With perfect balance, Hugh paced out as far as he could go on the metal limb and spread his arms wide, his maroon coattails whipping about him.

Below the airship, hundreds of people had gathered to see what was happening. Their voices rose as they questioned each other, the sound drifting to the ears of the airship's quartet of passengers.

"Coming up now," Algernon called, bringing the dirigible to a halt above the towering cathedral in the center of Luilekkerville with its dominant red window located like some fearsome all-seeing eye. He flipped a switch on his control pedestal, powering the rotor blades down to hold the magnificent craft he had built from junk he'd found in the Panamint ruins in place.

"Attention, people of the colonies," Hugh said, his voice booming loudly above the droning sounds of the ship's rotor. "Today you shall be civilized and become that greatest of all works of art—a society. Hear my words and love them."

Poised thirty feet below in the shadow of the airship, the people of Luilekkerville did not know what to make of the stranger's announcement. They stood and waited, wondering what would come next.

Hugh strode back into the passenger compartment and nodded once to his tiny audience of two. "Our tale begins with the ephemeral bubble that is man's civilization," he explained. "So fragile." He took up his position on the golden throne, brushing the loose strands of hair from his face where they had become dislodged by the wind.

"Create something, Hugh," Cecily urged. "Something we all can be proud of."

"No." Antonia laughed. "Create something scandalous that we might be magnificently ashamed of instead!"

Hugh smiled that terrible smile once more before closing his eyes to begin the mind meld. "As you will it."

Chapter 24

Luilekkerville was at war.

For the second time in almost as many days, the sleek, bronze-colored silhouettes of twin Manta craft swooped over the city's golden towers as Kane, Grant and Brigid hurried to the site of new devastation. Even from this high up, the high-walled settlement had become a picture of bloody carnage, smoke pouring from the buildings, men, women and children openly fighting in the streets. The populace used whatever they could find to maim one another, hunting lone unfortunates in packs, surrounding them and kicking or beating them to death before turning on one another, all sense of community and loyalty forgotten. They used knives and blasters if they had them, sticks, broom handles or merely their own blood-caked hands to kill their enemies. And their enemies were anyone who wasn't them—even their own children, husbands, *babies.* It was sheer, unmitigated hell. And above it all, watching from the slowly drifting silver bulb of their airship, the four Dorian soldiers applauded as each new horror emerged, as each travesty was committed by man on his fellow man.

Kane powered down the jets and brought the sleek-looking Manta around for a closer look, his mind in turmoil. "It's hell down there, Baptiste," he told his colleague.

"I see it," Brigid replied, her voice ringing with a kind

of emptiness that Kane could detect even through the Commtact. Kane brought the Manta around toward the airship where it loomed above the cathedral.

"I'm going in," Kane instructed over the Commtact.

Grant's aircraft followed in a wide, well-spread pattern, keeping distance while remaining close enough to protect Kane should things go awry.

There was no indication that the airship was playing any role in the destruction below, no great beams of force or thrum of noise or music. The airship simply waited above the ville, soundless, its rotors spinning as it remained stationary.

ABOARD THE AIRSHIP, Hugh was sitting in his broad-backed throne. It had been repainted from something that Antonia had found among the homes near Cecily's pleasure garden, and she had turned her artistic flair to it just to give this moment the appropriate sense of occasion.

Hugh's eyes were closed in deep concentration, manipulating each of the citizens-turned-madmen in his grand spectacle below, his tribute to man's inhumanity and the ephemeral beauty of war from which civilizations emerged. "How does it look?" he asked.

Cecily and Antonia peered from the open windows while Algernon continued to work the pilot's controls, holding the great airship in place.

"It looks glorious," Antonia assured her lover as the devastation spread across the walled city. The pleasure in her face was absolute, and Hugh could detect that joy in her voice. "A thoroughly modern marvel!"

"I like when they kill their own babies," Cecily remarked, fanning herself delicately with a hand fan of gold and lace. "Such a perfect comment on the senselessness of war, how it taints the very future they fight to hold."

Hugh nodded. "More baby death," he said with a grin. "Yes, let us see what we can do." He turned his attention to the youngest mewling babies he could detect in his mindscape, transforming them into figures of hate in their mothers' eyes.

Below, mothers turned on their children with wild abandon, stabbing them with kitchen cutlery, bread knives, carving knives, gouging their eyes with spoons.

Cecily squealed as she felt the waves of hate crash against her mental buffers. "Delightful."

THE LEAD MANTA streaked toward the airship like a bronze blur. Inside, Kane was analyzing the heads-up displays, magnifying specific areas of the airship as he did a quick scan on approach. It was a beast of the air, huge as a battleship, with protective spines dotted across its surface. An air assault would not be easy; it would take split-second timing and a whole load of luck to pierce the craft with his harpoon.

The airship's rotors were turning slowly, and Kane figured it should take a few seconds before they could be brought up to full speed. That might give him the window he needed, *if* he could get his hit in on the first pass. The Dorians hadn't given any indication that they had spotted him or Grant yet. If he moved quickly, stealthily, Kane might just be able to snag the top front of the craft with his harpoon and tow it away from the city. There was a small gap in the bristling spines there, enough that he could wedge the harpoon in if he could just get the right angle.

"Kane, look!" Brigid gasped from behind him.

"Where?"

"The underside," Brigid said, tapping Kane's shoulder to roughly indicate where she meant.

"I don't see…" he began, but he stopped. He saw it, all right. There was a shaft hanging beneath the body of the great airship, tubular and approximately the length of three men standing on each other's shoulders. "What is that?" Kane muttered. But he already knew.

"Bomb," Brigid said, confirming Kane's fears. "That's what I'd guess, anyway. Why else would it be placed underneath the craft like that?"

Veering to port, Kane brought up a magnification on the bomb, studying it with trepidation. A metal tube with fins, the thing looked a lot like a nuclear warhead. But its body was covered in a strange coating of jutting, cream-colored bands, and it took Kane a moment to figure out if they were of practical use or simply for decoration. Then he realized what they were, recognizing them from his prior experience with skeletal remains. They were ribs, piled up one after another, creating a kind of eerie protective cage around the length of the missile in sickening precursor to the death it was designed to bring.

"It's a bomb, all right," Kane confirmed as he dipped his craft down and away from the airship.

Over his Commtact, Kane heard Grant's voice raised in concern. "Kane, what's going on? You're veering off course."

"We're aborting," Kane instructed.

"Not me," Grant told him. "These sons of gene glitches almost killed Shizuka. I ain't about to let them get away.…"

"We're aborting," Kane repeated. "Grant, they have a bomb. It's too risky."

There was a long pause over their linked Commtacts

and Kane could feel the weight of the decision that Grant was having to make.

Finally, Grant's rumbling voice came over the Commtact again. "Following your lead," he confirmed. "Mission aborted."

Behind Kane, Brigid was analyzing the scope where Kane had patched through the scan feed of the missile. "The design is familiar," she said, drawing from her eidetic memory. Kane had seen her do this trick too often to be surprised. Sometimes it seemed that the distaff member of their little crew had an insight into just about everything. "That's an atom bomb. Rejigged a little, and the decorative flourishes are pretty way out-there, but the basic design is nuclear."

"Where would they have found that kind of device?" Kane wanted to know.

"Same place they got the airship," Brigid replied. "Built it themselves. They're geniuses, remember? Show them the designs for something and these supersoldiers can assimilate and recreate it, improve on it, even completely retool it so that it functions for another purpose."

"So, chances are we have a live nuke on our hands," Kane grumbled. "Well, that's just terrific."

ALGERNON WATCHED THROUGH the pilot's viewport as the twin Manta craft arced away from him. "It appears that we have some company at our little exhibition," he informed the others.

"Art for the masses," Cecily chirruped excitedly. "And they're just in time for your grand finale."

Algernon's hand wavered over the release control for the atom bomb, but he hesitated. "Not just yet," he announced. "Let's allow Hugh his moment in the sun before we create a second sun in the sky, shan't we."

The immortals watched as the Mantas whirled away like fireflies, their golden chassis catching the sun like glistening streaks of lightning.

"LIVE NUKE," GRANT REPEATED as he absorbed Kane's assessment over the Commtact. "This week just keeps getting worse, don't it?"

"Sure does," Kane agreed.

Grant's Manta followed Kane's path through the smoke-smeared sky, dropping close to Luilekkerville's walls.

Kane shook his head in irritation. "Damned if we do and damned if we don't," he muttered as he watched the expanding bloodshed below. The knock-on effects of a nuclear detonation would be catastrophic, never mind the immediate loss of life it would cause.

Kane spotted a group of young women attacking an old man who had been shot in the leg by a local magistrate as he tried to escape. The mag watched, smiling as the old man fell to the savage kicks of the young women—not one of them over fifteen—before turning his gun on the nearest of them and transforming her skull into a red smear atop her spurting stump of neck.

The ville was organized in a radial pattern around the central spire of the great cathedral, its single red-glass eye peering out across the current destruction like the sun seen through a haze of radioactive pollution. The "eye" was designed to remind people that they were safe, and it had been based on an older design used by the magistrates to represent the all-seeing eye of the authorities and so keep the population in check. Whatever they called it now, be it the eye of god or his grave, it overlooked a wide square within which hundreds of people were fighting.

"We're landing," Kane instructed Grant over the

Commtact. "Let's deal with each mess one at a time, see if we can't bring some order to the chaos."

With that, Kane brought the Manta down in a looping arc that settled it just outside the cathedral's main entrance, giving the deranged populace only a few seconds to scatter or be crushed. It was a risk, but a little shock-and-awe theatrics couldn't go amiss in a situation like this—get people thinking about something other than beating the living crap out of one another. He needed to capture their minds, snag them away from the influence of the Dorians the same way that Brigid had channeled the darkness in her past to force out the mind thief's thoughts.

Kane tapped on the Manta's external speakers and switched his Commtact to that frequency, using its pickup mic to relay his voice to the crowd. "Everybody cease and desist," Kane ordered. "You've been duped into this fight. Return to your homes. I repeat—return to your homes."

A moment later, Kane had the cockpit hatch open and his flight helmet off, and he and Brigid were scrambling down the wing toward the worst of the fighting. Brigid had shoved the interphaser into a backpack that she had slung over her shoulders. The weight would be an irritation, but she didn't want to get too far from it right now. It was critical if they were to trap the Dorians in the Cerberus mat-trans.

"We need to split these people up," Kane told Brigid.

"What do you suggest?" Brigid asked over the noise of chaos.

"You're the smart one," Kane told her.

"And you're the ex-magistrate," Brigid replied without missing a beat.

Kane thought about this for a half second before

reaching into one of the pouches in his belt and pluck-ing out a trio of small ball-bearing-like devices, each one approximately an inch and a half in diameter. "You have any flash-bangs on you?" he asked.

Brigid nodded. "And something better," she said, pull-ing out a similar-looking device.

Kane raised an eyebrow querulously as Brigid re-vealed the device.

"Lab boys call it a tearjerker," she explained. "Tear gas held in very dense mixture, expands as soon as the shell is broken."

Kane nodded in appreciation. "Like it," he said. "I really must start hanging out with the eggheads more."

Brigid rolled the tearjerker explosives around in her palm, sealing filters in her nostrils with her free hand while Kane did the same. "On three?"

"Sounds good to me," Kane said, leaping from the Manta's wing and wading into the crowd.

A moment later the square erupted with explosive bursts of light and a cloud of tear gas, startling the crowds. Kane turned his face away from the first of the explosions, screwing his eyes tight as the second went off yards away.

The ball-bearing-like flash-bangs contained a tiny ex-plosive charge but were not capable of making any no-table damage. Instead, they generated a bright flash like a lightning strike coupled with an extremely loud bang. To the unwary, the result looked for all the world like a massive explosion going off and it served not only to startle opponents but also to temporarily blind and deafen them if they stood too close. The Cerberus field teams had employed the devices in a variety of ways, but right now Kane hoped that the illusion of a bigger attack than the one that the crowds were engaged in would serve to disperse at least a portion of the frenzied attackers who had become caught up in the dangerous mental thrall.

Brigid's tearjerkers, meanwhile, generated an expanding cloud of smoke, irritating the eyes of anyone who caught a whiff of it. All around her, a whole section of the crowd doubled over, hacking and wheezing as their eyes began to stream with tears. Brigid watched as they tumbled to the ground, their immediate enmities forgotten.

Twenty feet from Kane's craft, Grant brought his own Manta down to rest with a resounding clank of metal on stone. As the Manta settled, Grant checked the sensor display, which gave a full 360-degree view of the remarkable aircraft. There was a group of magistrates attacking another group made up of young people, many of them pushing baby strollers at their attackers like rams. The babies were out of the strollers, thrown at the mags like weapons, and Grant felt sick to his stomach as he watched two tiny figures slapped to the ground with a thud.

Grant reached forward, tapping the control board of the Manta and bringing the cooling jets back to life. Before anyone realized what was happening, Grant's Manta spouted twin jets of air—using the same air-spike technology that powered the craft through the sky—sending the unwary assailants careening backward as if caught up in the grip of a hurricane. The move ended the battle in an instant.

Grant dislodged the cockpit bubble and pulled himself up from the pilot's couch. A moment later he was striding across the shimmering bronze wing amid the bloody chaos, strapping Shizuka's *katana* to his waist before he leaped to the ground.

Up above, the airship loomed like a brewing storm, waiting to rain down death on the unsuspecting population.

Chapter 25

The ville was arranged in a giant circle, with the highest building at the center. That building was the cathedral, a towering strut of stone with multiple entrances and a single red window placed close to the top like a second setting sun. With its open-door policy to outlanders—travelers who roamed the unclaimed lands between villes—Luilekkerville was full of three thousand people, the radial pattern of streets jammed to overflowing with people who had been wondering just what the airship was doing when Hugh's mental attack had begun. Now they had been turned into three thousand unwilling participants in Hugh's deadly art project, attacking one another in a nightmarish fight to the death; massacre in the name of art.

Kane, Brigid and Grant fought through the deranged crowds, working in tandem to split up groups and keep would-be killers away from one another. Kane and Grant were both ex-magistrates who had been trained since birth to handle such situations, and they dispersed the crowds using a combination of fear tactics and some well-placed shots from their Sin Eater pistols. They shot to wound, not to kill, taking the legs out from the more dangerous types who were running about causing mayhem, disarming those who had obtained firearms for the ruckus.

Brigid, too, acted to disperse the crowd, paying particular attention to protecting some of the more vulnerable members such as children and pregnant women. Luilekkerville was a "young ville," and while its population encompassed people of all ages the vast majority were under forty, drawn by the promise of religious salvation. Brigid's combat prowess kept her lithe on her feet, and more than once it allowed her to avoid a potentially lethal attack by one of the mind-controlled mob.

"We need to get these people away from here," Kane instructed, glancing up at the airship looming high above them.

Brigid shook her head. "It's impossible," she said. "Better we stick to the original plan and remove the Dorians from this place and into the containment facility at Cerberus."

Kane sidestepped as a blood-soaked figure came hurrying from the feverish mob around the cathedral, swinging a gold collection plate at his head. The man overshot, stumbling as his swing ended not in Kane's skull but in empty air. Brigid slid her foot back in the sand and tripped the man, sending him sailing away before striking a nearby wall with some force. She and Kane watched in satisfaction as the figure slumped to the ground, unconscious.

Grant joined the two of them a moment later, admiring their handiwork with a smile. "Nice," he said. "But if we stay down here much longer we're liable to get a mental bolt that'll send us as nutty as the locals."

"Good point," Brigid agreed. "From the way Reba explained it, the Dorians work their mental attack on individual minds, moving rapidly from one to the other and back again. We've probably missed the initial attack by dint of being late arrivals, but that can't last forever.

Sooner or later we'll be noticed—after which, it'll be every Cerberus man for himself, so to speak."

Kane glanced up at the airship thoughtfully, then at the cathedral tower where it almost nudged against it. If they could find a way up there, they might be able to board it and defuse that bomb—and the whole terrible situation with it. "Okay," he said, "here's how it's going to go down. We're getting nowhere fighting our way to exhaustion with the locals down here. We need to stop the Dorians at the source. So, we go with our original plan—grab them and hold them long enough to send them to a cell at Cerberus."

Grant looked at Kane querulously. "How do you suggest we do that? We get close and they're liable to trigger that A-bomb."

"Baptiste sets up the interphaser," Kane explained. "There's a parallax point somewhere around here, right, Baptiste?"

Brigid nodded. "To the south of the ville."

"Great, then Grant and I will handle the airship and bring you the immortal troublemakers," Kane told her.

"How?"

"Just get moving," Kane told her, "and let me worry about the how."

With a casual salute, Brigid turned and began wading back into the crowd, making her way slowly south down the panic-strewed streets.

Left behind, Grant looked at Kane with expectation. "Well?" he asked.

With detached professionalism, Kane popped a new clip into his Sin Eater. "You know, I can't remember the last time I went to church," he said with an air of casualness. "What say you and me go pay our respects."

Grant eyed the towering cathedral and smiled, sliding a new clip into his own weapon. "Yeah, I'm starting to feel some religious fervour in my soul, too, now you mention it."

Together, the two men entered the church, striding into a grand nave crammed with fighting maniacs.

BRIGID RAN ALONE through the war-torn streets. It felt like some nightmarish Mardi Gras, people running all about her with masks on. Only, those masks were their own pained expressions, some of them tempered with streaks of blood about the eyes, the mouth.

Brigid reared back in disgust as a woman came stumbling toward her with one arm outstretched as if she were blind. The woman's face was a patchwork of ripped skin, and she continued to run a razor blade over her features, gouging great chunks of herself away, slice by bloody slice.

Brigid hugged the wall as the blood-faced woman passed, reaching out and plucking the razor from her hand. The woman turned in surprise, unleashing a terrible shriek that sounded more like an animal in pain than anything that had ever been human. Brigid drove a straight-legged kick into the woman's kneecap, snapping her leg and dropping her to the ground. She slung the razor in a drain as she strode away, hurrying onward to the south gate of the ville.

The victims would start to fail soon, Brigid suspected. That was what had happened in Hope when the woman Antonia had tried to control people, because the pressure on the human brain was too great. And when that did start to happen, if Kane and Grant were too slow in removing the threat of the Dorian mind attack, then the whole ville would die from brain hemorrhages, vicious little war game or not.

SHINGLES COVERED THE CHURCH outside and in, creating a rough effect as if it had been eroded by time rather than constructed by man. There were great carvings in the wall and over the four compass-point doorways, each of them creating a man-shaped figure that stretched out across the floor in a huge shadow, a trick of the light. Not that the congregation noticed it right now. They were too busy fighting one another, moving between the pews like sharks scenting blood.

Kane and Grant fought through at least two dozen incensed "worshippers," each one turned mad by the mental bolts emanating from the airship high above. The crazies were vicious and relentless, but they were also disorganized and so caught up in the mental push to war that they walked into just about anything the two ex-magistrates set up. It took three minutes to clear a path through to the bell tower where the colossal red window loomed down on the ville like a bloody eye.

Finally, Kane and Grant stood at the staircase that looped around on itself, swirling up toward the bell. Above, the bell glistened like a drop of blood where red light streamed through the window. Kane led the way, blaster in hand, certain that there would be a roof access somewhere up there. Grant followed, Sin Eater ready, Shizuka's sheathed *katana* slapping against the side of his leg as he climbed the steps.

"Let's finish this," Grant told Kane as they began their ascent.

Chapter 26

The airship was low enough...*maybe*. Right then, as he stood on the cathedral roof staring at it, Kane didn't much care. All he knew was it was his only chance, so he had to take it. The airship was still thirty feet above the edge of the roof itself but it had trailing guy ropes hanging from its belly. One of those ropes whipped through the air just beyond the lip of the rooftop. Kane watched for a moment as it swung back and forth like a live snake.

Beside Kane, Grant clambered onto the rooftop, his eyes fixing on the swinging rope. "You think we can do this?" he asked.

In reply, Kane merely brushed a finger against the side of his nose in the 1 percent salute. Whatever the odds were, it was time they overcame them and put this thing to rest.

Kane took two steps back until he was at the farthest edge of the cathedral rooftop, high above the smoking streets of Luilekkerville. "Give me some space," he warned.

Grant watched as Kane sprang forward like a runner leaping off the blocks. He sprinted across the rooftop where the scarlet window peered down at the chaotic mess that was Luilekkerville, building his speed before leaping out into the ether.

Kane's feet kicked off as they left the tiles of the cathedral roof, thrusting him into the air high over the street, his arms poised forward to grab that flailing rope. It swayed tantalizingly ahead of him, a frayed knot swinging to and fro at its end. And then he had it, left and right hands grasping the dirty rope simultaneously, cinching around it and holding tight as he started to slip down its swinging length.

Behind Kane on the rooftop, Grant held his breath as he watched his partner slip down the dangling rope. "Come on, Kane," he muttered, "hang on."

Whether Kane had heard Grant or not, he somehow held on, slowing his descent as wisps of smoke burned from the rope and his hands. With a lurch, he brought himself to a halt. Without pausing, Kane began climbing up the rope the long thirty feet that stood between him and the observation gondola of the strange aircraft.

Kane was in the prime of physical fitness. Cinching his legs in place, working hand over hand, it took him a minute to ascend the rope, dangling high over the towering buildings of the ville. The wind billowed loudly up there, high above the ground, every huff and puff trying to derail him from his rapid ascent. He slowed as he reached the highest point of the rope. He saw now that it did not link to the bottom of the observation pod— instead, it was snagged on one of those porcupine spines that jutted out in all directions from the body of the airship. The spine poked upward and out at a ten-o'clock angle to the round cross section of the balloon itself, constructed of a framework of metal with a sharp end, twenty feet from the balloon's skin. The spines were connected to a frame that sat snugly around the airship like a cage, great metal protrusions presumably designed to keep an attacker at bay.

Kane yanked himself up onto the jutting spine, working his chest onto the narrow bar and heaving himself up so that he clung there. The bar was three feet across, enough for Kane to rest his chest against as he caught his breath. Down below, on the roof of the cathedral, he saw Grant sprinting over the tiles before launching himself out into nothingness, reaching for the rope. Kane saw Grant snag the rope and swing far out over the streets. The additional weight sent the airship swaying just a little in place, like a boat at anchor bobbing on the sea.

Kane waited, peering at the observation box where the silhouetted shapes of the Dorians could be seen at the open windows. He counted two of them, their profiles and hair giving away that they were the women. The men had to be on there, too, Kane told himself. To come this far and lose the chance to snag the whole group would be too much.

As Grant reached the bottom of the protrusion where Kane was hanging, Kane began to shimmy along it, drawing himself closer to the metal gondola.

THERE WERE PEOPLE groaning all around her. Brigid ran, zipping through the blood-strewed streets like a racehorse. The interphaser rocked to and fro in her backpack, its weight driving her on as she slipped around a corner, darting down another street toward the south gate in the ville walls. The gate was open—Luilekkerville had instituted an open-door policy ever since it had been rebuilt as a haven for the Worshippers of Stone.

There were people to the left and right of her, corpses littering the street in clumps, the agonized moans of the wounded prominent as she hurried past. Brigid ignored them, leaping over the fallen figure of a local magistrate, his head caved in on one side in a blood-colored bruise.

A figure stepped out from a doorway and made a grab for Brigid, but she danced out of the way, twirling in a graceful three-step before continuing on along the path to the ville's exit.

Another form, this one a woman in middle age sporting a bloody wound on her forehead and swinging a meat cleaver through the air like a kid with a kite, leaped for Brigid, slashing at her face with the steel blade. Brigid dodged back, dropping away as the cleaver swished through empty air where she had been a microsecond earlier.

The woman tried again, bringing the cleaver around in a downward swing that seemed destined for Brigid's shoulder. Brigid brought her arm out of the vicious blade's path in a blur of black leather, using her elbow to stab out at her attacker's solar plexus. The bloodstained woman tottered back with a gasp of painfully expelled air, dropping the cleaver with a clatter.

Brigid hurried on as the woman sagged to the ground, no time to waste. Kicking her legs out in distance-humbling strides, Brigid shot through the open gate, meeting the gravel path beyond in a shush of boot soles on stone, red hair whipping out behind her like a streak of flame.

There were two people just beyond the gates, an elderly man and woman, their hands clawed around one another's throats. Brigid lunged forward, striking the old man's elbow with the heel of her hand, snapping bone in an instant. The man sagged backward with a yelp of pain, breaking his grip around his partner's throat. The elderly woman let go as the man slipped out of her hold. She looked bewildered, as if waking from some terrible dream.

Brigid hurtled on like a rocket.

The path had been layered with loose gravel chips for just a dozen yards, a sort of "welcome carpet" to the ville. After that it turned rapidly to dirt, sloppy pools of mud slurping in indentations along its uneven surface.

Brigid sneaked a glance behind her to eyeball the airship where it waited, poised above the cathedral like some terrible cloud. It didn't seem to be moving; not yet. She hoped there was still time.

KANE WAS ALMOST at the gondola, a long box with windows that hung beneath the balloon of the airship, swaying slightly with the breeze. The wind felt stronger out here, whistling in his ears like crashing waves, thrusting against his body as he clambered along the metal needle. Close up, he could see that the pod was constructed of flimsy material, very thin sheet metal riveted together, doubtless to minimize the weight. There was a good chance he could break through it with a couple of solid kicks. It seemed like an option, anyway.

He could hear their voices now, bubbling over the sounds of the whistling wind, braying and laughing at the chaos they had generated.

"Let's end this," Kane muttered as he reached for the wall of the observation pod and pulled himself toward it.

Behind him, Grant had just reached the metal spoke where the rope swung, and he pulled himself onto it, bringing his legs up until he was squatting in a crouch. He looked around for a few seconds, judging the best way to get to the passenger bubble of the strange craft. "I'm going to go around," he told Kane over the Commtact, "and grab the pilot."

Kane turned back and caught Grant's eye, engaging his Commtact at the same time. "You want me to wait?" he asked.

"Negative," Grant replied, reaching up for another spine that stood out several feet above him. "Get in there now—don't lose the element of surprise. I'll meet you inside."

Kane grabbed the nearest upright bar lining the open windows of the observation pod. Then he pulled himself in, swinging his legs up and over the lip, smashing through the wall in a colossal crash of rending metal sheet. Rivets pinged everywhere as the delicate wall of the observation pod split in two with Kane landing amid the mayhem.

As one, the eerily handsome Dorians in the observation area turned, three in all, jaws open in surprise that was rapidly turning to anger.

Kane didn't stop for a second. Already, he was throwing the flash-bangs he had palmed from a belt pouch. He ducked away, turning his head as the flash-bangs went off in a carom of light and noise.

GRANT, MEANWHILE, was making his way around to the fore of the airship, utilizing the strange structure of spiny protrusions to move across the hull. He turned his head as the flash-bangs exploded inside the passenger bulb, blinking back the aftereffects of that bright shock of light.

"Little warning next time, partner," Grant growled into his Commtact. But he figured that Kane was too busy to worry about such niceties right now. Best to keep moving and get to the front section of the air clipper.

A LITTLE BEYOND Luilekkerville's walls, Brigid was almost at a ridge, her arms pumping back and forth, her legs pounding, feet striking the path in relentless blows. There was a line of trees up ahead, great redwoods that climbed into the air like the part-buried fingers of some ancient Titan. She knew that the parallax point was there—somewhere.

Brigid looked behind her again as she trotted along the path, slowing down for a moment to see what was happening above the ville. The airship still hadn't moved, but she watched in surprise as something appeared to explode within it. When no fire took hold, she felt relief and a touch of pride, realizing that either Kane or Grant must have set off another flash-bang to disorient their enemies.

Brigid renewed her pace, veered away from the path and started to ascend the ridge.

"SURRENDER," KANE ORDERED, raising his voice over the ringing in his own ears, "and we can end this thing now."

The Dorian women shrieked as they rubbed at their eyes, blindly bumbling around the deck. "What did he do to us?" Antonia hissed.

"I can't see," Cecily spit, batting against a metal wall. "Antonia? Hugh? Are you there?"

Kane, too, was suffering from the aftereffects of the flash-bang. While he had known when it would ignite, he had not had time to do anything more than turn his head, which meant that now his ears were ringing and there were luminous green patches affecting his vision. Didn't matter—Kane just had to do this quick, before these psychopaths dropped that nuke.

Kane heard Cecily shout as he charged across the deck, his feet striking a crashing tattoo on the wooden boards. "We're being boarded," she screeched. "We've been compromised, Hugh."

A moment later Kane was standing before Antonia where she continued to reel from his initial attack, and he barreled into her, driving shoulder-first into her midriff, using all his weight and momentum to shove her even harder against the flimsy metal shell of the observation pod.

Five feet away, the brunette was blinking rapidly to clear her eyes, sweeping at the air with her lace fan, so swift that it appeared to be a golden brushstroke hovering in the air, repeating her warning about the ship being boarded. Still moving, Kane brought the Sin Eater up as he dropped to one knee, keeping the weapon level so that he fired into Cecily's gut. She had not expected that, and Kane watched as the bullets impacted on the satin midline of her dress, shredding the material and scattering threads across the observation deck.

In his throne, Hugh Danner was concentrating on his grand art design—aka the citizens of Luilekkerville—as they slipped from his mental grasp. Some were still linked with him in the slip-nudge way of his telepathy, but most seemed to have been either too badly wounded or too hopelessly distracted to be brought back into line. The telepathy was not a natural thing. Antonia had discovered it quite by accident about a hundred years before, while she was trying to explain a dream she had had about the end of the world at the hands of the sailors of the Argo. She had been in the theater, speaking with Cecily at the time, when Cecily had begun to see the very things that Antonia was describing, right there, dancing in her head like animated paintings. At first she had put it down to her prodigiously well-exercised imagination, but when she had started describing Antonia's dream *to her* they had realized that something very strange was happening.

At first, the two women had assumed—quite understandably—that their closeness had somehow engendered the link, and that it was unique to them. They had spent an insufferable two weeks regaling one another with se-

cret thoughts and imaginings, Antonia thrusting each
new image into her friend's mind. The bond had been
especially useful during their bedroom sessions, Hugh
recalled, as they experimented with drilling sexual de-
sires into one another's heads with the resulting accu-
racy of William Tell's arrow.

It took a little longer before any of them realized that
they had achieved a kind of telepathy, and that the bond
was not limited to the two females in the group but rather
could be employed by all of them. It seemed that the
telepathic control was a by-product of their incredible
intelligence, an intelligence that had only grown and
matured as they had waited in their underground world,
Persephone-like, hidden from the eyes of mortals. Poor
Harold, of course, had come off rather the worse for Antonia's experimental probing, and Algernon had never
really shown much flair, but still the Dorian-class humans had discovered a new ability far beyond their cre-
ator's original plans.

However, the telepathy trick required a solid link and
was restricted by proximity. Hugh's ambitious project to
turn the whole of Luilekkerville against itself in an arch
morality play on the vulgar glories of war had rather hit
a snag with his main players turned away from him,
and the ill-considered death of many of the early stand-
out stars in his drama. Now, something was shaking his
airborne home, throwing the whole wretched thing out
of whack.

Hugh opened his eyes just in time to see Kane launch
a high kick into Cecily's proudly jutting jaw, sending her
floundering backward like a dancer who'd just been relieved of his date.

Antonia turned her attention toward Kane, trying to
fix him in her mental grasp, but the spots before her eyes

were confusing her. On the decking, Cecily was trying to do likewise, but bother!—the ringing in her ears. Both women connected at the same time, as Kane tossed another flash-bang to the deck at his feet and turned his head away. It was the last one he had.

You're mine, thought Antonia, directing the full extent of her mind powers on Kane.

You're mine, thought Cecily, directing the full extent of her mind powers on Kane.

Whoosh!—the flash-bang blurted out a great burst of light and sound between them.

UP AT THE FRONT of the hanging gondola, in the lower section where the pilot sat, Algernon was aware that something was occurring above and behind him. The controls remained steady but the airship jostled as if caught on a gust of wind, the cacophonous sounds of explosions reeling across the heavens as Kane set off the flash-bangs in the compartment above.

"Enough of this," Algernon spit, turning from the controls. The craft could take care of itself in hover mode, and he wanted to find out just what in the name of Her Royal Highness was going on up there.

He moved across the cramped pilot's booth and reached for the metal ladder rungs, barely a head's height above him. As he grasped the first rung, the front window of the airship came smashing toward him in a burst of splintering glass.

Algie brushed the glass away as shards slapped against his back and tangled in his hair. There was a man standing behind him. Algernon recognized him immediately, the dark figure he had tangled with in the burned-out factory where he had first constructed the airship, and the same man he had tussled with in the back alleys of Hope.

"It's over, pretty boy," Grant commanded as his Sin Eater materialized in his right hand. "Your reign of terror has finished."

"You have me at a disadvantage, good sir," Algie replied as he turned to face his would-be attacker. "I'm afraid I've forgotten your name."

Grant began to answer but already Algernon was moving, rocking across the cramped pilot's booth in a blur of phenomenal speed before driving the heel of his hand up toward Grant's nose. It was a move calculated to force the cartilage up into Grant's brain, killing him instantly. A combination of combat instinct and sheer luck prevented the blow from striking   Grant slapped out protectively with his right hand as he turned away from Algernon's blow. As such, his outstretched arm took the full impact of the Dorian warrior's savage strike, and Grant shrieked in agony as his arm went dead, the Sin Eater dropping from his grip and breaking free of its holster mechanism.

Algernon struck again without pause, bringing his other hand around in a tight fist that slammed against Grant's right shoulder with the power of a sledgehammer. Grant staggered back against the broken window, but with nowhere to go the only place left was outside. In an instant, Grant felt himself overbalance and begin to fall, slipping through the shattered remains of the windshield and into the evening air.

Chapter 27

Falling.

For a moment it was as if it hadn't really happened. It was so unreal, it was hard to take it in at all.

When Grant went crashing out the window high above Luilekkerville, pulling half the front panel of the metal shell with him, he had about one and a half seconds to go through all those emotions, get past the shock and get his head back in the moment.

Algernon's punch had been powerful enough to knock Grant back, but it had not been a good blow, not full-on the way he had intended. Instead, his fist had struck just a glancing blow to Grant's shoulder—albeit with enough force to leave his right arm nerveless and shunt him clean through the metal plate of the wall where the busted windshield had already weakened it. A direct hit would have thrown Grant so far out the front of the airship that he would have had no chance to survive; he would already be plummeting past the last of the ship and out into the great beyond.

Instead the ex-mag found himself tumbling backward, head and shoulders dropping as he fell through the gap in the pilot's cubby, his feet grazing across the last quarter inch of the deck before meeting with nothingness.

Grant reached out—blindly, hopefully, *desperately*—seeking purchase on whatever came into his hands. His right arm was numb from the blow but he forced it to work—the survival instinct is the greatest motivator a human being has, and a whole bucketful of adrenaline serves to provide as much fuel as that body might possibly need, high-octane rocket fuel.

Eventually, Grant's left hand clasped around something. In this instance, that "eventually" was maybe three seconds. Three long seconds where Grant's heart kicked into overdrive and he felt nothing but *nothing* beneath his feet. Three long seconds where he had fallen almost fifteen feet through empty air. Then he was swinging through the air on a rope, the coarse fibres hot against his one-handed grip as he was suspended in a wide arc over the cathedral tower. The red circle of window was glowing beneath him like the setting sun, beaming down on the ville like the eye of a cyclops. Grant watched it hurtle under him, bent his legs to lift then over the highest point of the cathedral tower lest he be pierced by it.

The rope was one of the guy ropes that worked as anchors when it came into dock. This one ran up to a strut not four feet from the front of the depending metal container resting beneath the balloon. Grant gripped the swinging rope with both hands, struggling to hold himself there as he swayed wildly over the smoking streets.

Above, Algernon—the blond-haired Dorian male—was standing at the break in the front of the airship's gondola box, watching as his foe miraculously cheated death. "Well played, old man," Algernon called, pulling something from the inside pocket of his frock coat, "but it won't do you a jot of good."

Swinging wildly in the air a dozen feet beneath, Grant tried to make sense of what the superman was doing. He held a pistol in his hand, a bulky thing with chimneylike vents placed at either side of the grip. Grant recognized it—it was the same pistol that Hugh had tried to blast him with back in the factory in Panamint, the heat beam weapon that had overloaded his shadow suit and almost fried him underneath.

Grant watched from his swaying position as the supersoldier took aim at him, sighting down the length of the blaster.

Pzzz-chow!

The heat beam blasted toward Grant in a line of lava-orange, burning through the air with a sizzle of fried molecules.

Grant winced, the heat beam missing him by inches rather than feet.

Above, Algernon was laughing as he blasted again, the hot beam burning up the air. "No escape now, old man," he bragged. "Your gun's gone and you'll be, too, in a moment."

Grant didn't doubt it as another red-orange line cut the air eight inches from his face.

KANE'S FLASH-BANG turned the interior of the gondola into a blizzard of light for a few seconds, and when it faded Kane could see nothing but glowing streaks of color across his vision. He should have used the protective lenses he had, but there hadn't been time. He had felt the mental touch of the two women as they probed into his mind, and he had reacted, survival instinct kicking in, a trapped animal lashing out.

The glow was fading now, not from the room but from his eyes. He was all out of flash-bangs, he knew that much, so whatever was left was going to need something else. The two women lay there, the brunette sprawled on the deck at Kane's feet, the blonde propped against the exterior wall, semisprawled against the low bench that sat snug beneath the open windows. Both women wore the same expression, a look of blank bewilderment. Their mouths were open and drool was forming on their lower lips, snaking slowly down their chins.

It took a moment for Kane to work out what had happened. The two women had tried to pierce his mental shell with their violent telepathic assault, but he had stepped out of the way, igniting the flash-bang. Somehow, in all the confusion, they must have latched on to one another instead, driving mental stakes into each other's brains, sending them both into oblivion.

Kane activated his Commtact, a smile twitching at the corners of his mouth. "Grant, I think I'm about wrapped up here," he said as he turned back to golden throne where the other one waited in his trance.

The throne was empty.

"What the—?" Kane began.

Something struck him from behind and Kane went tumbling across the cabin before slamming into the metal hide with a great clang of flesh on metal. The impact left a dent in the hull so deep that one could almost see Kane's profile in it.

Hugh strode across the passenger cabin and lifted Kane from where he had collapsed on the deck. The handsome dandy was swimming in Kane's blurred vision, and Kane could only barely hear the words over the sound of blood pounding in his ears as Hugh drew his face to close to his own. "You've ruined my beautiful performance, little man," he hissed, "and I don't respond well to critics. Any last words?"

"Surrender," Kane said through bloody lips, "while you still can."

With a snarl of anger, Hugh tossed Kane aside like a

rag doll. Kane sailed through the air and crashed into the thin metal shell of the passenger compartment. Into— *and through.*

JUST BELOW THE FRONT of the metal gondola, Grant was swinging wildly to avoid the fearsome blasts of heat from Algernon's ray beam. If just one of those hit him, he knew, it would liquefy his bones through the flesh, turning him into nothing more than a bubbling puddle contained in a shadow suit.

Pzzz-chow!

The beam blasted again, searing the air and leaving a shimmering heat haze in its wake.

Grant estimated it would take a moment for Algernon to get his eye in, such was the crazed loop through which his body was racing at the end of the swinging rope. But Algernon had other thoughts.

Algernon adjusted his aim, targeting not Grant but the end of the rope where it connected to the ship. Sighting down the gun, Algernon fired another blast from the heat ray, clipping the top edge of the rope in a burst of black smoke. Smart guy, Grant realized. He's going to burn the rope and let gravity do his work for him.

"Sorry, old fruit," he called down to Grant, "but I just don't care to lose."

"Yeah?" Grant snarled back, letting go of the rope with his left hand and trusting his right—already weakened from multiple blows—to hold him in place long enough for what he had in mind. "Well, me, either."

The heat beam cried again, setting light to the rope as Grant dangled below. But that didn't matter now. Grant's left hand was already reaching around and almost behind him to where he had strapped Shizuka's sword to his belt. In one single, swift movement, Grant had the blade free and he hurled it up, across his dangling body, up toward Algernon where the man was readying another blast of the burn beam.

Grant was swinging so wildly that he didn't see the blade strike home. But Algernon did, though he couldn't quite believe it. Thrown with incredible force, the *katana*'s twenty-five-inch steel blade drove straight into Algernon's chest where he leaned out over the side of the pilot's rig, burying itself to the hilt right through his heart. The Victorian supersoldier was launched upward with the force of Grant's blow, dropping the blaster. Pulled off his feet, Algernon was shoved into the low metal ceiling with a mighty clang as the blade pierced his chest and embedded itself in the gondola's roof.

But it wasn't enough. Hanging there, his feet eight inches above the deck, with the *katana* pierced straight through his heart, Algernon merely growled. If there was pain then he didn't show it, and no blood leaked from the wound beyond an initial trickle that seemed to coagulate almost as soon as it appeared.

Alone in the cabin, hanging from the ceiling like a piñata, Algernon reached mercilessly out for the control switch that would release the atom bomb, the final act of the great art project.

"All art is ephemeral," Algernon murmured as he reached. "Its perfect existence should be fleeting, and the artist should know when the performance has come to its natural end."

THE WRENCHING SOUND of tearing metal echoed in Kane's ears, shrieking through his skull like nails down a blackboard as he crashed through the metal shell of the gondola, landing on one of the scaffoldlike struts that acted as a cage around the balloon.

Kane lay on a narrow metal strut, winded and struggling to catch his breath. Far below lay the streets of Luilekkerville, waiting patiently like the dreadful punch line to a joke that began with him falling to his death. Kane turned his attention back to the gondola construction that hung beneath the balloon, watched as the dashing figure of Hugh Danner strode through the torn gap in the side of the gondola, giving no thought to stepping into the open air. Danner's face was red with anger, and his long hair and the tails of his maroon frock coat whipped about him with the wind.

"Philistine! Ingrate! You've ruined what was to be the most celebrated performance of all time," he snarled.

"Show's over," Kane told him, bringing his Sin Eater around to target the approaching Dorian. "Time to drop the curtain and take your final bow."

The Victorian supersoldier moved with astonishing speed. Eyeblink-fast, he was standing before Kane on the narrow skeletal arm of metal, his right foot kicking out and knocking the Sin Eater from Kane's hand. Kane heard something crack in his wrist, hoped that it was the retractable holster and not his ulna bone.

And then the immortal warrior was upon him, driving his hands at Kane's face as he threatened to throttle him. Kane felt the pressure against his throat as Hugh adjusted his grip to break his neck, just as Harold had done a few days before.

ALGERNON'S PALE HAND grasped for the bomb release lever—and missed. He was stuck fast against the cabin roof, the thrown samurai sword holding him there as effectively as a clothes peg. His fingers clawed at empty air, two inches away from the switch that would unleash certain nuclear doom on the people of Luilekkerville.

A moment later, Grant came scrambling through the makeshift hatch in the front of the cabin, breathing heavily, his face tense with worry. He eyed Algernon where the man struggled against the cabin roof like a pinned butterfly. "Things are looking up for you, huh?" he taunted as his gaze took in the damage to the cabin.

Algernon pierced him with a vicious look of hate. "You've absolutely ruined my shirt, you cad," he spit out.

"Yeah?" Grant asked. "Sorry about that."

With a howl of frustration, Algernon rocked against the sword that had him pinned to the cabin roof and kicked out, jabbing the heel of his shoe into the controls with a resounding crack before Grant could react. Sparks erupted across the control circuit. The Dorians were stronger than a normal man and while Algernon's last stab at victory had failed to launch the atom bomb, his kick sent the airship into motion once more, beginning a perilous descent toward the streets of Luilekkerville.

"They're dead," Algernon snarled through bloodied teeth. "The people, the project—all of it must end in death. When the ship strikes the ground, the bomb will go off regardless. And *I'll* survive. You can't stop it now, foolish man."

Grant struck the dangling figure a bone-crunching haymaker to the jaw, sending Algernon into a state of semiconscious delirium. "Shut up and let me think," he snarled, turning back to the sparking control board.

"Now," Grant continued, muttering to himself, "let's take a look at what we have here."

Grant's eyes roved over the controls, studying the strange collection of levers, dials and knobs. He had piloted a number of different vehicles in his time, from the magistrate's favored Deathbird Apache helicopters to the alien tech of the Mantas, but he had never seen anything like this. The levers were intricately carved with Latin identifiers, and the whole pedestal had been designed as much for decorative effect as for operation. Grant could guess that one of the flickering dials was the altimeter, showing even now the rapid descent of the craft as it plummeted earthward. No doubt another dial showed the speed, though he was damned if he could work out which on the cracked and sparking board. At least he had the experience to recognize the language, even if he could not read it.

"Latin," he grunted. "Huh. Where's Baptiste when I need her?"

With that, Grant reached for the controls and decided it was time to take a crash course in airship piloting—emphasis on *crash*. "Now, everybody just hang on," he said, engaging his Commtact and automatically broadcasting the instruction to Kane and Brigid.

The airship lurched as it began to turn beneath the clouds with a shudder of the rudder.

KANE HEARD GRANT'S instruction over the Commtact, but it was distant, as if coming from another room. There was something pushing against his throat, he realized, tight as a vise.

His eyes snapped open and he saw the figure before him. The once-handsome Dorian looked deranged now, his colleagues felled, his plan unraveled. Around them, the sound of rushing wind was picking up as the airship began to descend furiously toward the helpless citizens of Luilekkerville.

"They were to be my greatest performance," Hugh was ranting as he increased the pressure on Kane's throat. "A commentary on the wonder and hopelessness of war and progress." He glanced past Kane, down to the streets where some of the recovered locals were running for cover. "Perfect for a moment in time, remembered forever."

"Don't you realize?" Kane gasped through his closing windpipe. "Everything you did left corpses in its wake. Your chaos is killing them."

"Exactly," Hugh shrieked at Kane. "They were all to die in the name of art. It would have been *their* immortality.

"Oh, the songs they would have written about this day," Hugh snarled, increasing the pressure on Kane's windpipe with his superhuman hands. "But you and your colleagues ruined it. The death of art is upon us. You have killed the greatest dream man can ever hope to achieve."

Kane's left hand reached for a pouch in his belt where one last metallic sphere waited and with his last ounce of strength, shoved it into Hugh's open mouth, releasing its contents in a blush of white like snow.

"Yeah?" Kane croaked through his closed windpipe. "Have a new dream on me."

The powder burst forth in a great cloud from the tiny metal sphere, releasing a handful of glist into the superman's mouth and nostrils as he screamed at his enemy. Whatever happened after that, Kane wouldn't know—he had blacked out from the pressure on his throat.

Chapter 28

Brigid crouched amid a cluster of redwoods roughly a mile out from Luilekkerville, working at the controls for the interphaser. The setting sun had painted the trees a pinkish hue, and the same color danced across the mirrored sides of the interphaser where it rested on the dirt before her, its tiny display alive with lights. She had input the parallax point for this region, and it was set to open a gateway to Cerberus for a few seconds so they could send the Dorians to the makeshift holding station in the mat-trans chamber. Interphaser ready, Brigid brought herself to a standing position and scanned the horizon, impatiently tapping her boot's toe against the dry soil.

"Come on, guys—where are you?" she muttered.

Suddenly the Commtact in her head burst to life with Grant's voice. "Now, everybody just hang on," he said. His voice sounded urgent and strained.

"Grant, what's happening?" Brigid asked, engaging her Commtact's pickup instinctively. "I'm at the parallax point out in the woods but there's no sign of—" She stopped, her words catching in her throat as she saw the curiously styled airship lunge over the walls of the ville and begin a hurried passage toward her. "Grant? The airship's coming—and it's moving fast."

"I'm in the pilot's chair," Grant explained, "but the controls are shot. Long story. Suffice to say I'm doing all I can to hold her aloft. Where are you?"

"About a mile out from the south wall," Brigid told him. "Do you have the Dorians captured?"

"Not as such," Grant admitted. "I've got a live a-bomb under this thing and I need to get it out of the ville. I'm trying to figure somewhere to dump it after that. Any ideas?"

Brigid eyed the blot in the sky for just a moment, estimating its speed and the angle of descent. "I have one," she said, "but it's a long shot." Even as she spoke, she had crouched back down before the interphaser and began to tap in a sequence on the keys, searching the files for a new destination.

"Long shot's about where we're at at this stage of the game," Grant admitted. "What's your plan?"

"If I open a quantum window with the interphaser, do you think you could drop the nuke inside?"

Grant muttered something unrepeatable before he answered. "You weren't kidding about the long shot," he said. "Where are we looking?"

"Parallax point on the tree line, south of the ville," Brigid told him.

"Yeah, I used that parallax point once to help Domi out of a jam," Grant recalled, "but it was a while ago. I'm trying to remember where it was."

"Among the redwoods on the ridge," Brigid said.

CROUCHED OVER the pilot's podium of the airship, Grant was fighting with a control yoke that seemed determined to steer him to port. He peered up through the shattered window, saw the great line of redwood trees running across most of the right-hand side of his view. "Lot of trees out there, Brigid," he said. "You're going to have to be more specific."

"Try ten degrees to your starboard," came Brigid's

response. "I'll open the window when you're close and you should see it."

"I'm losing altitude here," Grant told Brigid. "Not sure how long we have."

BRIGID EYED the approaching airship, swiftly calculating its trajectory in her head. It was only forty feet off the ground now and moving at some considerable speed. It would be close.

Assuming Grant could navigate it through the outermost trees of the forest, he should pass over the parallax point in thirty seconds' time, at which point he would still be airborne—*just*.

"Keep coming starboard," Brigid told him. "You'll make it."

"THIS BIRD DOESN'T seem to like starboard awful much," Grant muttered, wrestling with the reticent controls. His dark eyes were fixed on the wall of trees that were rushing toward him as the vehicle dipped ever lower.

"Keep coming," Brigid instructed. "I'm opening the quantum phase window—*now*."

Grant grit his teeth as he pulled with all his strength at the controls, forcing the rudder around one last time as the ground and tree trunks came hurtling toward the viewport. Then, materializing from nowhere, he saw the quantum window bloom into life, a roiling swirl of colors like some magnificent flower budding, distant streaks of lightning cascading in its impossible depths. It was the interphase window, opening a gateway between here and beyond.

"I hope you planned this right," Grant muttered as he yanked the bomb release. Beneath his feet, he felt as much as heard something shunt in place as the catch slipped its hooks and the bomb began its brief descent.

A moment later leaves filled his view as the airship slammed into the trees, and Grant heard the great wrenching of metal as the undercarriage of the gondola tore through the topsoil in a howl of strained joints.

ON THE GROUND, Brigid had made as much space between her and the interphaser as she could, sprinting out from the trees and down toward the track that ran to Luilekkerville.

The interphaser was the product of alien science, and it relied on a complex web of linked points to connect the quantum windows it opened. These were dotted right across the globe, one here, one at Cerberus, numerous others all across the Earth. And there were also others, many others, located across the solar system and beyond, out into the deepest reaches of space.

In the thirty seconds she had had to reprogram the interphaser, Brigid had input a parallax point in phase with the moon, approximately 225,000 miles above the Earth.

Brigid hit the ground anyway as the atom bomb slunk toward Earth and into the quantum window, hands over her head in preparation for an explosion that never came.

The distance of the moon to Earth varies by as much as 20,000 miles depending on the time of year. At a different point in its orbit to the parallax point that the interphaser had accessed, the moon was thousands of miles away from where the window opened and the atomic bomb was suddenly dropped. As such, the moon witnessed nothing of the bomb's silent explosion in the vacuum, far away from human eyes.

THE AIRSHIP LOOKED as if it had been through hell. The deflated balloon was still spitting hydrogen in a whining hiss, and the protective cage around it looked like the mangled remains of so much roadkill. Brigid was the first on the scene, searching the wreckage for Grant and Kane, repeating their names into her Commtact.

She found Grant lying in a pool of blood in the pilot's cabin. As the lowest segment of the ship, the cabin had struck the ground first and taken the brunt of the impact. It had crumpled but survived, creating a protective box around Grant and his companion. The blood, thankfully, belonged to the Dorian called Algernon, who was still pinned to the cabin's ceiling by Shizuka's *katana*.

Grant roused after a few taps from Brigid, a tentative smile forming on his lips. Grant was tough; he could take a lot of punishment and still smile. "Did we do it?" he asked.

Brigid nodded. "Never doubted you for a moment," she assured him. "Kane's not reported in," she added.

Grant looked up and around. "I lost track of him. He was in the passenger compartment when I last saw him."

Together, the two Cerberus warriors clambered through the wreckage to said compartment, where the two Dorian women lay ensnared in one another's minds. They lay there with eyes wide-open, their skirts about their waists. They looked like victims of some hideous shell shock too traumatic to relate.

They found Kane shortly after that, caught beneath a cross of broken metal beams that had saved him from more serious harm. He lay beside the last—and first—of the Dorians, the dark-haired Hugh, who simply sat and babbled to himself, his eyelids closed against reality. It would be some time before Kane could explain how he had employed the dreamers' glist as a weapon against Hugh, an immortal soldier who could shrug off flames and outrace bullets, but who could never let go of his need to dream.

Chapter 29

The people of Luilekkerville were safe. Hurt, wounded and with a number of dead. Forty people had died in the bloody combat but none had died from the brain trauma they had suffered at the mind of Hugh Danner. And none had died from the atom bomb that had been diverted at the very last second by Grant and Brigid. Kane could live with that. All things considered, it was a good result, one the ville would recover from.

Now Kane stood marveling at one of the grandest storage facilities he had ever seen. The walls were decorated with ornamental red columns that towered to five times his height, with each face of each column carved with an elaborate beast, a tiger or a dragon or a snake whose tail curled around the height of the column in a dizzying spiral. Despite being located belowground, the ceiling was at least forty feet above him, and the echoes of voices as he tracked across the room flittered back to him like a church choir in song. "Quite the place you have here," he observed as he turned to the facility's owner.

Peering up from a datapad, Shizuka smiled prettily. There were dark circles under her eyes and her skin had lost a little of its glow, Kane noticed, but otherwise she looked to be back in the prime of health. The fact that Grant had spent every moment checking on her and running after her ever since she had awoken from her coma three days ago had helped her relax back into her role as leader of the Tigers of Heaven. Even now, Grant was busying along one of the Tigers as they set the installation up and ran through a final check of the equipment that Cerberus had brought to New Edo via mat-trans.

"I am honored that you approve, Kane-san," Shizuka deadpanned, but Kane caught a glimpse of her wicked smile as she turned back to her datapad. "Does Brigid know you are here?"

Kane shook his head. "Just on my way to see her," he said.

A dozen feet away, dominating a cordoned-off area beneath a set of bright lights, was one of the dream engines, its gnarled treelike growth expanding up into the air to end in a series of thick tubes that fed the data to the engine, six beds posed around its base in the familiar rose-petal formation. Five of those beds were occupied by the five Dorians, each wired up to the dream tech, their altered consciousness hooked into an ongoing simulation that could respond to their interactions in an ever-developing scenario; a lot like life.

A dozen Tigers of Heaven warriors, dressed head to toe in modern samurai chic—supple armor that looked more like biker wear, the curve of a sheathed *katana* blade resting at each man's left hip—bustled about the dream engine, running data checks and systems analyses under the supervision of Brigid Baptiste and Donald Bry, who had stripped, cataloged and remodeled the dream engines once they had been brought back from Hope. To see one of them back in use here, functioning as a trap for the minds of the immortal soldiers, sat uncomfortably with Kane, but he knew it would have to suffice until a better solution presented itself. In a few days, the Tigers of Heaven would take over the monitoring and upkeep of the dream engine themselves, holding the Dorians in this hidden facility beneath New Edo where they would remain safe from discovery. It wouldn't do to have them set loose again the way they had been from the Nevada installation. Better to leave them trapped in a dream than to run the risk of their getting loose and trying to run the world as some gigantic death-art exhibit again.

"Yeah," Kane muttered, "what the hell was *that* about?"

"Did you say something?" Brigid asked as she looked up from her programming work.

Kane brushed absently at his hair as he eyed the towering dream engine set amid the sealed crates and other odd items in this storehouse. "Nah," he said. "Just wondering what you did with them. In there, I mean."

"While you were sleeping things off?" Brigid teased.

Kane rolled his eyes. "I got pushed through an airship wall," he reminded her. "I think I deserved a few days' rest and recoup."

Brigid looked at him and laughed. "So, what Donald and I have done here is program a virtual environment that the Dorians should recognize," she explained. "Once we leave, the Tigers of Heaven will continue to tend to their basic needs—nutrition, hydration, etc."

"How's that work?" Kane queried.

"Controlled measures, intravenously," Brigid explained, lifting an IV line that was connected to the wrist of Algernon's sleeping form. The man's chest was still streaked black where he had been skewered, but the scar seemed to be healing nicely now. Seeing that reminded Kane how impossible these people were to kill. "Under Reba's scrutiny, we've added a very small dosage of glist to the cocktail, which should enhance the experience sufficiently so that they won't think to question it."

"You questioned it," Kane pointed out.

"I went in programmed to question it," Brigid told him. "That was why I was there, remember?"

"'Remember,'" Kane repeated with a grin. "Your idea of a joke, right?"

It was Brigid's turn to roll her eyes.

"Question is," Grant said as strode over carrying a large pallet of packaged glist in his arms, "what happens when the glist runs out?"

"Well," Brigid said, "we can't refine more, to do so would be inhuman. But we snagged a pretty big supply from Red O'Shumper, and Reba is even now working with the Cerberus lab techs to create an artificial substitute."

"So it could still be a problem?" Grant checked, concern in his voice.

"Not for a while," Brigid assured them, gesturing to several identical pallets of glist to the one Grant held, "and hopefully by then we'll have a more long-term solution."

Kane looked at the five dreamers as they relaxed in the embrace of the dream engine. "*Long-term* is right," he reminded his partners. "These psychopaths are going to outlive us and everyone else in this room, and everyone else on the planet."

"Except maybe Lakesh," Brigid said, lightening the mood.

"Sure," Kane agreed. But as he stood there staring at the dream engine burbling away to itself, he couldn't help but wonder what would distract an immortal soldier long enough to stop them breaking out of the false reality and trying to conquer the world.

THE WIDOW WORE BLACK. She had worn black since the day her husband has died in 1861, a tribute to their love eternal.

The widow glided among the Dorians, her long skirts swishing around her like black mist, a short figure yet still imposing. Her fearsome stare locked with each supersoldier she strode past as if in challenge. Lined up in the midday sun, the Dorians held firm, watching as the ultimate authority in the British Empire walked past them, surveying each of them in turn.

"This is quite the display, Professor," she said, turning to the scarecrowlike figure of Edgar Howard as he reintroduced his new breed of men, "seeing them all together like this after all that your Dorians have done."

"I trust you approve, Your Highness?" Professor Howard asked, his American accent seeming somehow too casual for the echoing surrounds of Windsor Castle's courtyard. The courtyard had been decorated with gold-trimmed red carpet and banners, and three battalions of Her Majesty's Royal Fusiliers stood stock-still waiting for the official ceremony to begin.

Queen Victoria halted before General Hugh Danner—always her favorite—and openly admired him, her eyes working from the beautiful, empire-made leather shoes of his feet right up to his perfectly coiffed brown hair and those crystal-bright eyes that burned like sapphires in the midday sun. "How could one not?" she asked in her always-regal tone.

Hugh felt himself begin to blush at that, but he held firm, meeting the queen's eyes and spying the trace of a smile at the corners of her mouth. "Black suits you, Your Highness," he said, keeping his tone low enough that only she heard the compliment.

Hugh stood beside his partners: good old Algie, his

right-hand man and the person responsible for saving his life twice over in India; Antonia, his would-be bride, whose strategic insights had annexed a whole slice of the Far East and absorbed it into the empire, leaving just a few local stragglers in their wake; Harold, ever dashing in his opera cape, the white dueling scar running down by his eye where he had fought with some jumped-up Prussian baron in the dining hall of his own ruddy keep; and Cecily—sweet "Silly"—who had tempted then married Czar Michael to further the empire's push into the new Anglo-Russian territories. Czar Michael was around somewhere, doubtless sampling Bertie's finest scotch or similar while the final preparations were made for the ceremony that would honor the Dorians for their work in creating a stable world under her majesty's rule.

"Together, these five have redrawn our map," the queen reminded the professor, "and to them each is owed a great debt by the British Empire and the world. Wars have been fought but so many others have been averted in the pursuit of perfection, creating a unity unknown since the heady days of Greece."

"All war is art," Hugh said, recalling the innumerable victories that had been performed on his watch as he drove the British Empire to greater heights.

"And all art is war," Algernon reminded the gathered peoples as they prepared to accept their knighthoods.

It was but a brief lull in the continued expansion of the empire. Tomorrow, pastures new would call. Even now, Howard and his team of scientists were working on new lung functionality for the immortal Dorians with the intention of conquering the ocean depths and perhaps outer space. That would take some doing, but from here, standing in the grand courtyard of Windsor Castle as the sun beamed down to honor them, nothing seemed impossible. A glorious future lay ahead. A dream come true, Hugh realized.

Long live the empire. God save the queen.

* * * * *